PRAISE FOR THE LARKIN DAY MYSTERY SERIES

"A smart, snarky series… Cozy mystery readers will adore Larkin Day."

BOOKLIFE, EDITOR'S PICK

"…an entertaining whodunit with a captivating amateur sleuth."

KIRKUS REVIEWS

"Ode to Murder is refreshing, and definitely recommended for fans of a good mystery. But it's also a great read for anyone who, like Larkin, is searching for a new story that can reach them in surprising, unexpected ways."

INDIEREADER

MURDER ON THE NERD CRUISE

MURDER ON THE NERD CRUISE

A LARKIN DAY MYSTERY

BOOK 4

NICOLE DIEKER

To all JoCo Cruisers—past, present, and future.

CHAPTER 1

"You know I'm not a nerd," Larkin Day whispered, as everyone in line moved one step closer to the enormous cruise ship. Ten sun-reflectant decks glared at her through a wall of windows, as if the vessel itself was responding to her thoughts—even though she hadn't told anyone what she was actually thinking.

Not since Chicago.

"I don't know any math past algebra, maybe pre-algebra, and I don't know anything about computers, and I fell asleep during *Lord of the Rings*." They were in the kind of metal-roofed, cement-floored space Larkin would have called an *airplane hangar* if they were traveling by air instead of by sea. A room that echoed, from one end of the line to the other, with in-jokes and ukuleles—and so Larkin kept her voice just loud enough for her best friend to hear. "Why did you bring me here?"

"Because I think you're nerdy enough to pass muster," Anni said. "Pun intended, as your boyfriend would say." She reached across the rope barrier to fist-bump a ukulele player. "Good to see you! This is my friend Larkin, she's new." Larkin held her fist over the rope; the ukulelist bumped it, and the serpentine line moved them in opposite directions before Larkin had to explain why she had agreed to a week-long nerd-themed cruise.

"Also because you need a vacation." Anni was wearing a cruise-branded T-shirt over her leggings and had towed her hair out of her eyes with a series of ship-shaped hairpins. "This might not be your ideal sailing, but it doesn't mean you won't be able to find activities that match your interests." Her lanyard, which she had been wearing ever since they boarded the flight to Orlando, was covered in buttons: SHE/HER, ALL THIRTEEN CRUISES, NOT TRISKAIDEKAPHOBIC, NO HUGS PLEASE. "Or you could spend the entire week in the spa."

"They said on the forums that the spa would be pretty near empty." That was from Claire, Larkin's mother's girlfriend—who was very definitely a nerd and had allowed herself to become even nerdier since they'd all booked their tickets. She'd spent hours on the online cruise forums, getting to know people who called themselves *SamwiseIam* and *WyvernandShirley*. "You can get your massage, and the rest of us can go to Adamantine Darcy's lecture on integrating artificial intelligence into sci-fi and fantasy." Claire was wearing white crew socks underneath her sandals, and continually calling out to all of the people she recognized from the internet. "You could get—hello!— a different spa treatment every day, if you wanted." Claire had also put on her cruise-branded lanyard before leaving Chicago; her buttons included SAY HI and FIRST TIME. "That's what I'd do—good morning!—if I weren't going to AI 'n' SF 'n' F."

"Or you could solve a mystery!" Larkin's mother said. Josephine Day had chosen to dress as if the ship she were boarding was setting sail in 1935. A loose, cotton sundress flattered her shoulders and hips; a wide-brimmed hat shaded the lines of her face. "Petty theft. Mistaken identity. Some kind of love triangle." Her lanyard was unadorned. "Maybe somebody will get murdered!"

"Nobody's getting murdered," Larkin said. "I told you to stop joking about the murders."

"Fine," Larkin's mother replied, her voice implying that Larkin had been the one who had overstepped—and, as they all took another step forward, inferred it was time to change the subject. "You know, I thought I would be one of the oldest people here." Josephine had just turned sixty, and she and Claire were counting the cruise as a birthday present. "But I see plenty of sexagenarians."

"Sexygenarians," Claire teased, squeezing Josephine's hand. "We won't be the only Boomers on the boat."

"You're barely a Boomer," Josephine said. Claire was a few years younger than Larkin's mother, and most of the time they pretended it didn't matter. "Demographically, I think you're Gen X."

"You're the one who said we're only as old as we feel," Claire said, "and I feel like someone who got way more excited about the moon landing than, like, *Reality Bites*."

"Linguistically, the fact that you just used the word *like* to *designate a metaphor* puts you firmly in the younger generation." Dr. Josephine Day had spent two decades as an English professor before transitioning to a career in academic administration. Now she was teaching again; at the library, at the community college, in the homes of the students whose parents wanted in-person college prep, and at the cruise port. "My generation only ever used *like* to designate a simile."

"Nerd," Claire said, smiling.

Larkin took another look around the *not-airplane-hangar*

to make sure she hadn't missed anything. There were, as her mother had suggested, nerds of all ages. Nerds of all sizes. Nerds of all colors and—Larkin watched a knot of turbans, a modest cluster of hijabs, a collection of necklaces bearing various crosses and stars, and one person irreverently wearing a hat shaped like a giant spaghetti monster—all creeds. Nerds with families. Nerds with extended families. Nerds with friend groups that were as close as family. A few nerds who stood, alone, waiting for someone to notice them. Larkin watched them all, looking at every masked and unmasked face.

"Statistically," Anni said, turning slightly to bring Ed and Elliott into the conversation, "someone could die on this sailing." She raised herself as high as her tiptoes could take her and waved to a nerd in a motorized scooter. "But it's highly unlikely that any of us will be murdered."

"Why?" Larkin asked. She couldn't tell Anni not to joke about the murders, because Anni hadn't actually made a joke. "Because nerds don't kill other nerds?"

"Nerds, both as individuals and as a group," Anni said, "are extremely non-violent."

"We fight with words," Elliott said, "not with swords." Elliott was Anni's boyfriend—or at least he would have been, if tiny, towheaded Anni and rangy, ginger Elliott had been anything like normal people. The freelance writer and freelance programmer had fallen for each other on the very first nerd cruise, nearly thirteen years ago. They had gotten back in touch after a decade of unexpected separation—the sort of story that only ever took place in the paperback novels Claire read by the stack—and their relationship had rekindled in kind. Now they were in the process of restoring an old farmhouse just outside of Pratincola, Iowa. They were also in the process of developing what Elliott called *a scalable, pattern-based tutoring system with an emphasis on 1:1 knowledge transfer* and what Anni simply called *magic school*.

"What about foam swords?" Ed asked, gesturing at two nerds who were both carrying orange-tipped, duct-taped, sword-shaped objects.

"Those are called *boffers*," Elliott said, "and they are rarely used to settle disputes."

Ed was Larkin's boyfriend. He and Larkin were exactly where a normal boyfriend and girlfriend should be, after a year and a half of dating each other. She had a toothbrush in his apartment. He had invited her to his niece's sixth-grade graduation. Neither of them had considered purchasing real estate together. They had talked about going on vacation together—again, perfectly normal—but hadn't even begun discussing where to go before Anni, with her accumulated cruise loyalty points, had solved the problem for them.

"Excuse me." The voice came from a young man in a slim-fitting cruise ship uniform. His eyes looked first to the tablet computer in his hand, then to the pronouns on Anni's lanyard. "Miss Morgan."

"Yes," Anni said, smiling, "this is she."

"Thank you, Miss Morgan," the man said. The first half of his sentence had gotten a lot more practice, as had the two sentences that followed. "Please, you and your group, come with me. I will help you board the ship more quickly."

"Thank you, Handoyono," Anni said, pronouncing the young man's name as carefully as he had pronounced hers.

"Oh no, Miss Morgan, please call me Handy," he said, as he led the six of them towards a shorter line, next to a sign that read SUPER ELITE STATUS. "For I hope to be very handy to you, on your relaxing cruise vacation!"

"Are you assigned to our stateroom?" Anni asked. "Thank you for taking such good care of us." She reached into her canvas satchel and pulled out what appeared to be a twenty-dollar bill, folding it in half and placing it in Handy's hand. "Has the luggage arrived?"

"Yes, Miss Morgan," Handy said. "I have made sure all is in order." He glanced at his tablet again. "Suitcases for Day and Jackson are in the main bedroom. Suitcases for Morgan and Fox are next to the convertible bunkbed in the main living space. The digital piano has been set up in the location you requested. All is well!"

Anni handed him another twenty. None of them—except Elliott, of course—had actually believed she was going to practice the piano on the cruise ship until they saw her wheeling the instrument case into the Cedar Rapids airport. "I appreciate everything you are doing for us, and we hope to be good guests."

"Wait," Claire said. "What about Novak?"

Handy noticed, for the first time, that there were two more passengers in front of him than there were on his tablet. "I am sorry, Miss Novak," he said, glancing at Claire's lanyard. "I do not have you in my stateroom. May I scan your badge?"

"Claire Novak and Josephine Day are in Interior 3689," Elliott said, making a twenty appear between his fingers. "They are traveling with us, but they are new to the cruise line and haven't had the opportunity to earn Elite Status. May they stay with us, and check in here? It would be an excellent way to introduce them to the hospitality this cruise is known to provide."

The twenty was in Handy's hand before he knew how it got there. "You do magic, sir?"

"Yes," Elliott said. "Can you do some magic for us?"

Handy nodded, thumbing at his tablet. He turned to

Claire. "You and Miss Day have been cleared for expedited check-in," he said, "and although Interior 3689 was not scheduled to receive service until later this evening, I have expedited that process as well." Then he looked at Josephine and Larkin, registering both the surnames and the resemblance, and smiled. "Are you two sisters?"

"Who taught you that?" Josephine said, laughing. She reached into her purse—an old, rattan handbag with a folded gold clasp—and gave Handy a dollar. "Thank you."

Ed, standing next to Larkin, unzipped the pocket of his athletic shorts and gave Handy a five-dollar bill. "You've been very helpful," he said.

"Thank you, brother," Handy said, giving Ed the kind of grin that was probably not included in his cruise employee training. Ed grinned back, mirroring Handy's delight. It was the kind of smile Larkin rarely saw; the one her boyfriend saved for the people who looked like him. "Enjoy your relaxing cruise vacation!"

Larkin was pretty sure that Handy was not Black—or, at least, not in the same way that Ed was. She could cast Handy as a Black man, if she were directing something like *Porgy and Bess* and needed a large number of plausible background actors, but she could also cast him as a Puerto Rican gang member in *West Side Story* or a Dominican salon employee in *In the Heights*. In reality he was probably Indonesian with North African ancestry—but what really mattered, when Handy looked at Ed and called him *brother*, is that they were both *brown*.

"You're very welcome, Handy," Ed said. "I'm sure I will." Larkin watched the young, uniformed employee find someone else to help. She watched her boyfriend's smile retreat from his face to his mind. She watched her mother's girlfriend Claire, a law enforcement professional who already knew the name of every other veteran on the cruise, complete another of one of her quick situational assessments. When Claire did it, she looked both professional and competent. When Larkin did it—because she had to check, one more time, for the face she wasn't sure she wanted to see—she felt Claire's hand on her shoulder and her voice in her ear. "Relax, kiddo. They've got this. I've been watching their security team. Everything is going to be fine, nobody is going to commit homicide, and you are going to spend at least one full day in the spa." Claire squeezed Larkin's shoulder before letting go. "Even if I have to book the appointment myself."

Everyone in the group knew that Larkin needed a break. She'd told them she was worn out from the summer she'd spent directing the Pratincola Shakespeare Festival, and everyone assumed it was because she'd solved two murders and one attempted murder, and nobody had ever said that she'd failed to save two people's lives, even though that was another way to tell the same story. But Larkin hadn't even thought about the murders—not in the way she usually thought about them—since they'd gathered in Cedar Rapids to begin their journey. She had been able to relax, then. She'd let her mother make jokes about Jessica Fletcher and *Death on the Nile*. She'd only started getting nervous when they flew out of Chicago, gripping the armrest so hard that Ed had laughed, leaned across the aisle, and asked Elliott to give her a lecture on aerodynamics.

"Are you worried about Ed?" Claire asked, quietly.

Larkin considered saying yes. It was close enough to the truth, but she didn't want Ed to spend his relaxing cruise vacation worrying that she was worried about him. Her boyfriend had spent the past year going through the complicated and stressful tenure application process, and he'd told Larkin that he didn't want her anxieties layered over his own. Ed was self-contained, a well-toned vocalist who was used to the uncertainty of academia. He was also used to being the only Black man in a room, and he'd made it clear that he didn't need Larkin's anxieties in that area either.

"He'll fit in just fine," Claire said. "We had a whole subforum just for Blerds. They're putting together their own tour of St. Maarten."

Larkin continued saying nothing. It was an old detective trick—it was also an old theater trick—and Claire, despite her officer training, kept talking. "Blerds are Black nerds," she explained, as if Larkin's silence had something to do with not being able to parse the portmanteau. "Ed's going to meet a ton of new friends."

Larkin continued watching Ed, who was removing his lanyard and badge and handing them to a security attendant. The former included HE/HIM, FIRST TIME, and SAY HI buttons. The latter read *Dr. Ed Jackson*, followed by a few words in his own handwriting: *Music, not medical.* The security attendant did not call Ed *brother*, but he smiled widely enough for everyone in the Super Elite Status line to get the message. "Let me take your picture before you board the cruise ship," the attendant said, and Larkin watched the flash brighten Ed's tightly coiled hair and nearly violet skin. "Now we'll be able to match your badge to your picture, everywhere you go—but I don't imagine any of us will have any trouble remembering you!"

"Thank you, Ahmad," Ed said. He turned back, blinking slightly, until he spotted Larkin. "Come on, cut the line," he said, winking at Anni and Elliott and Josephine as he waved Larkin forward. "She's with me," he said to Ahmad, who took Larkin's lanyard, badge, and photo—and then Ed took Larkin's arm, and the two of them walked through a pair of automatic double doors into the brilliant Florida sunlight.

"Wait," Larkin said. There were people on the gang-plank, and people on the decks, and she couldn't see any of them. "Is that a helicopter on the top of the ship? How often do you think they use it? Do you figure it's for mede-vac, or—"

"Who are you looking for?" Ed asked.

He knew.

He didn't know.

Larkin didn't know how he could know, since she hadn't said anything about it to anyone.

Not since Chicago.

"Anni and Elliott," Larkin said.

Not since she had seen both the face and the lanyard, in the second it took for the flight attendant to pull the curtain that separated them from First Class.

"They're right behind us," Ed said. "So are your mother and Claire."

"I know," Larkin said.

He didn't know.

She was still the only one who knew.

"Elliott!" Ed called. "Come on!"

Larkin blinked and rubbed her eyes and looked, one more time—*one last time,* she told herself, as the cruise ship glared at her—for Jaipal Malhotra.

CHAPTER 2

Larkin did not want to spend another minute of her long-awaited vacation thinking about her self-named nemesis. She turned away from the glittering ship, shifting her gaze from all the men who were not Jay Malhotra. Focusing her mind and her eyes on the man standing next to her.

"I can't believe it," she said, because it seemed like the kind of thing to say. "We're finally here."

"Finally," Ed echoed. He kissed her—or began to, before Larkin's mind and mouth twisted towards a tall, curly-haired man who was rushing past them on the gangplank. It wasn't Jay, of course; it was just another of Dutch Cruise International's multinational staff, and Larkin felt Ed's lips gently settle for her cheek.

"I know," Ed whispered, into her ear. *He couldn't know.* "It's kind of overwhelming."

"Right," Larkin said, because it was. She wondered if she should just tell Ed that she had seen Jay in Chicago. That would probably be the best thing to do. Ed knew

Jaipal Malhotra—they all did, although not as thoroughly as Larkin—and telling her boyfriend about Jay before they even boarded the ship would be the best way to neutralize the threat.

"Ed."

Now she just needed to think of the best way to say it.

"Yes?"

Maybe she should ask Anni first. Anni—who had corralled Elliott and Josephine and Claire at the double doors until it was clear that Ed and Larkin were no longer sharing an intimate moment—always knew the best way to do everything.

"Anni!" Larkin asked. "What do we do next?"

"We keep moving!" Anni answered, waving the rest of the group forward. "We are so close to being inside the ship, and even closer to being an obstacle on the gangplank!"

Larkin had no idea whether Anni knew that Jay Malhotra had been wearing a cruise-branded lanyard on the flight from Chicago to Orlando. Anni was the only person who knew that Larkin thought of Jay as her nemesis—and her advice, at the time, had been to *stop thinking that way*. "It's a distraction," she had explained—and even though Larkin hadn't been able to take Anni's advice at the time, she could start taking it right now.

"Kiss me," she whispered to Ed, "and then I'll stop being an obstacle."

Ed kissed her, as directed.

Jay, who never followed directions, would have said, *"But then I won't get to overcome you."*

———

"Wow," Claire said, after the six of them had successfully ascended the gangplank, scanned their badges, and passed through a pair of gilt-edged double doors. "It's just like *Titanic*." One of them had to say it, and since Anni and Elliott were used to cruise ships and Larkin was pretty sure her mother had never actually seen the movie, the job fell to the stocky, wide-eyed Claire. Larkin squeezed Ed's arm, hoping to nudge him into turning his head and sharing a knowing look, but his mind and his eyes were focused on the red-carpeted lobby with its enormous gold staircase—*wow*, Larkin thought, *it really is like Titanic*—and the cruise-uniformed photographer who stood eagerly at the bottom of the stairs.

"Welcome!" the photographer said, as if he hadn't said it a dozen times in the past half hour. "You look relaxed already!" he continued, as if he wouldn't say it five hundred times that day. "My name is Ismael. May I photograph your beautiful faces on our beautiful Grand Staircase?"

"It's like *Moby-Dick*," Josephine said. One of them had to say it, and this time Larkin was able to lean into Ed's arm hard enough that he winked at her.

"Ha ha, you are right!" The photographer was expecting the joke. "Call me Ismael! So many intelligent and well-read people on this cruise!"

"With guests like Adamantine Darcy," Claire said, "it goes without saying."

"Oh, yes!" Ismael's eyes crinkled to match his smile. "I took Miss Darcy's photograph an hour ago. World-famous author! So personable and so kind!"

"Have you read her books?" Claire asked.

"I saw the Netflix," Ismael said. He gestured towards the staircase. "Would you like to go first?"

Josephine glanced at her rattan handbag. Larkin could see her mother running the numbers in her head, adding up what she could afford to spend on their vacation and subtracting the dollar she had already given Handy. "How much does it cost?"

"Oh, madam," Ismael said, "do not worry. I take as many free photos as I can, of all the beautiful people enjoying their relaxing cruise vacation. You only pay for the photos you take home with you!"

"There's a kiosk," Anni explained, "where they display all of the photos. You don't have to buy them. It's just fun to see everyone, especially as you start to get to know people."

Claire grinned at Josephine. "Let's get our picture up on that kiosk." She ran her fingers through her cropped auburn bob. "Does my hair look all right?"

"You look beautiful," Ismael said again. "Come, stand right here."

He positioned Claire and Josephine next to each other on the second step. Larkin watched as her mother and her mother's girlfriend casually and comfortably assumed the classic prom pose: Claire at the back, with her arms around Josephine's waist. Then Claire leaned her head on Larkin's mother's shoulder.

"I love to see people in love!" Ismael said, snapping his photo and gesturing towards Anni and Elliott, who took their places and stood, side by side, the same way they always stood when they were next to each other. They didn't have to demonstrate their relationship through their posture. They didn't even have to look at each other. The photographer took his shot without comment, and turned towards Larkin and Ed.

"You lucky woman," Ismael said to Larkin, as Ed held

out his arm and escorted her to the second step. This was the response Larkin usually got when people figured out that the handsome, muscular music professor was dating the average-looking, extra-large, part-time theater director. Larkin had a few more muscles than she used to, though—thanks to twice-weekly exercise classes at the Pratincola Fitness Complex—and she extended her leg and braced her core as Ed effortlessly dipped and then kissed her.

"You two are like Hollywood!" Ismael said.

"No," Larkin said, "Broadway." Then she stood, on the second step, and looked over the photographer's head at the group of people coming through the door. One of them said "It's like *Titanic*!" None of them looked like Jaipal Malhotra. She wondered if Jay was on the ship yet. She wondered if he would be waiting outside the door of their stateroom. She wondered if he had planned, in advance, what he would say to her—just like she was planning, in advance, what she might say to him. *Stop thinking that way,* Larkin thought, pushing the words she wanted to rehearse out of her internal monologue.

Ed nudged her, gently, on the left shoulder. "We're being an obstacle again."

"Sorry," Larkin said, walking with her boyfriend as they followed Anni and Elliott and Josephine and Claire into a wide, windowed dining room. There were people, already, sitting at the tables or standing by the bar. Some of these people looked like nerds. Others looked—and Larkin recognized this, immediately, because it was what she wanted to be more than anything in the world—like professionals.

Larkin did not know, exactly, what *being a professional* meant. She suspected, in the part of her mind that she tried to keep silent, that it was the kind of status that had to be earned before it could be achieved. Larkin could see professionalism when it was in front of her. She could also see where she fell behind. She could not see—even though she had been looking, for years—how to cover the distance between who she was and who she wanted to be.

Maybe the people on the other side of the room could help her.

"Are those the guests?" she whispered to Anni.

"Yes," Anni whispered back. They were all guests of the cruise line, of course—in the weird, themed-event world where *guest* meant *person who had bought a ticket*—but the people who had been invited to entertain, perform, or lecture were Special Guests, with access to staterooms and lounges that were not available to the average cruisegoer.

Luckily for Larkin, Anni and Elliott were anything but average. "Would you like to meet them? We can say hello to Daniel and Moira Pennington," Anni said, leading the six of them towards the Special Guest tables as if she knew exactly what she was doing. "In fact, we *should* say hello to them. Let them know we're here." This was not the Anni whom Larkin had come to know, carefully, over the past year. Larkin's version of Anni was socially awkward. Unable to make small talk. The kind of person who memorized etiquette books and, when appropriate, recited from them.

"Daniel," Anni said, interrupting the guest—*interrupting him!*—and holding out her fist. He bumped it, which was clearly a Nerd Cruise thing that Larkin didn't yet understand. "Good to see you!" Her voice stumbled, then tumbled through the next set of sentences. "We should get together sometime and catch up. This is my friend Larkin Day, she's new, she's a theater director, and these are her boyfriend and her family, and of course you know Elliott."

Daniel, who had a blue porkpie hat and a deck of cards poking out of his shirt pocket, was the magician Elliott had met the first time he went on the cruise. The magician neuroscientist, if Larkin remembered correctly. That made Moira, who was sitting next to him with a pair of knitting needles and making patterns out of a ball of variegated yarn, *the magician neuroscientist's wife*. Anni had mentioned her before. She'd mentioned them both, when she told Larkin how she and Elliott had met—and why she and Elliott had spent more than ten years apart before getting back together.

"Scarbo," Daniel said. It had once been Elliott's stage name. Anni had given it to him the first time they fell in love. "Are you still working?"

"Always," Elliott said.

"Magic or tech?"

"Any sufficiently advanced technology is indistinguishable from magic," Elliott replied, quietly.

"Are you still thinking about teaching?" Moira asked, looking at Elliott as she worked her yarn.

"Always," Elliott said again. He seemed more nervous, in front of them, than Anni did. This might have had something to do with the ill-fated television career Daniel had pushed Elliott towards. It was a long story, and it had ended badly—but then Anni and Elliott had reconnected and bought a farmhouse, so it might actually have ended well.

"Elliott is building a scalable, pattern-based tutoring system," Anni said, "with an emphasis on 1:1 knowledge transfer."

That was when Larkin understood that Anni hadn't really changed. Part of Anni was trying to change, just like the rest of them—and part of that change involved setting up a conversation with a man she could not stand, just so the rest of them would benefit—but the rest of Anni was leaning on the systems that had helped her navigate the world thus far.

"I'd love to hear more," Moira said. The patterns kept repeating, under her needles. "I stopped teaching when it all went online. So hard to connect with people."

"That's the problem I'm trying to solve," Elliott said.

Daniel nodded. "Let's continue this conversation," he said. "Not right now, because we're waiting to hear when we can get settled in." He gestured towards a pile of hand luggage that included a gold-trimmed magician's case, a cruise-branded tote bag filled with even more yarn, and a medical-grade cooler. "Tomorrow, maybe, or Tuesday. I'll call you. What stateroom?"

"Verandah 213," Elliott said.

"213," Daniel repeated, memorizing the number. "The two of you, on the thirteenth cruise." He eyed Anni, carefully, before settling his gaze on her lanyard. "Good to know you're not triskaidekaphobic!"

"There's no reason to be superstitious," Anni said, crossing her arms over her chest, "unless you're interested in sustaining irrational behaviors in order to maintain a shared culture."

"There are plenty of rational reasons to walk around ladders and open umbrellas outdoors," Elliott countered. This was also a repeat; the two of them had carried this rapport through the Cedar Rapids Airport, and Anni was relying on Elliott to help her hold the current conversation until they could put it down.

"But there's no rational reason to be afraid of a thirteenth cruise," Anni said, reciting the riposte she had previously provided.

"I agree," Daniel said, assuming the conclusion. He nodded, again, and tipped his porkpie hat. "Good to see you both."

He hadn't even looked at Larkin or Josephine or Claire —and Ed had already turned his focus towards someone else.

"Is that Grandmaster Trey?" he whispered to Larkin, tilting his head towards a thin Black man with a thick gray Afro.

"I don't know," Larkin whispered back. Anni and Elliott were walking away from the Special Guest tables, as etiquette suggested after being dismissed. Claire and Josephine were following them. Ed was pushing forward, squeezing himself between the seats, holding out his hand.

"Hi," he said. "I'm a huge fan."

"Hey," the Black man said, turning his hand into a fist and letting Ed bump it. "They say we gotta do it this way, you know, because of the norovirus."

"Right," Ed said.

Oh, Larkin thought. *That's why.*

"Bunch of white nerds don't think you can get norovirus on the backside of your hand," the man continued, laughing. "Sit down. First time I've seen a brother all day who wasn't wearing a uniform. Where are you from?"

Elliott, who was nearly as observant as Larkin was, had turned around. "Looks like Ed's found a new friend," he said, quietly. "Don't let him stay too long."

"I won't," Larkin said. "Who is he, though? Grandmaster Trey?"

"He's an old-school hip-hop artist," Elliott explained, "back when everyone was still figuring out how to invent an entirely new kind of music. Trey was working with three turntables and three microphones. Cut one record, and then he went and got a computer science degree at U of I." Then he laughed, just softly enough for Larkin to hear. "I love his shirt."

Grandmaster Trey was wearing a T-shirt that read *Drop mics, not tables.* Larkin didn't get it. There was so much, about this cruise, that she didn't get.

She did, however, follow Elliott's advice to detach Ed from Grandmaster Trey—after scanning the room, one more time, for the man who could ruin their vacation. Not that she knew what she'd say if she saw the curly-headed, clever-minded Jay Malhotra. *Hello? How are you? Did you book a ticket on this cruise specifically to mess with me, and if so, can you let me know how you are planning to do it in advance?* She knew that Jay liked to play games with people, and she also knew that she was already one move behind—so she slipped in next to Ed and whispered, just loud enough for the Grandmaster to hear, "We probably shouldn't stay too long. I know Mom wants to get settled into her stateroom."

She watched Grandmaster Trey look her over. He was more subtle about it than most people, and he kept whatever he thought of her behind his smile. "You'd better not keep your girl's mama waiting," he said to Ed. "I don't want to be the cause of any trouble."

Then Trey winked at Larkin. It was so friendly that she couldn't help but be honest with him. "No," she said, "it's not that. Mom's fine. I was just making something up so we wouldn't take up too much of your time."

"I know," Trey said. "I saw you talking with that skinny white boy. He told you to come get your man before he wore out his welcome."

"He also said he liked your T-shirt," Larkin said. She could tell that Grandmaster Trey liked her, even if it was only because she was adjacent to Ed, and she wanted him to like Elliott too. "He thought it was a good joke. I don't know what it means."

Trey looked at Ed. "Do you know what it means?"

"Yes," Ed said, "but that's only because I used to read *XKCD*." He gestured over his shoulder to Elliott. "Our friend Elliott is the one who knows SQL."

"Him and half the nerds on this boat," Trey said. "Why do you think I wore it?" He looked at Larkin. "Would you have paid any attention to me if you thought I was just an old Black musician?"

"I like Black musicians," Larkin said. "I'm dating one."

"But you don't know who I am or what I've done, and neither do most of the people in this room, including most of the people *at this table*," Trey said. "So I put on this shirt, because it's got a programming joke on it, and maybe that'll get people to not skip my gig." He looked, carefully, at Larkin. "If you weren't dating Dr. Ed Jackson, would you have voluntarily gone to a hip-hop concert?"

"I flew across the country to see the original Broadway cast—"

Grandmaster Trey laughed. "Don't even say it." He turned to Ed. "Make sure she doesn't miss my set, and make sure you let me buy you a drink tonight." He wrote a few numbers on a napkin and passed them to Ed. "That's the passcode for the performers' lounge. Don't make me regret sharing it with you." He laughed again. "Now get out of here before the rest of your white friends come to drag you away."

Ed stood, starry-eyed, and let Larkin lead him towards the dining room doors. "I cannot believe that just happened," Ed whispered. "Did you know that Grandmaster Trey worked on one of the first MOOGs?"

"Tell me later," Larkin said, whispering back. "You can

explain all the acronyms once we're on our private balcony."

Then she kissed him—a current of contact, her lips against his cheeks—while watching her mother watch. Dr. Josephine Day liked Dr. Ed Jackson. She'd hired him, back when she was still the Dean of Howell College and Ed was still a recent PhD looking for a tenure-track job. Now Josephine and Claire were waiting for Larkin and Ed, impatient and delighted with the interaction.

"Come on, you two," Claire said. "I want to see the stateroom we aren't staying in."

Anni had been able to exchange her cruise loyalty points for a two-room verandah cabin that slept four people. She'd invited Larkin and Ed to join her, first because Larkin was her best friend and second because Larkin had just solved two murders and one attempted murder while simultaneously directing *Romeo and Juliet* for the Pratincola Shakespeare Festival. "The two of you get the bedroom," Anni had said, making both the plans and the decisions. "Elliott and I get the living room with the retractable bunkbeds, so I can practice the piano and Elliott can practice his magic."

Josephine and Claire had joined the group, booking a less-expensive cabin deep within the bowels of the ship, after Claire had learned that popular fantasy author Adamantine Darcy would be headlining the Special Guest lineup. While Larkin hadn't necessarily been thrilled that her mother and her mother's girlfriend were joining her on the first vacation she'd taken in nearly a decade—the cross-country flight to see *Hamilton* being the last trip that could even *technically* count as a break—she was secretly glad to have Officer Claire Novak on board. If Jay were planning anything that required legal interference, Claire would know what to do.

Claire would also know what *not* to do. "Don't engage," she had told Josephine, back when a group of Howell College students were leaving harassing signs on Larkin's mother's front lawn. "Every time you respond, you show the instigator exactly how much work they have to do to get a response."

Larkin wondered if Jay knew how much work she was already doing. She wondered if he expected her to respond in a certain way, and what he might do if she didn't. She wondered if she should say something to Claire or to Anni —*not to Ed, though, definitely not to Ed*—even though she already knew that both of them would offer the same good advice. "Ignore him," Claire would say. "Especially," Anni would add, "because we don't even know for sure that he's your nemesis. That was something you said, not something he said."

This was correct. Larkin had said to Anni: *I think Jay is my nemesis.*

All Jay had ever said, to Larkin, was: *My mother told me not to fall in love with you.*

So she kissed Ed again, and squeezed his hand, and said, to her friends: "Sorry we took so long."

"I met Grandmaster Trey," Ed said, still a little dazed. "He wants to buy me a drink."

"I want to meet Adamantine Darcy," Claire said. "But she doesn't drink. I read that on her website."

"She drinks *something*," Josephine said. "The two of you could have a cup of tea together."

Larkin watched Anni and Elliott exchange glances. "I think that our previous interaction with Daniel and Moira Pennington may have given you the wrong impression," Elliott said. "Most people on the ship don't get to spend any significant time with the Special Guests."

"You could get her to sign your books, though," Anni

said. "Adamantine Darcy's doing a signing line on Wednesday, right after she finishes her lecture on AI in sci-fi and fantasy."

"I know," Claire said. "That's why I brought her first book. She called it *How Now, Horatio*, because it hadn't yet become the *Time Tangent Gentleman* series. I bought it at a library book sale, before I knew how rare it was. I'm pretty sure they didn't know, or they wouldn't have sold it to me for fifty cents." Claire turned to Josephine. "Should I have brought all of my *TTG* books? Would she have signed all of them?"

"We couldn't have carried all of them," Josephine said. "I've seen your collection. There are forty books in the *Time Tangent Gentleman* series!"

"Forty-one," Claire said, "not counting the last one, which she's finishing right now." Larkin watched Elliott nudge his head towards hers. The six of them were blocking the path, and he wanted her to use her theater directing skills to move everyone aside—so Larkin took a big step to the right, and trusted *kinesthetic response* to do the rest.

Ed followed automatically. Elliott followed because he knew what they were doing. Anni followed because she saw Elliott doing it. Larkin's mother followed because she always had one eye on her daughter, and Claire, who was still going on about Adamantine Darcy's process—"She's got eighty pages left to write, and she's bringing her manuscript on the ship!"—remained where she was, her square shoulders and socked sandals forming a compact rectangle in front of the dining room's double doors.

Which was how—and why—Claire Novak and Adamantine Darcy met. The octogenarian author and her quadragenarian assistant entered through the double doors as Claire was extending her hands to demonstrate the ways in which Darcy's titular Gentleman tangented through time. Her right hand connected with Adamantine's left shoulder, knocking the author off balance. The woman gripped her cane and remained upright, but her octagonal glasses slipped from her eyes and ears and landed, silently, in the thick red carpet.

That was why—and how—Claire didn't know not to step on them.

CHAPTER 3

"Attention, all passengers," came the announcement, as Claire realized what she'd done. "We would like to welcome you aboard the MS *Kalmerende Zeeën*, courtesy of Dutch Cruise International, and invite you to join us on the Lido Deck for complimentary Champagne."

The voice was clipped and ship-shape; probably prerecorded. The voice that followed was not.

"Hello nerds!" This was a man, not quite middle-aged, with a cadence that suggested he'd made a lot of streaming videos in the early 2000s. "I know that most of you are either hiding from the sun or soaking up the last few hours of free internet you'll get for a week, but let me reiterate that you really should visit the Lido Deck and take advantage of some of that complimentary bubbly. I can't say for sure whether it is from the Champagne region of France, but it is going straight to the Champagne region of my head!"

"Who is that?" Larkin whispered to Anni.

"Xavier Torres," Anni whispered back. "He ran a math channel called *Solve for Xavier*. Now he runs the cruise."

Larkin had not spent any of her considerable time online watching math channels—but she had spent enough time with actors, influencers, and academics to get this guy's idea. "He's incredibly good-looking, isn't he."

"I couldn't say," Anni said.

"I could." This was Adamantine. She had righted herself, placing her left hand firmly against the curve at the top of her cane. It wasn't a typical curve, Larkin noticed; it was a sideways S, with Adamantine's curled fingers forming a clean line between peak and valley. "Francis Xavier Torres is more than typically attractive, if you are the kind of person who is attracted to symmetry. Unmarried, if you're interested—but no, you're not." She looked from Anni to Larkin, from Elliott to Ed, from Josephine to Claire. "None of you are, although two of you are unfortunately star-struck and one of you is star-struck *with me*." She stared at Claire. "Literally."

"I'm sorry," Claire said, her posture shifting into military precision. "Ma'am. Adamantine. Miss Darcy. I mean —ma'am—I did not mean to strike you."

"What is your name?" Adamantine asked.

"Claire Novak."

She turned to her assistant, who had picked the pair of glasses out of the carpet and was carefully eyeing the lenses. "Tom, please ensure that I do not collide with Claire Novak in the future, under any circumstances. Reroute me, if necessary, to prevent interaction."

The assistant, whose badge read *Eliza*, handed the author her octagonal glasses. "They should still work," she said. "There's a hairline crack in the left lens, so maybe only put them on when you need to use them."

"Thank you," Adamantine said. "I assume these people

are also in Claire Novak's traveling party?" She gestured towards Ed, Josephine, Claire, and Anni—but her hand stopped at Elliott. "I recognize you," she said.

Elliott was used to this. "You might have seen my television show."

The woman held her glasses up to her eyes. "Tom, what was this man's television show?"

"He used to be Scarbo," the assistant answered, holding out her fist for Elliott to bump. "The magician."

"You can call me Elliott," he said. "I assume we call you Eliza?"

"You assume correctly."

"Tom," Adamantine said, removing her glasses and folding the frames into the pocket of her crisp collared shirtdress, "please track the locations of all six passengers in front of me and ensure that none of their paths cross mine." The right lens of her glasses—the only part still visible—flashed green and then red.

"Sorry," Eliza said to Elliott. "It's probably for the best."

"It'll be a good test, anyway," he said. "Do you want me to push it to its limits?"

"I think we've been pushed enough for one day," she said, before placing her hand gently on Adamantine's shoulder and guiding her through another automatic doorway. Elliott followed, pausing in front of the closed glass doors.

"It works," he said—but Larkin was the only one who heard him say it. Josephine put her hand on Claire's shoulder, pulling her close. Anni reached into her canvas bag and handed Claire a packet of tissues. Ed looked to Larkin, who looked to her mother, who nodded—and all of them left, together, for the staterooms.

"Shouldn't we get our free glass of Champagne?"

Claire asked. They were halfway down a nondescript hallway; she was tucking a snot-covered tissue into her pocket and—Larkin understood— trying to stay on script. "Because it's free?"

"We can get that taken care of," Elliott said, as he tapped his badge against a door handle. The sensor, having recognized him, switched from red to green—and the door to Verandah 213 opened.

Inside was everything Larkin had been dreaming of. Literally, night after night, after watching enough videos of the MS *Kalmerende Zeeën*'s Verandah-class staterooms to allow her subconscious to envision the interior. The room smelled of coconut and sandalwood and strong Dutch soap. The carpet was thick enough to absorb drips of seawater and grains of sand, taking the wet and grit from foot to pile and yielding only to the weekly vacuum. The walls, two of which were mirrored, reflected art of both European and African mastery. The third wall was a window, with four white deck chairs waiting on the other side.

"Let's go out onto the balcony," Larkin said, turning to Ed and taking his hand—and then the doorbell rang. "Vacations shouldn't have doorbells," she whispered to her boyfriend, as Anni checked the peephole, raised the deadbolt, and opened the stateroom door.

It was Handy, the cruise ship employee who had guided them to the Super Elite Status check-in line. "Hello, Miss Morgan and guests!" he said. "I have come to see if everything is as it should be. Are you enjoying your relaxing cruise vacation?"

"I was," Larkin whispered, "for about three seconds."

"Yes," Anni said. "Thank you." She opened the lid of the digital piano and pushed the power button. A series of lights turned on, and she turned back to Handy. "Everything appears to be in working order."

"Is there anything I can get for you while I am here?" Handy asked—or began to ask, before he was interrupted by another all-ship announcement.

"Solve this equation," Xavier Torres said, his voice filling the stateroom.

"Vacations shouldn't have intercoms," Larkin heard Ed whisper, as Xavier continued his one-sided conversation.

"What do you get when you divide two hundred Champagne bottles by one thousand, one hundred sixty-three nerds? Not enough bubbly, am I right?"

He paused for a laugh. Larkin wondered if he got one.

"Good news," Xavier continued. "I just heard from the management team that every last passenger is now on board, which means we are on schedule for an amazing week of music, math, magic, and anything else you nerds can come up with! I've already stopped by the 24-hour Game Room, and it is packed! Wow! This is going to be the best cruise ever!"

"Let me guess," Larkin whispered to Ed. "He says that every cruise."

"But the bad news," Xavier said, "is that we're nearly out of complimentary Champagne—so get on up to the Lido Deck and get your free drink while you still can!"

"Is Champagne a *drink*?" Josephine asked. "I know that one drinks it, but I've always thought of Champagne—*real* Champagne, of course—as an experience."

"An experience that we're missing out on," Claire said, still sniffling, "because I wasn't aware of my immediate surroundings."

Larkin wondered, suddenly, if that was bothering Claire as much as the subsequent interaction with Adamantine. Officer Claire Novak, trained in situational awareness, had assumed she was in a situation that allowed her to drop her guard. For the first time in—well, Larkin didn't know, but it was an amount of time that could be counted in months, if not years. Claire had embraced this new world, flinging out her hands just like *Titanic* and striking her favorite author.

"Does your friend want some complimentary Champagne?" Handy asked. "I can go straight to the Lido Deck and bring back a bottle." He spoke not to Anni, but to Elliott. "We will consider it magic?"

Elliott took a step forward and placed one hand on Handy's shoulder. Even Larkin could see how this misdirection worked, but Handy still looked delighted to find the twenty-dollar bill in his pants pocket. "Thank you, sir!" he said, turning immediately towards the door. "I will be back before you know it!"

He left. Anni replaced the deadbolt. Josephine thanked Elliott. Claire wiped her face and attempted to smile.

"I should ask, right?" Larkin whispered to Ed.

"Ask what?" Ed whispered back.

Larkin tried to think of the best way to phrase it. "I thought it was supposed to be an all-expenses-paid cruise," she said aloud.

"It is," Anni said. "Unless you want to buy souvenirs, go on excursions, or drink alcoholic beverages."

"Or soda," Elliott said. The freestyle machines, which blinked and fizzed at every intersection they'd passed, charged fifteen dollars for twenty ounces.

"But you keep giving Handy money," Larkin said. She was trying very hard not to say *bribe*. "And he keeps giving you special treatment."

"That is correct," Anni said. She opened her suitcase and began arranging her neatly folded clothing into a series of drawers that were so well integrated with the wall that Larkin wouldn't have known they were there if she hadn't spent the past two months watching Verandah-class stateroom videos. "We budgeted one hundred dollars per day, for Handy."

"Why?"

Anni, having finished her own small suitcase, opened Elliott's. She looked towards him. He nodded, and she transferred the pile of shirts, shorts, and underwear into the drawer without disrupting a single wrinkle. "Because we want special treatment," she said.

"That sounds—" Larkin was trying very hard not to say *disgusting*. "Bad."

"It sounds very good, if you're Handy," Elliott said. "How much money do you think he's making? Our tips help him provide for his family back home."

"He has children?" Josephine asked. Handy was clearly younger than all of them. Probably a decade younger than Larkin, who—as the youngest person in the room—was thirty-six-and-a-half years old.

"Maybe," Elliott said. "Or parents, or brothers and sisters. Maybe he's helping someone in his family afford college. Maybe he's helping someone in his family afford food."

"So he has an incentive to help us," Anni said, "and we have an incentive to help him." She zipped up the two suitcases and tucked them under the sofa. "I've done the cruise the other way, where you don't bring a stack of twenty-dollar bills on board. It's perfectly fine, until you want a bottle of water or need a fresh bar of soap." She turned off the power to her digital piano and closed the lid. "Which you'll get, eventually. The cruise gives you exactly what you pay for, and soap and water are part of your all-inclusive package. But people like Handy are going to serve the people who tip well before they serve everybody else."

"*Well* before they serve everybody else," Ed said. "Pun intended."

"Exactly," Anni said. "And I don't want to spend my cruise thirsty and grungy."

"I don't know if this is capitalism at its worst, or socialism at its best," Josephine said. She, like her daughter, had begun gravitating towards the sun-dappled balcony. "May I?" she asked, with one hand on the door handle.

"Of course," Anni said. "The two of you are welcome to share our balcony at any time."

"We'll take you to the main office and ask them to add our stateroom to your badges," Elliott said. "That way, you can unlock the stateroom door and come in and out whenever you like."

Josephine had already figured out how to unlock the balcony door. "Give me the sunlight and the sea," she said, stepping out into the salty, humid air, "and who can take my heaven from me?"

"I don't know which poet you're quoting," Claire said, "but they left out a few words." She pulled herself into a form of composure—they all, except for Josephine, watched her do it—and briskly walked towards the thick glass doors. "Give me the sunlight, the sea, and the woman I love."

"Good," Ed whispered to Larkin. "She's back on board."

"Pun intended," Larkin whispered, squeezing his hand.

———

Larkin, following Claire's example, was on board with everything that happened over the remainder of the afternoon. Handy returned with the Champagne, which they drank—or, in Josephine's case, *experienced*. Then Xavier announced that it was time for the mandatory Lifeboat Drill, and all 1,163 nerds assembled at their designated lifeboat stations to pretend, for an hour, that the docked ship was sinking.

"Every time we hear someone say *it's like Titanic*," Larkin whispered, to Anni, "you should give Handy another twenty."

"I didn't budget for that," Anni whispered back. Then she turned to her boyfriend, who was pulling the ends of his ginger hair into a palm-sized ponytail. "Elliott!" she said, pitching her voice to match the classic film. "This is where we first met!"

"Best thing that ever happened to me," Elliott said, "followed by the worst."

"Daniel Pennington meant well," Anni said. The porkpie-hatted magician had, at the time, considered himself a mentor. He had pushed Elliott towards television, deciding it would be the best thing for both of them. Anni, at the time, had decided not to be the girlfriend who held Elliott back.

"We could have had an extra ten years together," Elliott said, shading his eyes and tucking an errant strand of hair behind his ear.

"And instead, we both worked hard and built our careers and saved our money and now we have a farmhouse," Anni said, "and we're developing a pedagogy so we can start a school, and we might not have had any of this, if we'd done something else with those ten years."

Larkin thought about what she'd done with the past ten years, most of which she'd spent mastering and doctoring her life in an attempt to become an academic. Now the only three letters after her name were ABD, her six thousand-word dissertation last opened six months ago. She knew she'd never finish it. She hoped, one day, to finish paying off her student loans.

But she had a job, now—well, she sort of had a job, since her stint as Interim Artistic Director of the Pratincola Summer Shakespeare Festival had not yet resolved into a full-time appointment, although Sahil Malhotra assured her that the Board was very enthusiastic about keeping her on. In fact, they'd already hired her to direct *The Winter's Tale*, next summer, while they conducted a national search for the person who might end up replacing her.

"Not that we want anyone to replace you," Sahil had said. "It's merely a formality."

"Tell that to the hundreds of people who are filling out their applications," Jay had said. Jay Malhotra was Sahil's son. The cynical surgical resident had spent his summer vacation hanging around the Shakespeare Festival, ostensibly to spend time with his fiancée—Larkin had seen the ring, heard the announcement—but insensibly spent his afternoons in his father's office, holding court over Sahil and Larkin's conversations.

You're not paying attention, Jay had told her.

It had been opening night, *Romeo and Juliet*, an hour before curtain.

What do you want me to pay attention to? Larkin had asked.

Me, Jay had said—the word appearing not on his lips, but in his eyes.

Then he'd gone back to Chicago. The incisions he'd made in Larkin's life had healed. She had started referring to him as her nemesis, since Larkin and Jay had yet to have an interaction that didn't end badly, and then she had stopped referring to him at all. He was far enough away that Larkin didn't have to think about him.

But she kept thinking about him anyway.

And now he was here.

On the ship.

By a lifeboat—but not *this* lifeboat, which was all that mattered. If the MS *Kalmerende Zeeën* were going to sink—and it wouldn't, Anni had already assured her of the statistical impossibilities—Larkin would go down with Ed by her side.

———

Later, after they had stowed Josephine and Claire in their tiny interior cabin—no windows, not even a porthole, although the cruise line had thoughtfully hung a portrait of the horizon above the double bed—and returned to Verandah 213 to dress for dinner and check their emails one last time, Larkin was finally able to join Ed on their shared balcony.

"What's a MOOG?" she asked. "You said you'd explain all the acronyms to me."

"It's an early synthesizer," he said. "Developed by Robert Moog, which means it isn't actually an acronym."

"See?" Larkin said. She was wearing a dress that her mother had picked out for her, which meant that it was blue and flowing and had pink-and-white flowers printed all over it. "I'm learning."

Ed was also wearing blue, pairing his freshly steamed shirt and trousers with a pair of tan boat shoes and a pink bow tie. Anni had told them that the other nerds made a big deal out of dressing for dinner, and they didn't want to disappoint. "Some of the most brilliant minds in the music industry worked on that project," he said. "Do you know who Wendy Carlos is?"

"Nope," Larkin said.

"Well, you probably know her work," Ed said. "She did the score to *The Shining*, the Kubrick one, and a bunch of other stuff, really famous stuff, to prove that the MOOG was just as real as any other instrument. People were being jerks, you know, about how classical music only counted if it came from a human, not a transistor. It had to be fingers and air, not voltage and switches. Definitely not ones and zeroes, which came later."

"Right," Larkin said. She could see Ed, in his classroom, telling this story to his students. She loved that he was telling it to her.

"But at the time, which would have been the late 1960s and early 1970s, Wendy Carlos took the MOOG and the orchestra and, well—"

"Synthesized them?" Larkin said. She knew how Ed's mind worked.

"Pun intended," Ed said. "But you knew that."

"I didn't know any of it," Larkin said. They were facing east, away from the sunset; all they could see were the sea and the stars. "That's why I asked."

"She's a trans woman," Ed said. "Wendy Carlos." He shifted his weight with the ship. "I never know whether I'm supposed to say that or not. She didn't tell people until after she'd done all of the work that made her famous. Everyone assumed she was a woman, which, I mean, she *was* a woman, but—"

"Dealing with the transistor-exclusionary radical musicians was hard enough," Larkin said.

"Right," Ed said.

They stood, side by side, as another pair of stars twinkled into visibility—and then they heard the familiar crackle of the all-ship intercom.

"Good evening, nerds!"

"He broadcasts on the balcony?" Larkin asked, as Xavier informed the entire ship that dinner was about to be served.

"There's a speaker," Ed said, pointing. "I wonder if it has an off switch."

"I wonder whether we could pay Handy to destroy it," Larkin said.

". . .and proceed to the Main Dining Room," Xavier continued, his voice rattling the glass, shattering all hope of a quiet, relaxing evening. "We can't wait to see what you're wearing!"

Larkin turned around. Anni and Elliott were clearly visible through the glass doors. They were also—*very clearly*—dressed as chessboards. Anni had found checkered fabric, or maybe she'd had their outfits custom-made, and Elliott's jacket and her gown were both covered in green-and-white squares. She had pinned the white pieces into her hair, like a tiara; Elliott was wearing the black pieces on his shoulders like epaulets.

"Anni!" Larkin said, opening the balcony doors and pushing her way into the stateroom. "When you told me that people *dressed for dinner*, what exactly did you mean?"

They found out soon enough, as a thousand nerds—"one thousand, one hundred sixty-three," Anni reminded them —descended the Grand Staircase, paused for photographs with Ismael, and took their places in the Main Dining Room. The room, which had seemed wide when Larkin first saw it, had since been crammed so tightly with tables that Larkin had no idea how the servers could squeeze through. To her relief, she quickly realized that she and Ed were not the only nerds dressed in "normie clothes," which was a phrase she overheard from a nerd dressed as a TARDIS—but most of the attendees had chosen to costume themselves, dressing in allegiance with a fandom or a special interest. There were historically authentic doublets, futuristic space leotards, an abundance of super-heroes and wizards, and one man who had a fully-functioning model train running in circles around his torso.

And then, once they had all been seated—

"Please stand, or raise a hand," Xavier said, his voice coming out of a tiny speaker embedded in the centerpiece of every table, "as we welcome our Special Guests!"

Larkin stood. She was tall enough that she could see over most of the costumes; she spotted the man she assumed was Francis Xavier Torres—who was beautifully symmetrical, Adamantine's description had been accurate —holding a microphone and gesturing to each guest in turn. The shouts and applause would have drowned out the names, had the speakers not been distributed throughout the dining room; as it was, the setup allowed Xavier and the nerds to amplify each other, and Larkin saw more than one nerd reach into a purse or bag and pull out a pair of noise-canceling headphones.

Larkin also saw—and this was what she wanted to talk to Anni about, later—that none of the Special Guests were in costume. Professionals had the privilege of dressing as themselves, because they had already done the work of becoming someone worth looking at. It made Larkin, who had done enough work to have retained an Interim Artistic Director position for two consecutive summers, feel a little better about wearing the dress her mother had bought her. *I don't need to be a nerd*, Larkin thought, applauding just hard enough to look as if she were part of the group. *I don't even need to be a Special Guest. I can be Larkin Day, and that will be enough. It has to be, because I can't be anyone else.*

When Adamantine entered, followed by her assistant, Claire turned to Josephine and said something that Larkin couldn't hear. Larkin watched her mother put her arm around Claire's shoulders—both of them dressed in normie clothes, neither of them uncomfortable about it—and then Larkin realized that she was not only *enough*, as *herself*, but also that she had enough professional skills to solve Claire's problem.

You know how to get people to do what you want, Jay had said. *But when you do it, nobody thinks you're an asshole.*

She would not think of Jay. She would not even look for him. She'd learned, last summer, that she could choose where she put her attention, and—

"And if you'll all turn your attention towards the port side of the ship," Xavier continued, interrupting her thoughts, "you'll be able to watch the beautiful Florida coastline disappear."

The ship's horn hooted, a single long blast that was louder than anything they'd yet heard.

"That's right," Xavier said, "we are leaving the dock! As soon as we finish our dinner service, I hope you'll join me on the Lido Deck for our Sail Away Dance Party! Will it be Enya or Styx this year? You'll have to find out!"

Larkin waited just long enough for the nerds to stop laughing—and then she started thinking again. "Ed," she whispered, as a server pushed a cart of entrées towards her and she nodded towards the plate that looked like it had chicken, "do you still have the passcode to the Performers' Lounge?"

CHAPTER 4

arkin and Ed entered the lounge together—Ed providing the passcode not to a lock, but to a uniformed Dutch bouncer—and after exchanging a few pleasantries with Grandmaster Trey, Larkin gracefully exited the conversation.

"I'll leave you to it," she said, squeezing her boyfriend's hand. He knew what she had come to do and was happy to discuss turntables and vacuum tubes until she was done.

Larkin was also—finally—happy. She was, just as she had been last summer at the Shakespeare Festival, standing in a room full of people who did what they did for a living. It was the kind of room that had excited her ever since she was five years old and had figured out that all of the actors in a college production of *Camelot* were *real people*, who had learned how to pretend to be Arthur and Guinevere and Lancelot and Merlin so well that everyone else believed it was the truth. By the time she was seven-years-old she'd figured out that it wasn't quite true, nobody really believed that a college sophomore was actually a centenarian wizard, but by the time she was ten she'd put together what was actually going on. The sophomore found the one true thing about Merlin—not that he was a wizard, which was only ever a metaphor, but that he could see both the sequences and consequences of his actions—and shared it with the audience.

It was what Larkin had written down, on a piece of paper, when she was in the seventh grade: *I want to work in the theater because it is the best way to tell the truth.*

It took Larkin until she was thirty-five years old—after moving from Los Angeles to Pratincola, connecting with a community, reconnecting with her mother, and solving her first murder—to start learning that there were even better ways of telling the truth.

The best of which was, simply, *to tell it.*

"Hello," Larkin said, sitting herself on the edge of a coffee table. She faced Adamantine Darcy and Moira Pennington, the two of them sharing a sofa with Moira's needles and yarn.

"Tom," Adamantine asked, "who is this?"

The assistant, whose badge still read *Eliza*, said nothing. Her asymmetric silver hair was the brightest thing in the dimly-lit room; the kind of metallic dye job that came not from a nine dollar bottle, but a $900 salon appointment.

"I'm Larkin—"

"You're Larkin Day," Adamantine said, as if Larkin had interrupted her. "I am not supposed to be in the same room as you." She turned to Eliza. "Why was she not rerouted?"

Eliza looked from Larkin's badge to Adamantine's glasses. "Because the passcode is analog," she said, opening a notebook and quickly writing something down. "They don't scan badges at this door." She closed her notebook. "I'm sorry, I should have thought of that."

Larkin expected Adamantine to reject this apology; instead, she accepted it. "We are all learning to think in new ways," she said. Then she turned back to Larkin. "Why are you here? You are not a Special Guest. You're a theater director." The creases in her forehead sharpened. "You're also a detective."

"Amateur detective," Larkin said. "Professional director."

"What kind of detective?" Moira asked. Her hands moved silently, continuously.

The kind of detective who cannot wait until nobody ever asks her this question ever again. "It isn't important."

"It may be the most important thing about you," Adamantine said. "Larkin Day solves murders," she explained to Moira. "It seems that one of her previous cases was only a metaphorical murder, since it only involved the destruction of an online identity, but otherwise she has been quite successful at identifying those who might commit homicide."

"Only after they've already committed homicide," Larkin corrected quietly. "I haven't, like, been able to prevent any murders."

"My sources indicate that you prevented exactly one death," Adamantine said, "although one never knows if such information is to be fully trusted." She looked at Eliza again. "Write that down." Then she looked back at Larkin. "You feel guilty," Adamantine said. "Something's troubling you."

"No," Larkin said. *Tell the truth.* "I mean, yes, something is troubling me, but it's not me who feels guilty. It's my friend Claire Novak. She bumped into you earlier today. It was an accident, and I wanted to ask—"

Adamantine suddenly looked confused. "Somebody bumped into me?"

"I mean, it was more like you bumped into her," Larkin said, keeping her voice casual and companionable. "If the rules for traffic accidents also applied to people, your insurance would have picked up the tab for the collision. But Claire's the one who feels bad. She's been crying—"

"Tom," Adamantine said, digging a pair of octagon-shaped spectacles out of her shawl-covered bosom and tilting her head towards the ceiling, "help me recall—what was the name?"

"Claire Novak," the assistant said.

"Thank you, Tom, *Claire Novak*."

Larkin looked at Eliza—because her name *was* Eliza—and then at Moira, who had stabbed her knitting needles into her ball of yarn and balanced it carefully in her lap. The woman reached down, stretching both hands into a patterned bag at her feet. Sorting its contents by touch. Selecting, and removing, a deck of well-worn tarot cards.

"I remember," Adamantine said. "It appears that I walked into her, although she was clearly blocking the way."

"Right," Larkin said, "and you told your assistant that you didn't want to have any contact with Claire for the rest of the cruise."

"I told Tom," Adamantine said.

"Right," Larkin said, again. "Claire feels really badly about everything, and she's been crying, and she owns all of your novels, I've seen them, and I wanted to ask if you would still let her come to your lecture and book signing on Wednesday."

Adamantine considered this. "You're doing this to assuage your guilt," she finally said.

"I'm doing it to help my friend," Larkin said—which was just as true as Adamantine's conclusion—"and to correct the record."

The famous author removed her octagonal glasses and stared at Larkin. "You are here when you have no reason to be here, which means that someone must have given you the passcode to the lounge."

"Yes," Larkin said, "we covered this already." She glanced at Eliza. "Something about analog."

"By process of elimination," Adamantine continued, scanning the room, "it appears that the young man sitting next to Walter Johnson Murray the third, otherwise known as Grandmaster Trey, must have given you the code that the Grandmaster gave him."

"He's my boyfriend," Larkin said. "The younger man, not Grandmaster Trey."

"Of course he is," Adamantine said. "It's obvious from the way he looks at you. It's also obvious, from the way you don't look at him, that—"

"Addie," Moira said, placing her hand on the author's arm, "let's let the cards tell the story."

The magician neuroscientist's wife nodded towards the tarot deck in the center of the coffee table. "Pick them up," she said to Larkin. "Hold them to your heart. Then shuffle them, as many times as you like."

Larkin had never touched a tarot deck before. The cards felt warm; slightly oily, like human skin. Like they were alive.

"I don't believe in tarot," Adamantine said, as Larkin touched the deck to the center of her chest. The dress her mother had bought for her was just low-cut enough for the deckle edges to brush her decolletage.

"You believe in artificial intelligence," Moira said. "Tarot is the same thing. It stores what we know and reveals it to us when we ask."

Larkin shuffled the deck seven times, the way Anni had taught her. "It takes seven shuffles before a deck is fully randomized," she explained, as Adamantine and Moira watched. "Otherwise, there are still clusters of cards that remain in predictable patterns."

"I read that article," Moira said, "but I think you'll find that tarot cards have meaning no matter how many times you attempt to depattern them."

Larkin finished the seventh shuffle. Moira's hand landed, rough as wool and cold as needles, on top of hers. "That's enough." The magician neuroscientist's wife slid the deck towards her. She turned over the top card, placing it to Larkin's left. "The Chariot," Moira said, as if it meant something.

Larkin looked at the card in front of her. The man on the chariot looked a bit like Elliott. The black-and-white sphinxes at the front had lipstick and breasts. "What does this mean?"

"The past," Moira said. "It often represents a decision. A choice that must be made, between two opposing forces." She turned over the second card, placing it directly in front of Larkin. "Death," she said, as if she'd known what it was going to be before she revealed it. "The present."

"Well," Larkin said, "at least I know that the death card doesn't really mean death." She pulled her face into a smile before pushing it towards Adamantine and Moira. "It's extremely statistically unlikely that I'll have to solve any murders on this cruise!"

"You solve murders?" Adamantine asked. Moira glanced at her, quickly and concernedly. "I meant to say," the author continued, "that you are very experienced at solving murder."

"Not really." This record also needed to be corrected. "I'm not like"—Larkin tried, quickly, to think of a detective who wasn't fictional—"Hercule Poirot."

"I never cared for that waffley Belgian," Adamantine said, putting her left hand on top of Moira's and extending her right hand to Larkin. "Would you like to have tea with me tomorrow? You might be able to help me with my current project."

Larkin wasn't quite sure how Adamantine had gotten from tarot to tea, and she wondered if she should ask at least one question about the project before agreeing to help —but she didn't want to give up her one chance at a negotiating advantage. "Only if you admit that you bumped into Claire, not the other way around," she said, taking and shaking Adamantine's hand, "and let her come to your book signing."

"Tom—" Adamantine began.

"I've got it," Eliza said, jotting in her notebook and reaching for her phone. She turned to Larkin. "What stateroom?"

"Verandah 213," Larkin said.

"We'll be in touch," the assistant said. Then Moira, gently, touched Larkin's knee. "There is still one more card," she said. "The future."

She placed the last card, face-up, on Larkin's right. It was covered in lightning bolts and fire. One person was diving towards what appeared to be a bottomless pit; the other was falling, headfirst, in the same direction. "The Tower," Moira said, with finality. She looked directly at Larkin. "If you proceed with the choices you are currently making, you will lose everything."

Adamantine laughed. It was an octogenarian laugh,

bone-shaking and skin-cracking. "This is the most ridiculous tarot reading I've ever seen," she said. "All Major Arcana cards? Death and the Tower? Moira, I expected better from you. The Ten of Swords, at least."

"We both saw the same thing," Moira said, holding out her hands as if she had no control over what had just happened. "The cards just told the story."

"Not the whole story," Adamantine said. She tapped her fingers, sharp-nailed and soft-knuckled, against the remaining cards. "Pick up the deck, Larkin Day. Turn it over. Let's see your Shadow Card."

Larkin did as she was told. The card at the bottom of the deck—the one that faced her, when she flipped it—showed a pair of people sharing a pair of cups. The woman was tall and dark-haired, like her. The man was tall and curly-haired, like Jay. A caduceus—the symbol of surgeons, of healing, of broken and restored hearts—hovered between them.

"The Shadow Card," Adamantine said, "reveals what you are most trying to hide."

Larkin stood up. She looked towards Ed, who was still talking and laughing with Grandmaster Trey.

"He doesn't know," Adamantine said. "Yet."

The ship lurched; Larkin's stomach clenched; she reached for the edge of a chair—Eliza's—and attempted to restore her equilibrium. "I'm sorry," she said, trying to think of what the truth was, action-reaction, sequence-consequence, *I get to choose where I put my attention*, "but I don't believe any of this."

She left the lounge, her stomach churning, her mind roiling, a cold sweat collecting under her arms and at the back of her neck. She told herself—she even told the Dutch bouncer—that she needed some fresh air.

What she needed—

What she wanted—

What she feared—

Was the man who stood against the railing as if he had been waiting for her.

"Larkin Day," Jaipal Malhotra said, smiling. "I wondered how long it would take for you to find me."

CHAPTER 5

arkin stared at Jay Malhotra. He was as tall as she was, which shouldn't matter—she had spent her entire postpubescent life telling herself it didn't matter—but it meant that she could look at him, eye to eye, without having to adjust. He was wearing a T-shirt with words on it, something she'd read later, after she'd won the contest and could drop her gaze.

Jay would blink first.

He had to.

They couldn't stand there staring at each other for the rest of their lives.

But Larkin understood—

As her stomach continued to churn and her eyes began to water—

That Jay Malhotra didn't have to do anything.

"What did you say?" she finally said, when the ship rolled just enough to shift her off balance. To push her towards the railing, which she grasped, gratefully, with both hands. *Force majeure* didn't count as losing. It didn't count as blinking. It didn't count as—

"Are you going to be sick?" Jay's hand was on her back. Concernedly. Clinically. He had never touched her before, and it felt both professional and impersonal. Maybe he wasn't here to torment her after all. Maybe none of it meant what she'd thought, when she saw him on the plane in Chicago. "Come, sit down," Jay said, leading Larkin to a pair of white-slatted deck chairs. "My mother insisted I pack ginger chews," he said, unzipping a pocket on his cargo pants. He was wearing expensive German sandals, the curly hairs on the ends of his toes poking out against the smooth, soft leather. She still hadn't read his T-shirt.

"How is Rupa?" Larkin asked, as she accepted and unwrapped a ginger candy. It was shaped like a baby, for some reason; soft and squishy and brown, like Jay would have been when he was born.

"My mother is doing well," Jay said. "She'd have told me to say hello, if she knew you were here." He looked at Larkin—a glance she felt rather than saw, as her eyes were fixed on the horizon. "Then she'd have told me to stay away from you."

"So stay away, then," Larkin said. "This ship has ten decks and a thousand nerds. We could go the entire week without seeing each other."

She heard Jay laugh. Then she felt another candy land, carefully and quietly, in her lap.

"If you don't want to see me," Jay said, "I'll leave."

Larkin hated the way Jay played games, taking words out of people's mouths and putting ideas into their heads. She'd seen him do it to his father, when they were working together to save the Shakespeare Festival. She'd seen him do it to Anni, before the two of them had a conversation that resolved into a truce. Now he wanted her to think that she was the one who wanted him next to her, on this deck chair, under the moonlight, eating his ginger babies.

"You are affianced," Larkin said. It was the best way to tell the truth without having to tell it.

"Actually," Jay said, "I'm not."

He said it as if he almost sounded sorry—although Larkin couldn't tell if Jay felt badly for himself, for his former fiancée, or for the families that would have benefited financially by the merger. The Malhotras and the Yangs had treated the engagement as a business arrangement, exchanging power for dowry, and Larkin could see —because she finally felt secure enough to turn her head— that Jay was recalling all of the actions that had gotten him both into and out of his predicament. She chewed her ginger and waited, letting him make the next move.

"You know I liked Beatrix," he said.

"I know you didn't love her," she said.

"You know I don't know if I can love anyone," Jay said.

That was the truth—and it was something they had both known since they first met. Jay operated the way he did because he knew how people put themselves together. He knew where they believed themselves to be whole. He saw the holes in their belief systems. He studied their outsides and understood their insides and asked himself, every time he cut or sutured, why he would not interact with the world in the same way.

"Then your mother doesn't have to worry about you being here with me," Larkin said. It was another truth—*told slant*, as Josephine Day would have put it. Larkin had not told her mother much about Jay. She hadn't thought she'd have to.

"I will tell my mother that her concern is unnecessary," Jay said. Then he laughed, his deep voice echoing against the endless sky. "But what are you going to tell Ed?"

"I'm not going to tell him anything," Larkin said, standing up. Whatever those ginger chews were supposed to do, they'd done—and she knew exactly what she needed to do next. "You're going to." She looked at Jay, drawing him off his deck chair with her gaze. His T-shirt had a slim silver starship printed on it, the rocket flames resolving into the words *I Need My Space*. "I know the passcode to the Performers' Lounge," Larkin said, "and we're going inside, and you have until we get through the door to figure out what you're going to say to my boyfriend."

———

"So it was all right?" Anni asked, the next morning.

"Of course it was," Larkin said. The two of them were on the Lido Deck, Larkin wrapped in a ship-branded bathrobe and Anni wearing a pair of shortie pajamas printed with sheet music. Larkin had heard Anni practicing the piano, when she woke up—the sun managing to work its way into Larkin's endocrine system despite her five-star blackout mask—and waited patiently until she could no longer hear the clicks and thumps of keys and pedals. Then she slipped out of bed, leaving Ed to snore his way through the morning, and asked Anni if she wanted to get a cup of herbal tea.

"I brought my own," Anni whispered, holding up a plastic baggie filled with teabags. "But let's go to the Lido Deck and get you some coffee."

The two of them had been drinking coffee and tea together for nearly two years. They'd discussed murder investigations, farmhouse renovations, and the best way for Larkin to pay off her student loans. Now—and Larkin couldn't believe how cliché they were sounding—they were talking about boys.

"Men," Anni had said, when Larkin had made the joke. "Ed and Elliott and Jay are all men, and we don't want to diminish them."

"But then I have to take them seriously," Larkin said, "and it's much more fun for me to complain about how Jay ruined my vacation."

"But you just said he didn't," Anni said. "You said that Jay went into the Performers' Lounge and said hello to Ed, and then he said he didn't want to get in the way of Ed and Grandmaster Trey's conversation, and then he said he hoped we could all get together for dinner sometime."

"Right," Larkin said, "and you remember what that was like the last time."

"You mean last summer?" Anni sipped her tea and watched as a family of nerds introduced a water-winged toddler to the shallow end of the pool. There weren't a lot of people on the Lido Deck, at eight thirty in the morning; the Sail Away Dance Party had still been going strong when Larkin and Ed finally left the Performers' Lounge and went back to the stateroom.

"Trey's going to teach me how to turntable," Ed had said—as if Larkin hadn't been sitting next to him for the past hour, listening to Grandmaster Trey give a one-person masterclass—"and I'm going to write a course proposal for a History of Hip-Hop seminar, we won't be able to get it on Howell College's schedule for the spring, but maybe for next fall, and he says he'll do a guest lecture. In person, if he can. If there's the budget for it."

"That's wonderful," Larkin had said. It had been. Ed hadn't mentioned Jay at all; it was as if their brief interaction had never happened.

"Last summer Jay was being pressured into an

arranged marriage," Anni said, "and he was doing everything he could to make himself as unattractive a prospect as possible."

That wasn't what Larkin remembered. She recalled an afternoon, in the Pratincola coffee shop, Jay balancing on two chair legs as he interrogated Elliott and Anni. Showing off for Larkin, the way boys did. Ignoring Ed completely.

"Jay and I had a conversation about it," Anni said, "after the engagement was dissolved. He apologized for being so antagonistic."

"Wait," Larkin said, "he apologized?"

"Yes," Anni said, "and he brought us a tomato plant."

"He came to the farmhouse?"

"Yes," Anni said again. "He helped Elliott install the porch swing. Then he asked if I would sit with him for a minute, because he had something he wanted to tell me."

"Did Elliott mind?"

Anni looked at Larkin. "Why would Elliott mind?"

"I don't know," Larkin said. "I think Ed would have minded."

Anni continued to look at Larkin. It was as if Larkin had said the wrong line, and she was waiting for the right one—and then Anni sipped her tea and continued the scene. "Jay asked me how I functioned so well. I asked him what he meant. He told me that I was like him, except I was on a spectrum, and he was facing one of two paths. I told him that if he was suggesting that I was aspie and he was ASPD, he was looking at the entire thing incorrectly."

"Wait, *what*?" Larkin asked. There was something about this ship that made everyone talk in acronyms, or words that sounded like acronyms. SQL, MOOG, ASPD. She was beginning to regret not having become a nerd when she had the chance.

"It doesn't matter," Anni said. "Jay was afraid that a psychological diagnosis was going to affect the way he interacted with people, and he was asking me how I had handled it."

"You have a psychological diagnosis?"

"I don't, actually," Anni said. She put her empty cup on the edge of a glass table; a cruise employee transferred it to a bus tub. "Thank you," Anni said, as the man disappeared. Then she turned back to Larkin. "Most people would say I'm neuroatypical, and enough people have asked me whether I'm on the spectrum to make me wonder whether I should have an answer for them."

"But you didn't get one," Larkin said.

"I didn't want it to be the way in which I experienced the world," Anni said. "I had already constructed enough rules, for myself, to ensure I could make it through the day. The last thing I needed was a net of words between *me* and *not-me*." She opened the canvas bag she always carried with her and took out the notebook that was always by her side. This notebook had a glittery dolphin on the cover; Anni removed two pages and handed one to Larkin.

"Make a paper airplane," she said. "I'll make one too."

Larkin had a general idea of how paper airplanes worked. Anni's was more specific, and when the two crafts were complete it was Anni's that flew, directly, towards the water-winged toddler. The child squealed, reaching up one chubby hand to catch the paper plane.

"All right," Anni said—after bending over to pick up Larkin's attempt, which had flown approximately eighteen inches. "So we know two things. One of them is that I am good at making paper airplanes. What's the other?"

"That I am bad at making paper airplanes," Larkin said.

"Wrong," Anni said. "You just don't know how to make one *yet*." She unfolded Larkin's paper. "I could teach you, and it wouldn't take more than five minutes, and then it might take another five minutes for me to teach you how to throw one." She began refolding Larkin's paper more carefully. "But that's not the point. The point is that you think you are bad at making paper airplanes, and because of that, you're going to treat every paper airplane you make as *something you are bad at doing*."

"This is a metaphor, isn't it?" Larkin asked.

"It's an analogy," Anni corrected. "If I had gone in and gotten a doctor to tell me I was on the spectrum, and if I had gone online and learned that I might have difficulty navigating interpersonal relationships, I would have treated every person-to-person interaction I had, from that point on, as *something I was bad at doing*."

She flew the new plane towards the toddler, whose fingers did not quite close around the craft before it hit the surface of the swimming pool. One of the adults rescued the plane from its unexpected water landing. Another comforted the child.

"That little kid, the one who caught the first plane but didn't catch the second one," Anni continued, "at some point someone is going to tell that kid that they're either good at catching things or bad at catching things, dependent entirely on how many things they've successfully caught thus far." She pulled her knees up to her chest, which was an Anni way of indicating anger. "Even though nobody has taught the kid that there's a way to catch things! The kid is just guessing, and if they're good at iterating their own work they'll guess correctly more often than not, but there's a way to teach them how to know!"

Larkin considered this. "You're saying that there's a

way to teach people how to know how to interact with other people."

"I'm saying that if you tell someone they're bad at something, they're going to treat it as something that will never improve," Anni said, "and yes, I'm probably saying that there's a way to teach people to know how to interact with other people, although I haven't figured that out yet." She unhooked one knee, letting it dangle off the edge of the deck chair. "I'm still learning. Elliott's helping me." Then she looked at Larkin. "But you were one of the first people to help. I didn't ever think I could have a real friend, until you."

"Awww, shucks," Larkin said. She put her empty cup of coffee on the little glass table; she thanked the man who took it away. "So Jay was asking—"

"He was asking me how to live, for the rest of his life, through this filter of *I am incapable of connecting with others*," Anni said, "because he assumed that someone had once assigned me the same attribute."

Larkin thought about Jay, sitting next to Anni on a porch swing, asking her how to love.

Then she realized what Jay had really been asking.

"You know it's me," Larkin said, "who minds that you're having private conversations with my nemesis."

"I know," Anni said. "That's why I didn't tell you before."

"What changed?"

"Jay did," Anni said. "Or, at least, I think he did. We'll have to see what he does next."

That was when they were interrupted—not by Jay, not by Ed, but by a cruise-uniformed employee holding a telephone.

"For Miss Day," the employee explained, passing Larkin the receiver.

"Hello?" Larkin said. She couldn't remember the last time she'd held an old-fashioned analog telephone. She couldn't remember the last time she'd taken a call without knowing who was on the other end of the line.

"This is Adamantine Darcy," the voice said, loudly and distinctly, into her ear. Larkin had forgotten how telephones used to sound before they went digital. It was as if Adamantine were standing right next to her. "Have you had breakfast?"

"Just coffee," Larkin said.

"Appalling," Adamantine said. "You may join me in my stateroom, in half an hour, for a proper meal. I assume you have no other plans?"

"I'm on vacation," Larkin said.

"I am not," Adamantine said. "You will find me in the Koningin Suite, Deck Nine, forward, on the starboard side. Eliza will meet you at the door."

CHAPTER 6

Adamantine's stateroom was even statelier than Larkin's. The Koningin Suite had a crown on the door instead of a number; inside, Larkin saw portraits of monarchs and a glass case filled with bees and butterflies.

"They're fake," Adamantine said, when she caught Larkin staring. "Doubly fake. Neither insect nor gemstone."

Larkin looked more closely. The wings glittered; the proboscis sparkled. "The feathers are made of metal and glass."

"Scales," Adamantine corrected. "On lepidoptera, what you read as *feathers* is best written as *scales*."

"A scale model, right?" Larkin said, turning to look at her host. "Pun intended."

Adamantine did not acknowledge Larkin's wit; instead, she sat patiently in the center of the room, waiting for her guest to join her. Eliza had retaken her place by the door, waiting for their breakfast to arrive.

"I don't know why the service is so slow," Adamantine

said, gesturing to the chair next to hers. Larkin thought about telling Adamantine—or her assistant, maybe—that they should slip their stateroom attendant a twenty. Then she thought better of it. She still didn't know why she was here, after all. It was too soon to presume to offer advice.

"Thank you for inviting me," Larkin said, as she settled herself next to the famous author. After she'd received the call from Adamantine, she'd raced back to Verandah 213—waving at Elliott, who was doing something with his laptop, and kissing her boyfriend, who was just starting to consider getting out of bed—and quickly put on a set of clothing that she considered presentable. Another outfit her mother had chosen, when Josephine had suggested they go shopping together. The loose, rectangular dress both looked and felt like a burlap sack, but it was better than showing up in the glittery *Theater Kid* tank top and nubbly terrycloth shorts she'd planned to wear that day. Adamantine was wearing a bathrobe, nearly identical to the one Larkin had worn an hour ago—except Adamantine's robe had a tiny crown embroidered over the cruise line logo, and she appeared to be wearing nothing at all underneath. Larkin could see the pale veins tracing their way over Adamantine's frail skin. She could see Adamantine's pulse, quivering the vein on the left side of her neck. She could see what looked like confusion, transformed—with a deep breath—into what looked like resolve.

"You are both a director and a detective, are you not?" Adamantine asked.

"I am," Larkin began, "but—"

"You don't need to explain your bifurcated career," said the author, clutching one hand around the curved arm of her chair the way she'd gripped the top of her cane. "I am familiar with your work. In fact, I spent part of the morning speaking with two of your former clients."

She looked at Larkin, as if it were a test.

"Blythe and Bonnie Cooper," Larkin said. It wasn't that difficult to figure out whom Adamantine had spoken with. In most cases, the murderer and the victim were taken to the ends of their respective stories. In this case, both the good and the evil twin—and Larkin still wasn't sure which had been which—had been allowed to begin again.

Adamantine nodded. "Larkin Day understands how people work," she continued, as if quoting the twins directly, "and she's fun to work with!" The exclamation point fell out of her mouth as easily as she put it into the mouths of her characters—Larkin had done her research, too, peeking into one of the *Time Tangent Gentleman* paperbacks that had been stacked, attractively, in one of the ship's many stores—and Larkin wondered if she was watching a version of Adamantine that had been written in advance.

"That's what they said on their podcast," Larkin said. Blythe and Bonnie had spent much of the first season recapping the not-quite-murder, not-quite-crime that had brought them back together. They had even interviewed Larkin, for one episode—which had received forty-seven downloads, when Larkin last checked. "How did you get them on the phone?"

"Tom took care of it," Adamantine said. Larkin looked, automatically, towards Eliza—who was opening the door to allow a wheeled breakfast tray. The uniformed cruise employee pushing the tray looked familiar; Larkin was about to check his nametag to make sure, and then Handy greeted her personally.

"Good morning, Miss Darcy, Miss Day," he said, greeting Adamantine with civility and Larkin with a smile. "If I had known it would be you, Miss Day, I would have moved the ticket to the front of the line!"

"It's all right, Handy," Larkin said. She wished she'd stashed a twenty-dollar bill in one of her pockets. She wished her dress *had* pockets. "We've been having a lovely conversation, and the breakfast you brought looks delightful." Now Larkin was the one playing a version of herself. Improvising. The conversation hadn't been lovely—if anything, it had been interrogatory—and the breakfast looked as if it were intended to induce a coronary. Butter, imprinted with the Dutch Cruise International logo; chocolate, imprinted with the same crown that adorned Adamantine's bathrobe and door. Scrambled eggs, as yellow and reflective as the sun; toast, as white and fluffy as the clouds. A single strawberry, sliced and splayed like a taxidermied butterfly.

"I have brought green tea for Miss Darcy," Handy said, "and now that I see Miss Day is here I will return immediately with a pot of fresh coffee!"

"Thank you," Larkin said. "I'll make sure the rest of my stateroom knows how well you took care of us."

"It is my job," Handy said, turning towards the door, "and your job is to have a relaxing cruise vacation!"

"You know the help," Adamantine said, as soon as he had gone. "More interestingly, the help knows you."

"His name is Handoyono," Larkin said, watching Adamantine wave her hand over the tray of steaming, gleaming food. "I wouldn't say we know each other, not beyond pleasantries." It was obvious that Adamantine would not serve herself until Larkin took something, so she released a piece of toast from its metal grating. "He services our stateroom."

"I should have known," Adamantine said, loading her own plate with eggs and bread before buttering both. "Tom, compile a list of all staterooms currently serviced by my attendant." Larkin turned towards Eliza, who was sitting quietly on an armchair; she turned back towards Adamantine just in time to catch the light flashing off the author's dangling octagonal glasses. Light was supposed to flash off glasses, especially in staterooms that were eighty percent windows. It wasn't supposed to flash green.

Adamantine took a careful bite of her breakfast, wiping the dribbling fat off the edge of her lip. "You occupy an interesting place on this cruise. Not quite a Special Guest, as they call us—but not an ordinary guest, either."

"I'm very ordinary," Larkin said. "I'm not even a nerd."

"But you have managed, in less than twenty-four hours, to befriend one of the highest-ranking stateroom attendants," Adamantine continued. "To access the passcode to the Performers' Lounge. To be invited to have breakfast, in the Koningin Suite, *with me.*"

"My friend Anni was the one who befriended Handoyono," Larkin said, "and my boyfriend Ed was the one who got the passcode to the lounge." There was a soft knock on the door; Eliza allowed Handy to enter and set a coffee service next to Larkin. "Thank you," Larkin said as Handy left, pouring herself a cup and adding a packet of nonfat creamer. The sugar had been cubed—brown and white, like the toast—and as Larkin eschewed the cubes for a sachet of saccharine, she returned to her story. "Did you know what I used to do before I became a director? I poured coffee. I served coffee. I carried trays just like this one." She stared into Adamantine's unspectacled eyes. "I'm not special. I'm just a thirtysomething woman trying very hard to be her Best Self."

"That, in itself, makes you different from your peers," Adamantine said, using the crust of her bread to wipe up the last of her butter.

"I only knew how to do it because of my peers!" Larkin

retorted, using the end of her finger to combine the additives in her coffee. "They're the ones you should be having breakfast with, not me."

Adamantine smiled. "I did not ask your star-crossed lover," she said, "nor am I interested in the failed magician and his success-driven wife."

"They aren't married," Larkin said, "and Elliott is way more than a failed magician."

"They're as good as married," Adamantine said, "and if he presents as more than his failures, it is because she is putting everything she has into *giving him something to be.* If I were to have breakfast with them, it would turn into a lecture."

"They'd probably like that," Larkin said, still wanting to defend her best friends. "They're both nerds."

"And you are not," Adamantine said, "by your own admission." She finished her cup of green tea and followed it with a piece of chocolate. "Which is why you are the one who has been admitted into the Koningin Suite."

Larkin took her own piece of chocolate—rich, filling, and surprisingly bitter—and suddenly understood what was really going on. "That's not true," she said. "You invited me here because you wanted to hire me." She took a second piece. "You said, last night, that you needed my help on a project."

For a moment, Adamantine looked completely bewildered. "Tom," she finally said, her hand shaking as she sliced off another pat of butter, "please help me remember the relevant conversation with Larkin Day." Her glasses flashed, again. Then Larkin saw a similar flash, in a device Adamantine was wearing in her left ear.

"Ah," Adamantine said, transferring the butter to her mouth and wiping her fingers. "I wanted your help on a project."

"I just told you that," Larkin said.

"I know," Adamantine said. "Let me finish."

She poured herself a second cup of tea.

"I want you to tell me how to hide a body," Adamantine continued, "so that no detective could ever find it."

Larkin did not know what to say. Nor, it appeared, did Adamantine—but Eliza, from her armchair, finally spoke. "It's for a book."

"Yes," Adamantine said, reassuringly. "It's for my final *Time Tangent Gentleman* novel." Reassured. "He needs to disappear forever, but in a way that might allow him to remain alive." With assurance. "Just in case, you know."

"An author always needs to be prepared to revive her favorite characters," Eliza explained.

"Right," Larkin said. She eyed Eliza, who was on the edge of her cushioned seat. The woman, whom Larkin had assumed was Adamantine's assistant, appeared to be more than she seemed. "I suppose it would depend on where the novel took place," Larkin said, choosing each word in turn, watching both Adamantine and Eliza for clues. "Would it just happen to be set on a cruise ship?"

"It would," Eliza said.

"I told you she was a detective," Adamantine said, laughing. "Look at what she's already figured out!"

"I've figured out more than you think," Larkin said. She stood up, taking one more piece of chocolate before turning towards the door. "I know at least two of your secrets, Adamantine Darcy—and I can guess yours, Eliza, *if that is in fact your real name.*"

Now Eliza looked confused. "Why wouldn't it be my real name?"

"She thinks you're Tom," Adamantine said.

"No, I don't," Larkin said. She didn't tell them that she had—until that last piece had fallen into place—been not quite sure. "I know what Tom is." She gestured towards the octagonal spectacles. "I know what your deal is." She gestured towards the device in Adamantine's ear. "I'm pretty sure I know what you're asking me to do."

Eliza looked even more confused. "How could she know?"

"Even an amateur detective could have figured out that I'm trying to hide my own body," Adamantine said. "I was hoping she'd be professional enough to have understood that I must have a very good reason to want to do it."

Larkin did not want to hear any more of this conversation. "It doesn't matter." She turned towards the closed door, trying to hide the lie. "Professional, amateur, I don't care."

She put her hand on the doorknob.

"I'm still not going to help you."

Then she pulled.

"You have to release the deadbolt first," Eliza said, quietly. "And undo the chain."

"Fine," Larkin said. She fumbled, fat-fingered, with the slick loops of metal.

"Help me," Adamantine said, her voice quivering, her words landing like arrows in Larkin's back, "or I'll end up dead before I'm ready."

CHAPTER 7

Larkin told her friends how her conversation with Adamantine had gone—the butter, the butterflies, the size of the suite—but did not tell them how it had ended.

Larkin wasn't sure she could ever tell them how it had ended.

She had answered Adamantine's question—the one about making a body disappear—and fled what she had called *the scene of the not-crime*, returning first to Verandah 213 and then, after reading the note Anni had left on the table, joining the group on the Lido Deck. She had decided, in the time it took to change her clothes and arrange her hair into a messy bun, what she would say.

"The whole thing was, like, *death by butter*, you know?" Larkin joked. "She put it on her eggs. On her toast. In her green tea. That's, like, the best way to have a heart attack, right?"

"Not necessarily," Elliott said. "The current research indicates that saturated fat is much less harmful than we thought, and eating large amounts of butter may be the best way to ensure optimal brain functioning."

"I thought it was ginseng," Josephine said. She turned to Claire. "When did it stop being ginseng?"

"I have no idea," Claire said. She squeezed Josephine's hand and grinned at Elliott. "I guess that means I get to order the pork belly tacos for lunch."

"So she was doing it to improve her mental capacity?" Larkin asked. That, at least, made sense—especially with what Larkin now understood about Adamantine's mind. She shifted forward in her deck chair, placing her elbows on her terrycloth-covered thighs. "Um, can you all keep a secret?"

The trick fooled Elliott and Ed—who kept looking around for Grandmaster Trey and what he hoped would be his first turntabling session—and puzzled Anni, who knew Larkin better than either of their boyfriends. "Is everything all right?"

"Yeah," Larkin said. If Anni suspected Larkin was acting according to a plan—which she was, finalizing the details as she'd slipped into her glittery *Theater Kid* tank top—they could discuss it later. Right now, Larkin had to reveal a piece of information about Adamantine in order to conceal the information she'd both given and received. Directors knew almost as much about misdirection as magicians did, after all—more, in this case, since Elliott hadn't spotted the tell.

The failed magician and his success-driven wife. They could discuss that later, too.

"So what's the secret?" That was from her mother, who knew that Larkin was up to something and was nudging her to get to whatever it was. "Is Adamantine Darcy having mental difficulties?"

Josephine had guessed it—and Larkin wondered if her

mother had seen the truth in her body language or, given yesterday's encounter, Adamantine's—but she hadn't guessed all of it. "I think so," Larkin said. "She's operating almost entirely off an AI assistant."

Now she had Ed's attention. "An AIA? Which one?"

"Wait," Larkin asked, "how do you already know the acronym?"

"It's kind of obvious," Ed said. "Plus, I'm part of this pilot program at Howell. We're comparing the top three AIAs to see which one would be best for basic desktop work. It's interesting to see where people reach their limits—like, some of the people on the committee think it's okay for an AI to write a syllabus but not to reply to a student email, and other people think it should be the other way around."

"The one Adamantine is using is called TOM," Larkin said. She had begun capitalizing it, in the part of her brain that turned thoughts into words, once she'd understood what it stood for. "Top of Mind."

Now she had Anni's attention—or, at least, the part of Anni's attention that had been formerly focused on *what Larkin was hiding*. "She's got TOM? With the implant?"

"Yes," Larkin said.

"Nobody told me there were going to be implants," Ed said. "I thought these things were, like, the next level of autocomplete."

"Stochastic parrots," Josephine said. "Able to repeat what generations of humans have previously generated, in patterns that only have meaning when they are observed by other humans."

"That's not what TOM is," Anni said. "It's not a parrot, and it's not an autocompleter, and it's not a search engine that uses natural language processing. It's the closest thing we currently have to an external, networked mind." She turned to Claire. "Do you remember when Adamantine asked TOM to route her through the ship in a way that would allow her to avoid you?"

"Yep," Claire said. "I remember it like it was yesterday."

"Okay," Anni said. "Elliott can probably explain this next bit better than I can."

As Elliott told them all how TOM would track Claire's badge as it passed from stateroom to dining room to Lido Deck, keeping the information it learned to itself—"because sharing Claire's location with Adamantine would be a breach of privacy, and everyone's really concerned about privacy right now"—while giving the author instructions that would allow her to travel through the ship without encountering her biggest fan, Larkin wondered why Anni had told them all that Elliott would be able to explain the AIA better than she could. Anni was a freelance writer, specializing in the intersection of tech and finance. Explaining this stuff was literally her job.

If he is more than his failures, it is because she is working as hard as she can to give him something else to be.

"But this must be costing Adamantine an enormous amount of money," Josephine said. "To be continually networked? I asked Handy how much it costs to access the ship's onboard Wi-Fi, and he told me I could pay ten dollars for five minutes or forty dollars for half an hour."

"Those are the rates for people who don't have Super Elite Status," Anni said. "Elliott and I only have to pay fifty cents a minute. Adamantine probably got an even better deal."

"Which means that the money you pay for Wi-Fi is subsidizing Adamantine's use," Elliott said, "even though Adamantine is taking more of the network's resources."

He swept a stray strand of his hair into his ponytail. "Socialism at its worst, you might say."

"I'm not paying any money for Wi-Fi," Josephine corrected, looking as if she wanted to correct his politics as well—so she looked out, instead, at the rest of the passengers on the Lido Deck. "But a lot of them are." Many of the nerds who had chosen to spend the morning in the sun had also chosen to turn their eyes towards their devices. Some nerds were wearing full VR headsets, attaching themselves to a reality that appeared even more rewarding than what was otherwise in front of them. The sun, the swimming pools, the starboard bar that hummed and whirred as it churned out hurricanes. The sky, on either side, cloudless and endless and blue. The ocean, in all directions. *At sea,* the onboard newspaper had called it. *Today we are at sea.*

"Adamantine Darcy's wearing a robot that sends messages to her brain?" Claire asked. "That's the big secret?"

"I think the real secret is that your favorite author is dealing with the early stages of dementia," Ed said quietly. "I've seen how that ends. I don't think the AIA is going to help her. I'm not sure if there's anything that can help her, now that the beta-amyloid hypothesis has been proven false."

"Not necessarily false," Anni corrected. "It's just that the initial research was at best sloppy and at worst fraudulent."

"And Adamatine's diagnosis isn't a secret," Claire said, adding her own correction to Anni's. "She wrote about it on her blog." She turned to Larkin. "If the robot's telling her everything she needs to know, then why did she want to talk to you?"

"She finds me interesting," Larkin said. It was close

enough to the truth—but not close enough for Officer Claire Novak.

"I would have put money—not real money, Jo—on Adamantine wanting you to help her with the ending of her last book," Claire said. "Everyone on the forums knows that Horatio Bonheur has to die, except we're all pretty sure that he's going to die in a way that allows him to come back, you know. In the future. When another author takes over the *Time Tangent Gentleman* series, or when all the books are written by robots."

"Are you saying that Adamantine Darcy asked my daughter for advice?" Josephine asked, almost laughing. "One of the most famous popular authors in the world, wanting to know how Larkin Day would kill off her most famous character?"

"No," Claire said. "She's figured out how to kill him, or at least how she's going to make it look like she's killed him. I read it on her blog." Now she grinned at Larkin, her smile widening as she figured it out. "She needs Larkin, who thinks like a director and a detective—great combination, by the way—to tell her how to hide the body."

Larkin tried to keep her face still. It would be the easiest thing in the world to say *yes*. It would also be a lie, and she was pretty sure at least one of the people in front of her would notice.

"Am I right?" Claire asked.

The hurricane blenders whirred; somebody splashed, cannonball-style, into the pool.

Help me, or I'll end up dead before I'm ready.

"Hello nerds!" It was Xavier, of course; his voice omniscient and omnipresent.

Deus ex machina, Larkin thought. *Thank God.* "It's almost time to gather in the Main Theater—that would be the Gehoorzaal, for those of you who plan on spending your vacation learning Dutch—for our first big event! We're gonna meet, we're gonna greet, we're going to have a keynote speech, and if you know anything about how we do things on this cruise, you already know that we have a few surprises planned! We've got a little over an hour, so there's still time to have lunch in the Main Dining Room or make a quick stop at the taco bar on the Lido Deck—or, if you are the kind of nerd who prefers snacks to meals, make sure you stop by the twenty-four hour Game Room for candy, popcorn, and a literal aquarium of fish-shaped crackers! Maybe even play a game while you're there! Our librarians have built a database of board and card games that can be sorted by time-to-complete, so pick one that doesn't take much longer than half-an-hour—and I'll see you in the Gehoorzaal in one hour and seventeen minutes!"

"Thank you, one hour seventeen," Larkin whispered to Ed. It was what they used to say when they were working the Shakespeare Festival together. Ed smiled softly, but kept his eyes on the crowd, looking for Grandmaster Trey, presumably. Larkin wondered if that was what she had looked like yesterday, when she was scanning every face they passed for Jay Malhotra.

Now she had something more important to do with her time—all seventy-seven minutes of it—and someone else to watch out for.

Phase One, Larkin had said, to the two women in the Koningin Suite.

Keep Adamantine alive.

The Main Theater was—like every other interior space on the ship—a sophisticated imitation of its audience's expectations. The seats were upholstered in red velvet; the curtains were trimmed in gold fringe. There were Corinthian columns and Rococo cupids, and three tiers of box seats on either side of the stage. That was where Ed finally spotted the Grandmaster, waving to get Trey's attention, squeezing Larkin's hand as the Special Guest waved back. It was barely a wave, of course. The lift of a hand. An acknowledgement—which, to Ed, meant everything.

"I'll see if I can catch him afterwards," he whispered to Larkin, "to talk about turntabling."

Larkin nodded. The six of them settled into a row, house left: Larkin and Ed, Anni and Elliott, Josephine and Claire. Larkin wondered if Claire had taken the aisle seat on purpose; if it was part of her training, to always choose the seat that allowed her the most freedom of motion. Larkin was trapped, in the center, with Ed on one side and a redheaded nerd on the other.

"Hi," the nerd said. She had a row of rainbow-colored piercings in her right eyebrow. "I'm Eirwen." This was the name of a character in a chapter book that had been popular when Larkin was a child. A girl who cut off her hair and dressed as a boy because she wanted to be a knight, losing herself on the way to the castle, and finding shelter with an old woman. The woman, who is of course *more than what she seems*, treats the girl as she would treat a boy—the hardest work, the hardest bed—while teaching another group of girls about herbs and households. By Chapter Nine, the curious, envious Eirwen has given up both her pretense and her secret. In Chapter Ten, the old woman reveals herself to be a witch—which the clever reader will have already guessed—and tells Eirwen that she will teach her not only about maintaining a home, but also about the magic that all women possess and a privileged few learn to access. "The bravest girls grow into the wisest women," the woman said, on the last page, after redressing Eirwen and tying a ribbon around her shorn hair. There had been a pen-and-ink drawing, below the paragraph, of Eirwen churning butter. Preparing for the adult she would become and the wisdom she would learn.

This nerd had a ribbon in her hair, too.

"Hi," Larkin said. "I'm Larkin."

Eirwen, however, had become distracted—and Larkin watched as the bow in the red hair tilted upwards, following the eyes. The box seats, where Ed had just been staring. The Special Guests. Professionals, in conversation with each other, pretending not to notice the faces turned in their direction. Two seats empty; Adamantine and Eliza had not yet arrived.

"I wish they did this cruise without the guests," Eirwen said. She turned to Larkin, assuming an eyebrow lift. "Why do we have this cruise where we're all supposed to be accepted for who we are, except for the part where there are all these people who are better than us?"

Her voice was superficially snarky. Her face—despite the eyebrow—was profoundly sad.

"I think they're just the entertainment," Larkin said. "I don't think you're supposed to think that they're better than you."

Now the eyebrow lifted for real. "We all know that they have something we don't." Eirwen tilted her head back towards the guests. "Otherwise we'd be up there instead of them."

This was the truth, or at least close enough to the truth to hurt. Larkin had felt it herself, the first time she'd seen the Special Guests.

"Or there'd be no *up there* at all, and we'd all be *here*,"

Eirwen continued, as if that were her preferred solution. "We could all get to know each other and share our work."

Eirwen looked older than Larkin. She seemed younger, somehow.

"We can still do that," Larkin said. "What's your work?"

"I write short stories," Eirwen said, pulling out what appeared to be a printed manuscript. "My work deals with the intersection of technology and identity. I want to expand SF into SIF"—she looked at Larkin, noting the lack of understanding—"that's *science fiction* into *science identity fiction*, because the way we create and interact with technology consistently neglects the experiences and needs of marginalized people."

"All right," Larkin said. She flipped through the printout, her eyes landing on a page that included a reference to *teledildonics*. "I'll take a look." She glanced at Eirwen, who clearly expected her to take that look *right now*, so she began skimming through the stories. A robot dog, abandoned by a person who could only take one possession to Mars. A pair of long-distance lovers communicating through networked sex toys, until a series of software updates allowed the newly-sentient devices to take control of the situation. She doubted that any of these entries would help Eirwen expand a genre, the way Wendy Carlos had. The way Grandmaster Trey had. Getting themselves into rooms with the smartest people they knew—and then getting to work, undisturbed, in a room of their own. That was what Eirwen wanted. It was what so many creative people wanted. The Gehoorzaal, packed with *not-special guests*, smelled of sunscreen and mixed drinks and ambition.

"Hello, nerds!" It was Xavier, microphone in hand,

taking his place at the center of the stage. "We are so excited to welcome you to our thirteenth cruise!"

The lights flickered ominously. There was a thunder-crack, for some reason, followed by a run of clichéd organ music. *Standby Cue Three,* Larkin thought, automatically, right before the lights restored. *Cue Three go.* She wanted to visit the people in the tech booth, to tell them how much she appreciated their work.

"How many of you are afraid of the number thirteen?" Xavier called out, pausing for the smatter of applause. "Not a lot of triskaidekaphobes? How about thalasso-phobes? How many of you are afraid of drowning?" This time a few more people joined in. "Wow," Xavier said, the one-liner entering everybody's minds before it exited his mouth. "Guess you picked the wrong vacation."

"Of course," Xavier continued, after the obligatory laugh, "we already know that in this community we rise above phobias. Homophobia, transphobia, fatphobia, ableism, and racism *have no place on this cruise!*" This time his words were met with cheers. "But—and I have to be honest with all of you—we all know that there is one thing that everybody in this room is afraid of." He picked a few faces out of the crowd, staring at each one in turn; it was a trick Larkin had used, every time she'd had to address the audience at the Summer Shakespeare Festival. "Something each and every one of you is afraid to lose."

"Onboard Wi-Fi access!" The heckle came from a head-setted nerd, his face embraced by his VR helmet. Larkin wondered what he was watching, and whether he thought it improved on what would have otherwise been in front of him.

Xavier—just as Larkin expected he would—handled the outburst with aplomb. "Losing access to information is pretty bad. But there's one thing that's even worse. *Losing access to your own mind.*"

Larkin glanced automatically at the box seats. Adamantine and Eliza were still not among the Special Guests. "I'm glad our featured author isn't here to hear this," she whispered to Ed.

"Yeah," Ed whispered back. "It's a little *above the nose.*"

"Neuroableist," Larkin whispered as Xavier continued his monologue: "That's why we're bringing out our favorite stage magician, Daniel Pennington, to allow one of you lucky nerds to experience your greatest fear."

Daniel, porkpie-hatted and hacksaw in hand, entered stage left. Upstage, Moira arranged a vertical contraption that resembled a torture chamber.

"Daniel," Xavier asked, after the applause, "what are you going to do to one of these people?"

"I'm going to cut off their head," Daniel said. His next joke, like Xavier's previous quip, landed before it left his lips: "Don't worry, I'm going to put it back on again!"

What followed was a somewhat pedestrian demonstration of the classic *saw-a-lady-in-half* trick. Even the way it began was predictable—Xavier filled Daniel's hat with slips of paper, each one containing the name of a nerd; after drawing out a single volunteer, Daniel turned his hat over and let Xavier act surprised that the rest of the papers didn't come tumbling out. Larkin found herself wondering why Daniel hadn't done something more interesting. More innovative. She'd seen enough of Elliott's magic to know that tricks could still contain surprises, and that illusions— like all theatrical arts—worked best when the audience was invited to suspend their disbelief. When Daniel finished his business with the hacksaw and tilted the vertical box just enough to allow the volunteer's head to slide off their shoulders, no one gasped. They laughed, instead, until the box and the head were restored.

"Thank you," Xavier said, after affixing a special pin to the nerd's lanyard in honor of their service to the cruise. "Let's hear it for Daniel Pennington!"

Daniel bowed and exited. The lights flickered, again— something was wrong about that, although Larkin couldn't tell what it was—and the theater filled with a thumping techno rhythm. As the lights came back on, Larkin watched the nerd in front of her take off his VR headset and push a few of the buttons on its side. She could swear he swore, although she wasn't close enough to overhear the obscenity. The nerd next to him shrugged, took out his phone, and used his front-facing camera to check his hair.

"And now," Xavier said—he knew something had gone wrong, Larkin could tell—"it's time"—someone in the audience whooped, in advance—"for the Parade."

The beat got louder; the houselights got brighter. Xavier began singing, and everyone who knew the words sang along:

Identity parade
Affinity parade
Some are born and some are made
Identity parade
Affinity parade
Show your pride and take the stage

"Let's start with NATS!" Xavier said. Whatever had happened with the lights—and something had happened, Larkin was sure of it—didn't seem to bother him anymore. "That's neuroatypical! Autists, attention deficits, whatever spectrum you're on, get on up here!"

Larkin watched a group of nerds parade their way across the stage. Two of them hugged each other. Two of them made a joke out of not hugging each other. Xavier fist bumped anyone who wanted the connection.

"Next, let's do RATS!" he continued. "That's the rationalist community! Did Bayes predict you'd end up on this cruise?"

Most of the NATS were also RATS, which allowed them to remain on stage and fist bump Xavier a second time. Larkin looked over at Anni, who was both rational and atypical—but Anni was leaning into Elliott's side, tapping what appeared to be a Morse Code message into his forearm. Elliott nodded, concernedly, and responded in kind.

"Now let's do LGBTQ," Xavier said, his voice raising with each of the first four letters so it could drop to the octave on the last one. "LGBTQ!"

Claire said something to Anni, who nodded distractedly, and then she said something to Josephine, who nodded excitedly, and then Larkin watched as her mother and her mother's girlfriend took to the stage. They looked thrilled, the two of them, to share space with at least three generations of queer nerds. Claire immediately started dancing, shrugging her shoulders, and shifting her weight from one sandaled foot to the other—careful not to intrude into anyone's space, Larkin noticed—and Josephine twisted and twirled until her sundress flared around her speckled legs.

Eirwen, on Larkin's left, also left her seat—but instead of dancing, she walked right up to Xavier. After a fist bump that turned into a negotiation, Xavier yielded the mic to Eirwen, who began chanting, in rhythm: "Trans. Train. Reclaim the word. Trans. Train. Reclaim the word." Larkin knew—everyone knew, except people like her mother who didn't spend a lot of time online—which word Eirwen wanted to reclaim. Not *trans*, which was already theirs to use, but *train*. The slur that had been created to evade the censors. Intelligent readers understood when a train was a train and when it was a trans person, but artificial intelligences did not—and so Eirwen led a conga line of transgender nerds around the theater, up and down the aisles, the chanting getting louder with every step. "Trans! Train! Reclaim the word!" Larkin watched—everybody watched—as Eirwen reclaimed center stage. "Fuck TERFs," she said, dropping the mic and accepting the applause.

"I got that." It was Grandmaster Trey, who had made his way into the parade without anybody noticing. He picked up the microphone that Eirwen had dropped and examined it for damage. Then he smiled. "You all don't mind if I freestyle?"

Xavier, quick to understand that his role had shifted from major to minor, took a second mic from a stagehand and said, "Give it up for Grandmaster Trey!" The sexagenarian hip-hop artist began rapping over the techno beat:

Where my blerds at

I know that people don't call us that anymore

But when I was young they called us freaks, or geeks, or worse

So where my blerds at

The portmanteau isn't going to go anywhere

And Black nerds always been here

Always been here

Always been here

My people have been technology ever since we were installed

We arrived in slave ships, leaving on spaceships

Blerd flight, Black magic

When the aliens come, when the AI come

We're the ones who have already honed the skills to survive

Where my blerds at

The words succeeded without artifice; the syllables flowed out of the Grandmaster as everyone in the audience listened and watched, motionless except for the rocking of the ship and the pulsing of the beat. It was her heart, Larkin realized, once her mind caught up to her body and her hand went to her chest to confirm. The rhythm and the meaning and the sea and the blood pumping through her veins all matched, and if one had sped up to meet the others, it was how art worked.

Why art worked.

"Well?" Grandmaster Trey finally asked. "Will all the beautiful Black nerds please join me on stage?" He turned around, smiling at the LGBTQ group. "Most of you are going to have to leave."

That got a laugh, which allowed the audience to shift into the ovation the Grandmaster was owed. The applause only paused when Grandmaster Trey said, "All of you back there, working the bar, working the doors, come on up here too. If you're a nerd, and you're Black, I want you here with me. Don't let the Dutch control the African."

That got the gasp that Daniel Pennington had missed. It got even more applause—and as Larkin watched Ed and the other Black nerds join Grandmaster Trey on the Gehoorzaal stage, she wondered if this would in fact be the best cruise ever. There was something about the way Ed looked at Grandmaster Trey—and then, over the footlights, *at her*—that made her love him more than she'd ever loved him before.

It might be the first time she'd actually loved him.

It might be the first time she'd actually seen him.

Ed, on that stage, bumping fists with the ship's photographer. Whispering something to Grandmaster Trey. Stepping aside to allow Adamantine Darcy—*wait, why was*

Adamantine there—to cross in front of the Grandmaster and take the microphone out of his hand.

"I have an announcement," the octogenarian author said. The microphone squealed with feedback. Somebody shouted, "Get off the stage!" Adamantine thumped her cane until it was quiet enough to continue.

"As you may know, I am currently writing the final volume of the *Time Tangent Gentleman* series." A few people cheered. Adamantine glared. "This morning, I finished the final draft and printed out the full manuscript."

"Let us read it!" one nerd shouted.

Another repeated "Get off the stage!"

"I would like to inform you that the manuscript has been stolen from my stateroom," Adamantine continued, as if neither nerd had responded.

"Oooh, a mystery," Claire whispered, leaning past Josephine so her voice would reach Larkin. "I wonder if she'll ask you to solve it?"

"I would also like to ask Larkin Day to join me onstage," Adamantine said.

"My daughter, the detective," Josephine said, as Larkin pushed her way past her mother and Claire and Anni and Elliott.

"Something's wrong," Elliott whispered, just as Larkin entered the aisle. "Look at the way her glasses are flashing. I think TOM reset itself during the power outage."

Adamantine's octagonal glasses were in fact pulsing red—not so much that anyone would notice, if they weren't looking, but Elliott had known enough to see it, and knew enough to warn Larkin about it, and that should have been enough for Larkin to pause before taking the stage. To ask herself *what else to look for, what else to notice*—and to see the Dutch cruise employee, white-skinned and blonde-haired, who had taken his place behind Adamantine.

"Are you Larkin Day?" the cruise employee asked. It was perfunctory. He was already matching Larkin's badge and photograph to the image on his tablet. Holding up the tablet to scan the badge. Watching as it beeped, and then stowing it under his arm.

"Yes," Larkin said.

"Larkin Day has stolen my manuscript," Adamantine said, pointing to the document Larkin was still holding. Eirwen's short stories, rolled into a tube and trapped between her fingers. Adamantine's wrinkled hands grabbed at the pages, sliding them out. Slicing the loose skin between Larkin's index finger and her thumb.

"Ow!" Larkin said, examining her paper cut. "You drew blood!"

"Take her into custody," Adamantine instructed. The Dutch cruise employee immediately gripped Larkin's left forearm. A second bead of blood emerged from the palm of her hand. "I'll take this"—the author continued, gripping Eirwen's manuscript—"back to my stateroom."

CHAPTER 8

"No, Miss Day," the Dutch cruise employee said, "we do not refer to this room as *the brig*."

"The jail, then?" Larkin asked. "Do you spell it with a *g*, like the Brits do? Or is there a Dutch word for *cruise ship prison* that I am not aware of?"

"Sit down, Miss Day," the Dutch cruise employee said, gesturing towards a tiny metal chair at a tiny metal table. "You may consider yourself in temporary custody."

As Larkin sat, she saw—for the first time—the words dangling from the man's lanyard.

Aart Van der Voort

Chief Security Officer

Dutch Cruise International

Larkin had thought, earlier that morning, that her biggest fears were *death* and *spiders*. This was something new to be afraid of—the lack of agency, the absence of options, the surrender to a system that held little room for humanity. The *little room*, not much larger than her mother's stateroom, that held herself and a uniformed man who had enough stripes and loops decorating his shoulders that Larkin suspected he was a pretty big deal.

He, in turn, suspected her.

A terrible mistake, followed by a terrible joke—and Larkin hadn't meant to ask whether they were putting her in *the brig*, the words had slipped out of her as she stumbled through the metal door. Officer Van der Voort had been kind about it; he'd held her arm as the ship swelled, ignoring her lack of both sea legs and tact. Letting her comments stand, as she sat—and then sitting, waiting for her to continue. Larkin scanned the room for hidden cameras, wondering if anything she said could be held against her in a court of maritime law.

Then she spoke. "I know how to prove I didn't do it."

The man, seated on her right, remained silent.

"Are you aware that Adamantine Darcy is wearing a device that records everything that happens in front of her? Audio and video?"

The Chief Security Officer was aware of many things. Larkin could tell by the way he looked at her, both eyes daring her to continue what she knew would be a one-sided conversation. She'd been on the other side of this conversation herself, allowing a suspect to speak until she understood what they were trying not to say. "I'm actually kind of a detective," Larkin said, hearing the thoughtless sentence fill the silence. Wondering what she would say next. Knowing the trap that Officer Van der Voort had set and talking into it anyway.

"Look, it should be very easy to figure out whether I have Adamantine's manuscript. You probably already know that I was in her stateroom this morning. You probably know everywhere I've been on this ship, because my badge has RFID in it or something." Larkin had no idea what RFID stood for. She would ask someone—she could probably ask any other passenger on the cruise—as soon as she made it safely out of *the not-brig*. "You should also have, like, a record of when Adamantine printed her manuscript, and you can compare that to when I was in her stateroom. Maybe she didn't even print it until after I left!"

Officer Van der Voort remained silent. Larkin wondered if he'd already done all of this, and if the evidence had proved—well, whatever the opposite of *exculpatory* was. *Culpatory*, probably, with Larkin Day as the culprit.

"And you know that manuscript that Adamantine took from me, the one that gave me this paper cut?" Larkin held up her hand, which was much less dramatic now that she was no longer bleeding. Maybe more dramatic, since it implied she was feigning injury. "I mean, it's fine now, it's just a paper cut, but the point is that it wasn't Adamantine's manuscript. Those were a bunch of short stories written by Eirwen Wald." Larkin decided not to mention the subject matter, since she wasn't sure she could say *teledildonics* with a straight face. "You can prove it, since those are the papers that have my fingerprints all over them."

Silence.

"And Eirwen's fingerprints."

Silence.

"And probably some of my blood."

That was when Larkin started laughing. She couldn't help it. She hadn't been able to help, in any way, not since Officer Van der Voort had taken her into temporary custody—and she'd failed so badly at being both a detective and a suspect that she couldn't think of anything else to do but let the tension collect in her throat and release itself not in words, but in bursts. Sounds that bounced off the walls and compounded as her laugh got louder.

No, not just *her* laugh.

The Chief Security Officer had started chuckling as well.

"Miss Day," he said, "you are a very entertaining interrogatee. Unfortunately, we neither have the equipment nor the interest to conduct a forensic analysis on the manuscript Miss Darcy took from you. Nor can we review the audio and video stored by Miss Darcy's intelligent assistant."

"Why not?" Larkin asked.

"Because"—said a familiar voice, from behind Larkin's left shoulder—"TOM is committed to maintaining the privacy of its users."

Larkin knew without looking that it was Jay Malhotra. She looked anyway. He was leaning against the open door, wearing a shirt that read *I can regurgitate more pi than you.* It looked like he might have gotten the shirt in high school; there was fraying around the neckline and a tiny hole above the screen-printed words. It didn't match his expensive German sandals. It didn't match anything about Jay that Larkin thought she knew.

"How did you get in here?" Larkin asked.

Jay shrugged. "Same way you got in."

"By being falsely accused of stealing another person's creative work?"

"No," Jay said. "Through the door."

He turned to leave the little room—Larkin saw a year and a list of names on the back of his T-shirt, proving that her guess had been correct—and closed the door behind him. Then he opened it again. "It isn't locked," Jay said. "I figured you wouldn't have figured that out yet."

"As I told you, Miss Day," Officer Van der Voort said, "I have not taken you to *the brig*."

"Where am I, then?" Larkin asked. She looked around —the simple metal table, the framed map of the Netherlands, the four-legged stand that held a fake potted plant —and then she knew. "This is your office." She looked at the officer. "Sir."

"It is a bit more accommodating than a cell," Officer Van der Voort said, "but not quite. I will forgive you the misunderstanding."

"And we'll forgive you the misunderstanding," Jay said, standing at what immediately became *the head of the table*, "as soon as you let Miss Day go."

The Chief Security Officer turned towards the tall man in his worn-out T-shirt. "I do not believe we have been introduced."

"Jay Malhotra," Jay said, holding out his hand. Officer Van der Voort shook, automatically. Then he opened a tiny drawer on his side of the metal table and took out a tube of hand sanitizer. "I'm a friend of Xavier's," Jay continued, accepting the squeeze of goo the officer offered. He rubbed his hands together and twisted around to show them both the back of his shirt. "We were roommates in high school." He pointed, as well as he could, to the pair of names: *Jaipal Malhotra* and *Francis Xavier Torres*. "Yes, I went to boarding school, yes, it was one of the ones you've heard of, and yes, I was roommates with Xavier before he was famous." He twisted back around. "I convinced him to join the Mathletes, and twenty years later he convinced me to come on this cruise."

Then Jay smiled, wryly, at Larkin. "You probably thought I was stalking you."

"You kind of are," Larkin said, wrinkling her nose in return. "How did you find me?"

"Seriously?" Jay said. He sat on the edge of the table, crossing his legs and letting one ankle bounce against his knee. "We were in the theater, he escorted you off the stage, and I just got up and followed you. It wasn't hard." He winked, conspiratorially, at the officer. "She was making a lot of noise, after all."

"Americans always do," Officer Van der Voort said, attempting a wink of his own.

"Be careful," Jay said. "I'm an American."

Larkin watched, not sure whether to be astonished or appalled. Jay was charming the Chief Security Officer, the way he seemed to charm everybody, and in less than a minute Jay had gotten not only the officer's nickname— "Aart Van der Voort? May we call you Artie?"—but also his apologies.

"I did not know what to do, when Miss Darcy gave me my instructions," Officer Van der Voort explained, tapping a piece of the wall until a panel opened. He removed an electric kettle and an enormous plastic water bottle. "May I make you both some cocoa? It is very good, from home."

"That sounds delightful," Jay said, his crossed leg twitching with anticipation. "Thank you."

Officer Van der Voort began preparing the cocoa, setting a tin of biscuits on the table as the water boiled. "Miss Darcy insisted that Larkin had stolen her manuscript. She said it could not be anybody else."

"Let me guess," Larkin said, taking a biscuit from the tin. She was feeling a bit more comfortable, now that she knew she was not in jail. "Adamantine printed the document right before I arrived for breakfast, and after I left, it was gone."

"Wow," Jay said, aiming another wink at his new friend Artie. "That sounds exactly like something a manuscript thief would say."

"It was exactly what Miss Darcy said," Officer Van der Voort said, attempting another wink back. Larkin watched both of his eyes close. "Miss Day was the only other person to have been in the same room as the manuscript. Therefore, it was my duty to lock her up." He opened his eyes and looked at Larkin. "Her companion, Miss McFarlane, suggested I simply remove you from Miss Darcy's presence for a little while. That's why I brought you here." He smiled, his lips pressing together the way his eyes had done. "I hope you don't mind."

"Not now that you've brought out these cookies," Larkin said, taking a second one. "They're amazing."

"My mother made them," Officer Van der Voort said. "I will pass along your compliments."

Larkin finished her buttery Dutch shortbread and almost reached into the tin a third time—but then she thought of something. "I wasn't the only other person in Adamantine's stateroom," she said. "Eliza was there. That's Miss McFarlane, right? Adamantine's assistant?"

She heard Jay laugh. "You thought Eliza McFarlane was Adamantine's assistant?"

"What?" Larkin said, annoyed at the assumption in Jay's voice. "Did she invent TOM or something?"

"Yes," Jay said. "Or something." He winked, one more time, at Artie. "Eliza McFarlane is one of the top three minds working on artificial intelligence right now."

"I see," Artie said, both of his eyes squeezing closed.

"It doesn't matter who she is," Larkin said, even though it was clear that it did matter, and Jay was still laughing at her, and she really should have become a nerd when she had the chance. "The point is that *she was there.* In Adamantine's stateroom. So was"—Larkin almost said *Handy,* but caught herself in time—"one of your employees. I don't remember his name."

She watched Jay register the lie. She watched the Chief Security Officer accept it as the truth. "But you remember that he could have taken the manuscript?"

"No," Larkin said. "He couldn't have. He brought us breakfast and left. I saw the whole thing."

The kettle squealed; the boiling water bubbled. "I can easily find out who serviced Miss Darcy's stateroom," Officer Van der Voort said, turning to prepare and pour the cocoa. Larkin glanced quickly at Jay, who waggled his foot as if he knew exactly what she had accidentally done. "We've had some trouble in the past with theft," the officer continued, placing a gold-rimmed teacup in front of each of them. "It usually isn't the person who services the Koningin Suite, though. Those are our most trustworthy attendants." He sipped his cocoa and considered. "Perhaps this man was—how do you say it?— *playing the long game.*"

"But why take a bunch of paper?" Larkin asked. "If you're a stateroom attendant looking for something to steal, a printed-out manuscript is fairly worthless. It's not even like it's the only copy. Adamantine could print another one."

"The final draft of the final book in an extremely popular series is worth a lot more than you think," Jay said. "He could upload it and sell copies, or he could keep it to himself and use it to make bets on those prediction market sites. Which characters will die, which characters will end up together, how the book will end, that kind of thing."

"People are betting on how this book is going to end?" Larkin asked. There was so much about the nerd world that she didn't understand. "Like, real money?"

"Not just real money," Jay said. "Serious money."

"We need to find Miss Darcy's stateroom attendant

right away," Officer Van der Voort said. "Thank you for giving me this information. I will move as fast as I can towards a satisfactory resolution."

Larkin also needed to make her next move—and quickly. "Am I free to go, then?"

"Not before you drink your cocoa," Jay said. "It's even better than the shortbread."

"Can't be," Larkin said, giving Jay the kind of smile she would have given Ed, back when they first started flirting. "Officer Van der Voort's mother didn't make it." She had to be very careful, to ensure both men had an incentive to support her moves as she played her half of the game—so Larkin gave Artie a wink before sipping the drink he'd prepared. "Wow," she said. "That's the best cocoa I've ever tasted." It was, actually. She took another sip. "It's incredible."

"The Dutch know chocolate," Jay said.

"And you know how to prepare it," Larkin said to Officer Van der Voort, who had finished closing and opening his eyes. He'd have the winking thing down, as soon as he could keep his other eyelid up. "I used to work in the coffee industry," she explained. "There's a skill to this." Then she turned to Jay. "But we really should go. We're missing the keynote speech, right?"

"Probably," Jay said.

"And if we sneak into the back, we can keep out of Adamantine's sightlines," Larkin said.

"Probably," Jay said again.

"And even if TOM registers that our badges are close by," Larkin said, "Eliza will have programmed the AIA to keep Adamantine a safe distance away from us." She remembered, suddenly, what Elliott had said about TOM resetting itself. She'd have to ask him what that meant— but she'd have to ask him something else first, and he'd have to say yes, otherwise none of this was going to work. Elliott had always been part of her plan, even though he didn't know it yet, and Adamantine's life depended on—

"TOM will keep Adamantine away from *you*, not from *us*," Jay corrected, talking over Larkin's thoughts. "I haven't been accused of any manuscript theft." Then he looked at Officer Van der Voort. "You'll find the employee who serviced Adamantine Darcy's stateroom?"

"Of course," the officer said. "I will make the call immediately." His left eyelid wobbled but remained in place as his right eyelid descended. "This man, Miss Day" —he chuckled again—"may end up in the brig!"

"I hope he doesn't," Larkin said, swilling the last of her cocoa, swallowing her thoughts, and standing up. "My guess, and this is from one detective to another, is that Adamantine Darcy simply left her manuscript somewhere on the ship." Having both flattered and impressed Officer Van der Voort by equalizing their ranks, Larkin turned to Jay. "Was she in the Main Dining Room at lunch, do you remember? I was eating tacos on the Lido Deck, so I wouldn't have seen her."

"She may have been," Jay said. "There was a lot of applause." Larkin watched him watch her, putting it together. Deciding to play along. "You might not get it, Artie," he explained, subtly negging his new friend, "but Xavier does this thing where we're all supposed to applaud any time a Special Guest enters a room."

Artie thought about how to *get this*, since it was clear that was what Jay wanted. "Very American," the Dutch cruise officer finally said.

"I know, right?" Jay turned back to Larkin. "So you think the manuscript is in the dining room?"

"I don't know," Larkin said. "Someone might have picked it up and taken it to the Lost and Found." She looked at Officer Van der Voort. "That's in the Main Office, right?"

"Yes," the officer said, opening another panel on his wall and removing an old-fashioned telephone receiver. "We can call them right now and ask."

"You've got more important things to do," Larkin said, focusing her eyes on the gold-braided loops that adorned Artie's uniform. She was not quite manipulative enough to touch them. "Surely that's the kind of thing that a Chief Security Officer would delegate?"

Officer Van der Voort, who must have been trained in neurolinguistic programming at some point, still responded exactly as Larkin hoped he would. He blushed, then straightened himself into the attitude he had taken on the Main Theater stage. A man in charge, doing something he internally disagreed with because a powerful woman had asked him to.

"I will have my staff look into it," he said.

"Good," Larkin said, adjusting her own posture until she was as tall as both men, feeling Jay's eyes on her back and Artie's eyes on her *Theater Kid* tank top. "You've already handled one crisis today." She let her right hand run, carefully, over the part of her left forearm that the officer had gripped as he escorted her from the stage. Her eyes flicked, quickly, towards the *not-bruise*. "You handled it very well, all things considering."

"I think he handled it even better than that," Jay said. Larkin couldn't see the expression on his face without turning her head—but his voice, passing her left ear, came across as someone who cared about her very much. "This could have been a real problem, if you had decided Larkin was responsible, but now it's all taken care of."

Jay paused—but Larkin already knew that Officer Van der Voort had been trained not to fill a pause, so she applied a bit of Meisner instead. "It's all taken care of," she repeated, looking directly into the Chief Security Officer's eyes, and hoping that he had never taken an intro-to-theater class.

"It's all taken care of," Artie said, as if scripted. Then, as if he had just discovered this truth for himself—which was the whole point of these theater exercises, Larkin would have to write the Meisner Institute and thank them —added "and, of course, you're free to go."

"Thank you," Larkin said, smiling at her own ingenuity. She was both a director and a detective, after all—and Jay had helped, for once, instead of getting in the way. "I'll make sure the cruise line knows how helpful you've been. Thank you for your hospitality, Officer Van der Voort, and for being so thoughtful of everybody's needs." Then she turned, trying not to analyze the expression on Jay's face. He still looked like he was pretending to be the romantic lead. "We really should go. Shouldn't we go, Jay?"

They said their goodbyes—handshakes followed by hand sanitizer—and as soon as the little metal door closed behind them, Larkin began walking as quickly as she could towards the Main Theater.

"We're going to check our badges at the door," she said, quietly, "and then we're going to lose them."

"Ooh, fun," Jay said. He finally sounded like himself; an antagonist, her nemesis, the kind of character that would nudge her into better behavior and then, conveniently, disappear. "What are we going to do, Detective Day?"

"We're going to ask Elliott to help us break into the Koningin Suite," Larkin said, "and we're going to figure out what happened to Adamantine Darcy's manuscript."

"This sounds like an extremely complicated way of clearing a stateroom attendant's name," Jay said. His voice was one step behind her. His mind was two steps ahead—or, at least, he thought it was—but for once, Larkin wasn't afraid of what might happen if Jay found something wrong with her plan. She was only afraid of what could happen if neither of them were able to figure out the best moves.

"It gets even more complicated," she whispered, entering the darkened theater and flashing her badge at a cruise-uniformed attendant holding a tablet. "If the manuscript is where I think it is, we're going to have to steal it."

CHAPTER 9

The first step was to get rid of their badges—or, as Larkin explained to Jay, to place them carefully in a pair of empty theater seats. "That way, the ship's computers will think we're watching the show."

Onstage, a Special Guest was riding a unicycle while playing a ukulele. The tune was familiar, but—as the guest began to sing—all of the lyrics had been reworked to incorporate Dungeons & Dragons. "Make sure you remember this guy," Jay whispered, "just in case the computers ask what you saw."

"I'll tell the computers I fell asleep," Larkin whispered back.

"You fell asleep next to me?" Jay whispered incredulously, as the two of them walked quickly and quietly down the aisle. "Head on my shoulder, the whole deal?"

"No," Larkin whispered back. "Just the ordinary way. Head flopping forward and jerking awake and then falling asleep again."

"Good," Jay whispered. "Otherwise, we'd have to

come up with one story for the computers and another story for your boyfriend."

Larkin wanted to tell her boyfriend the real story. She was ready to ask Ed if he wanted to be a part of the plan she had started putting together that morning—a carefully plotted series of events that now included what she was already thinking of as *the heist*—but when she reached the left-side aisle where they'd all been sitting, she found Anni and Elliott and four empty seats.

"Where's Ed?"

Anni nodded her head towards the box seats, where Ed had found a spot next to Grandmaster Trey. The two of them were having some kind of a private conversation, their words obscured by the audience's laughter as the ukulele-player made a joke that everyone else got. "Where are my mother and Claire?"

"They've gone to the Main Office," Anni said, "to try and get you out of jail."

"If they come back," Larkin said, "tell them I got myself out." Then she turned to Elliott. "We need you for a thing. Can you do a thing? I don't want to say what the thing is, not right now, but it's a very important thing, and you're the only person on the entire ship who can do it."

She watched Jay's hand descend, carefully, onto Elliott's shoulder—the first brush of fingers asking permission, the second and third fingers tapping out a series of dots and dashes. Elliott reaching up to cover Jay's hand as he transmitted the message, ensuring the conversation remained private. As Elliott clasped Anni's hand to continue the chain of communication, Larkin whispered, "When did you learn Morse Code?"

"As soon as I saw your friends using it to talk shit about me," Jay whispered back, as Anni nodded at Elliott, and he gathered up his things. That had been last summer;

Jay joining the group at the coffee shop where Larkin used to be a barista, Anni and Elliott tapping out messages on each other's wrists. Ed and Larkin, who had studied art instead of cryptography, had reverted to Pig Latin.

"Anni doesn't talk shit," Larkin whispered, following Elliott and Jay up the theater aisle. "She talks *shiitake mushrooms.*" Another code, designed to communicate one message to the adults in the room and another to the children—although everyone in Anni's family, including her sister's eight-year-old twins, knew exactly what was being said and unsaid.

"Not in Morse Code she doesn't," Jay whispered, as they exited the theater. Nobody scanned their badges on the way out, and Larkin and Jay remained—at least in the eyes of the ship's many iPads—in the aisle and next-to-aisle seats where they'd stashed their lanyards. "Too many letters."

"And yet you found the time to learn them all," Larkin whispered, the three of them walking quickly down the length of the ship's Promenade. There was a swimsuit store; a coffee shop; the kind of wine bar that had a locked piano in the front of it. It might have been the piano Elliott unlocked for Anni, ten years ago. She'd have to ask him later, when they had time for non-plan-related questions.

"Do you have everything you need?"

"Yep," Elliott said. "I have sufficiently advanced technology at my disposal."

"What does that mean?"

"I can do magic."

A parfumerie, in French; a chocolade winkel, in Dutch. A blinking soda machine attempting a universal language.

"How did you know it was a power outage?"

"The emergency lights went out," Elliott explained, as if it were obvious.

"Of course."

A kiosk of snapshots, posed and candid, taken by the ship's photographer—and that was when Larkin stopped.

"Wait," she said. "Look."

"At what?" Jay asked. Elliott, who already understood Larkin's instruction, began scanning the pictures that filled the hut-shaped frame. He found Adamantine almost immediately, pointing to a photo in a row labeled *Main Dining Room—Lunch—First Day at Sea*.

"Good," Larkin said. She'd guessed correctly. "Adamantine Darcy ate lunch in the Main Dining Room, with Eliza McFarlane and Daniel and Moira Pennington." She left out the part where she hadn't known who Eliza McFarlane was, aside from assuming she was Adamantine's assistant, and Jay—surprisingly—didn't add it. Instead, he pointed to a cluster of photos under the heading *Lido Deck*. "There you are." The photographer had captured all six of them—Larkin, Ed, Anni, Elliott, Josephine, and Claire—eating their poolside tacos. Claire had her feet in the water. Josephine was trying to catch a paper napkin before it blew away. Ed had just made a joke —a pun, more likely—because Larkin and Anni and Elliott were looking at him and laughing.

"It's an excellent photo," Jay said. Larkin wondered if part of him wished he were in it. She wondered if the other part of him knew that she couldn't remember what her boyfriend had said. She had been following along, relying on kinesthetic response to get her through the experience, her body acting automatically as her mind ran manually through the events of the morning.

What Adamantine had said to her—*Help me, or I'll end up dead before I'm ready*—and what she had said to Adamantine.

What she knew.

What Adamantine didn't know—which was why she needed to solve this manuscript mystery before Adamantine put the next phase of her plan into action.

"So we have proof that Adamantine was in the Main Dining Room while I was on the Lido Deck," Larkin said.

"Not necessarily," Jay corrected. "You could have spent part of your time in the dining room and the other part at the taco bar, just like the photographer did."

"His name is Ismael," Larkin said, "and we have proof that Adamantine was in the Main Dining Room."

"I don't see a manuscript, though," Elliott said. "Not in any of these pictures."

"It doesn't matter," Larkin said, *"because we have proof that Adamantine was in the Main Dining Room."* She started walking, quickly, towards the pair of glass-front elevators at the end of the Promenade. Jay, still one step behind and ahead of her, whispered "they're badge-operated," so Larkin swerved around a pair of nerds who were filling the Promenade's decorative fountain with hundreds of uniquely patterned rubber ducks—Larkin saw an Incredible Hulk duck, an Einstein duck, a duck that looked like the one Doctor Who she recognized, and a duck with a twenty-sided die for a head—and made a sharp turn onto the starboard deck before ascending the white, wooden stairs that allowed badge-free passage up the ship's exterior.

"There'll be a locked door at the top," Jay whispered, his cork-soled sandals clumping against each step. "Badge-only. It's like a floating hotel."

"I know," Larkin whispered back. She hadn't known, but Jay didn't need to know that. "We're not going in that door." Then she stopped—to give herself time to think, but Jay didn't need to know that—and turned to Elliott. "Do you have, like, your tools? Should we stop by our stateroom first?"

"I'm good," Elliott said. "I got what I needed out of Anni's bag before we left."

If he is more than his failures, it is because she is trying as hard as she can —

"Okay," Larkin said. She looked, carefully, at their surroundings. An exterior staircase that would take them to the Lido Deck if they couldn't find a way to get inside. A set of Verandah staterooms, each with its own private balcony—and Larkin allowed herself to imagine the three of them climbing from one balcony to another, clambering up the corners until they reached Adamantine's cabin, before she dismissed the scenario as both implausible and probably dangerous—and a subset of cruise-uniformed employees who were rearranging Verandah deckchairs and putting wet towels into wheeled canvas hampers.

Then Larkin knew how she would get where she needed to go.

"You two," she said, to Jay and Elliott, "wait by the Deck Nine door. I'll open it once I'm on the other side."

"Larkin," Jay said, giving her one of his most insouciant looks, "we are not doing the Mr. Bundles scene from *Annie*, are we?"

"What?" Larkin said, watching Jay's tousled head gesture towards the same laundry hamper that had given her the idea. "No. I wouldn't even fit in there. My plan's much simpler. I'm just going to, like, go up to the Lido Deck, pick up a bunch of wet towels, look for someone who's pushing a hamper through a badge-only door, carry the towels to the person with the hamper, drop them in, make a little conversation, and *hey would you look at that,* I'm suddenly standing in the hallway."

"The nerd who just wants to be helpful," Jay said.

"The nerd who uses a physical phishing scam to trick someone into opening the door for them," Elliott said.

"The *not-nerd* who should be *the only person on this boat* who knows *the Mr. Bundles scene from* Annie," Larkin said, ignoring whatever Elliott had just said about fishing and hooking her eyes on Jay. "How do you know that she hid in a laundry hamper? Did they stage it at your rich boy boarding school? Is there a picture of you somewhere, holding a bucket and singing about your hard-knock life?"

"Nope," Jay said. "Never saw the stage show." He winked at Larkin, taking in her fluster and bluster with his wide-open eye. "But when you figure out why I watched the 1982 film version so often that my mother had to replace the VHS, let me know."

Larkin allowed herself to climb three steps towards the Lido Deck before tossing her hair and calling back her answer: "Ann-Margret."

"Wrong," Jay said.

"It can't be Carol Burnett," Larkin said, "even though she spends most of the movie wearing a negligée."

"Larkin," Elliott said, his voice like the noise her first computer used to make right before she was about to do something she'd regret. A simple, descending chord, as a bicycle with eyeballs turned into a paperclip with eyeballs and reminded her to save her work. "Be careful." Maybe it wasn't a chord if the notes were played separately, the way Elliott had spoken them. She'd have to ask Ed, which is what Elliott had meant, wasn't it, *be careful about Jay and Ed* —because Elliott couldn't have meant *be careful gathering up towels*, that was the easy part, nerds were not known for their picking-up-after-themselvesness, she already had, like, twelve towels in her arms, she was practically to the door, she was through the door, she was thanking the stateroom attendant who had held it open for her, she was down the hall and down the stairs—yes, good, she didn't need a badge to enter the interior staircase, the ship still operated off the model that all staircases had to double as freely-descendible fire escapes, even though Larkin was sure that you'd want to go *up*, not *down*, if you were on a ship that were on fire, or sinking, or sinking while on fire —and then she was at the Deck Nine door and then she was opening it, no badge required, and then Jay and Elliott were inside.

"Told you it would work," Larkin said.

"We also told you it would work," Jay said. "There was literally no disagreement about this."

"Be quiet, both of you," Elliott said. "Follow me, and walk like you belong on this floor."

"It's a deck, you landlubber," Jay said, "and I do belong here. My stateroom is at the other end of the hall from Adamantine's. I'm sharing with Xavier, just like old times."

"Wait," Larkin said. "You mean—" She thought over everything that had happened in the last half hour. "We could have used your badge to access the elevators? We could have gone straight up to the ninth floor without having to trick a stateroom attendant into letting us in? We could have done all of this in, like, *two minutes*?" She stared at Jay, trying to arrange her face into something that resembled fury. "Why did you let me let you leave your badge in the Main Theater?"

"Because you're the detective," Jay said, "and if you were careless enough to ask me to leave my badge behind without asking me what it accessed, I certainly wasn't going to volunteer that information."

"I thought you were on my side!" Larkin said. "That means sharing all of the information you have!"

"It didn't last summer," Jay said—and this time he

looked at both Larkin and Elliott. The two of them had decided, as they'd worked together to solve the murders that had taken place during the Pratincola Summer Shakespeare Festival, to keep Jay on the outside of the investigation. It had been Larkin-and-Ed, Anni-and-Elliott, their four minds fitting together into a perfect square of artistry and nerdery. The director, the connector, the technician, and the magician. There had been no room—or rhyme—for Jaipal Malhotra.

"You were also careless enough," Jay continued, "to assume I dropped my badge next to yours." He reached into his pocket and pulled out his lanyard. "You should have checked, Detective Day."

Then he began walking down the hallway. "I'm going into my stateroom," he said, "to call the security office and report two suspicious individuals." He turned back to Larkin, running one hand through his curls. "Don't worry, I won't identify either of you by name—but if you're going to break into the Koningin Suite, you're going to need to get it done before the Chief Security Officer arrives."

He held his badge over the panel on the front of his door until it beeped, flashed green, and unlatched. "Or, you know, maybe Artie will delegate someone else to do it."

"Jay!" Larkin called out, as the door opened. She couldn't believe the words that were about to come out of her mouth, and they came anyway. "I thought you were my friend."

"You thought I was more than your friend," Jay said, "which gave me the advantage." He opened the door. "And I," he said, imitating the vowels of Officer Van der Voort, "was only ever—how do you say it? *Playing the long game.*"

CHAPTER 10

Larkin watched Jay close his stateroom door behind him. Then she turned to Elliott, who was crouching in front of the Koningin Suite. "We should go," she said. "We can figure out another way to clear Handy's name." She looked left, then right, then left again. They were still the only two people in the hallway. "I mean, I was pretty sure we'd find Adamantine's manuscript in her printer queue, she probably tried to print it and then something got in the way, maybe the printer was out of paper, or maybe the printer doesn't communicate with TOM." She looked right again. "I mean, my mom's printer refuses to accept ink cartridges that aren't, like, proprietary, and it'll stop printing if you close your laptop halfway through the job, so what if Adamantine did something like that by accident, and then forgot?" She looked left, her eyes pausing on Jay's doorway. "I just figured that was what happened, and I figured that if we found the manuscript and gave it back to Adamantine, Handy wouldn't get into any trouble."

"Okay," Elliott said, unwinding a long piece of wire

and twisting one end into a thumb-and-forefinger-sized loop. "Then we have a plan." He curved the wire, carefully, before slipping the looped end under Adamantine's door.

"We should go," Larkin said again. "I don't want you to get caught picking locks."

"No, we should stick with the plan," Elliott said. He pulled, slowly, on his end of the wire. "It's a good plan, and anything you come up with in the next four seconds is likely to be less good."

"Why do I only have four seconds?" Larkin asked.

"Because that's how long it takes me to unlock a standard lever-mechanism door," Elliott said. Larkin watched the door handle begin to pull itself downwards, as if by magic. Elliott, one hand still on his wire, pushed gently against the door of the Koningin Suite as the latch released. "Ta-da," he said softly, gesturing Larkin inside.

"Wow," Larkin said, as the two of them entered the suite and closed the door behind them. It still smelled of Adamantine's bacon-and-butter breakfast and the dregs of Larkin's coffee. Handy must not have hurried to clear Adamantine's tray, knowing that there wouldn't be any extra cash folded between the sugar packets or tucked under the carafe. "Will you tell me how the trick works?"

"Magicians never tell," Elliott answered, unhooking his looped wire from the handle on the interior side of Adamantine's formerly locked door, "but I bet you can figure this one out on your own."

"Well, sure," Larkin said, watching him coil his wire into a tight figure eight before tucking it into his back pocket, "but how'd you know how to get the loop around the door handle?"

"I did it a thousand times," Elliott said, "give or take." He stood in the center of Adamantine's sitting room, looking carefully at its layout. "Then I did a hundred takes in a row." His eyes paused on a panel in a cabinet. "Then I did it another hundred times until I could unlock a door in under five minutes." He opened the cabinet, revealing the same matte-black printer that Larkin's mother had in her home office. The light on the printer was blinking red.

"Okay," Larkin said, watching Elliott navigate the printer's touch-screen console, "but why did you spend so much time learning how to get a loop around a door handle? There's no reason to know how to do it except to, like, solve or commit crimes." Her mom's printer had the same console, and Larkin and Josephine knew how to tap their way around its three basic commands: *Print, Copy,* and *Scan.* Elliott had swiped his way into some kind of sub-menu she didn't even know existed.

"Why did you spend so much time studying theater?" Elliott asked. "There are even fewer reasons to do that." He entered a command into the printer's console. The red light turned green, and the machine began grinding.

"I wanted to understand how it worked," Larkin said.

"So did I," Elliott said. The first piece of paper made its way onto the printer tray.

"I wanted to know how to do it," Larkin said.

"So did I," Elliott said, handing the title page to Larkin.

The Yet Unknowing World

A Time Tangent Gentleman Novel, #42

By Adamantine Darcy

Larkin watched Elliott as he watched the printer. He was wearing slip-on sneakers with worn-out socks. His shorts were held up with a woven leather belt, and his shirt—which was both wrinkled and tucked in—had some kind of programming joke on it that Larkin was completely unable to parse. He'd worn his hair loose, today; the ginger strands and the gray ones tangling as he brushed a strand behind his ear. The ponytail holder was wrapped around his wrist, waiting for its moment—so Larkin took hers.

"I was also lonely," she said. It was the sort of thing she would have said to Anni, which was why she wanted to say it to Elliott—even though he, like Anni, would probably just tell her that loneliness was an easily manageable biochemical reaction. "I mean—"

"I know," Elliott said. "So was I."

The two of them listened to the printer as it wheezed; they watched as each successive page emerged and flew, on the energy of its potential and the momentum of its departure, before falling into place on the top of the growing stack.

"Do people have to be lonely to do what we do?" Larkin asked. "Or, like, sad?" She stared at the back of Elliott's T-shirt, which read *!front*, and decided it still didn't make any sense. "Is the tortured-artist thing real?"

"A famous magician once said that the best cure for sadness was to learn something," Elliott said, turning on his heels to look at Larkin. The front of his shirt read *!back*. "If there's nothing else to catch your interest, you might as well learn how to catch a handle on the end of a loop." He removed the first section of Adamantine's novel from the printer tray. "Or catch a ball in the cuff of a sleeve." Elliott passed the papers to Larkin. "But there's a difference between learning and creating."

That sounded like something Anni would say. "I'm much better at making things than I was," Elliott continued, "before we bought the farmhouse." He turned back to the printer tray, nudging the edge of a page that had fallen askew. "Mostly I'm better at making choices."

"I thought I was, too," Larkin said. "Because of Ed, and you and Anni, and directing the Shakespeare Festival."

She looked at her half of Adamantine's final draft. "But now I'm not so sure." Something about the title was familiar. She knew it.

"Ah," Elliott said. "Because of Ed, and me and Anni, and no longer being in a space where you're surrounded by people who do what you do best."

"Right," Larkin said. It always surprised her how observant Elliott was. Anni was observant too, but never about anything to do with people or feelings. Larkin wasn't sure Anni believed people had feelings. In Anni Morgan's mind, humans perpetuated *motion*, action-and-biochemical-reaction, and *emotions* were simply the stories they told themselves about the zip-zap-zops. "But what do you mean, when you say *because of Ed*?" she asked Elliott. "Is it the same thing that I mean, when I say it?"

"I don't mean anything," Elliott said. "I only meant to say that I knew it was troubling you."

"Right," Larkin said again. "Which means now I have to tell you what I mean—"

"No, you don't—"

"Good, because I'm not sure about that either." Larkin looked back down at Adamantine's title: *The Yet Unknowing World*. "And I don't want to make any decisions right now because I'm not sure they'll be my best ones."

"Because you're in a place where you don't belong," Elliott said.

"Right," Larkin said for the third time. "*Literally*, in this case."

Ed would have held up the remaining pages of Adamantine's manuscript and made some kind of quip about *literally* and *literature*. Elliott simply handed them to her. "Well," he said, checking and changing a few more printer settings before closing the cabinet, "we have what we came for. As long as the hallway isn't filled with Dutch Cruise International security officers, I think we're free to go." He stood up, running his fingers through his thinning ginger hair. "What's the next phase of the plan?"

"I'll put the manuscript in the Main Dining Room," Larkin said, tucking the pages carefully under her arm, "and make it look like Adamantine left it there."

———

Larkin had expected, after successfully collecting Adamantine's manuscript and retrieving her badge from the back row of the Gehoorzaal, to return to her stateroom and dress for dinner. She had expected to see Anni and Elliott put on some kind of costume, and to suggest that she and Ed *follow suit*—which might require borrowing a few playing cards from Elliott, but he wouldn't mind, he had at least four decks already spread out on what would otherwise have been the coffee table but had become, in just under twenty-four hours, *Elliott's workspace*. Larkin didn't have a workspace. She hadn't expected to need one.

She hadn't expected Ed to need one either—but when she made it back to the stateroom, she found the mirrored dressing table in their shared bedroom turned into a place where Ed could watch himself turntabling. He'd gotten a pair of old-school record players from somebody—Grandmaster Trey, presumably—and was busily twisting and scratching and whispering snatches of rap to a beat that was leaking from the earmuffs on his old-school headphones.

He didn't notice Larkin until she stood behind him and waved.

"I got Adamantine's manuscript," Larkin said, holding up the document.

Ed nodded—in time, more than anything else—and slid his left-hand record back.

"I'm going to dress for dinner," Larkin said, opening the panel that revealed their closet and looking for an outfit that might pair well with a playing card. The ankle-length dress with the oversized hibiscus print, probably—another of her mother's suggestions, and Larkin would have to remember to thank her mother for encouraging her to buy something so ridiculous—and she'd probably have to use tape to stick the cards to the shoulder straps, but Anni would probably have tape in her bag. Anni would also be able to clarify what a *follow suit* was, just in case it needed to be the clubs or something.

Larkin lay the rayon dress on the made bed, and then turned towards Ed's half of the closet, taking out something black, short-sleeved, and silky. He looked at her and shook his head.

"I'm practicing with the Grandmaster tonight," he said, each word matched to the scratch of a record. "You're going to have to eat without me."

"Okay," Larkin said, louder than she probably needed to. She left her dress on the bed and went into Anni and Elliott's half of the stateroom, where she found two laptops, three chessboards, the aforementioned decks of cards, and a neatly folded note next to what appeared to be a piano-keyboard-shaped headband.

The ink was pink, and the writing was legible, which meant Anni had written it.

Larkin—

You've figured out that Ed will be spending the evening with Grandmaster Trey. Elliott and I are having cocktails with Daniel and Moira Pennington, and although we hope to make it back to the Main Dining Room in time for the main course, this may turn out to be an all-night conversation. If you'd like to dress for dinner, you may have the costume I planned for myself tonight. It's quite simple—just a hair accessory, since I don't like full-body costumes that inhibit my range of motion—but it functions as a player piano, and is programmed to play the first eight measures of Für Elise. Press the button on the right-hand side to make it go.

Anni

P.S. Call your mom. I told her you got out of jail, but she probably wants to hear the whole story.

Larkin dialed Interior 3689. She told both her mother and Claire, who were cheek-to-cheek against the single receiver like two teenage girls, about her brief and largely positive interaction with Officer Van der Voort. She explained that Eliza had asked the security officer to keep her out of Adamantine's way for a while—"Hey," Claire said, laughing, "I remember when that happened to me!" "I remember it like it was yesterday," Josephine giggled, and Larkin wondered if the two of them had stopped for drinks on the way to their stateroom—and then Larkin explained that she knew where Adamantine's manuscript really was and was going to return it to her at dinner.

"My daughter, the detective," Josephine said, for the second time that day. There was an unnecessary *s* in *daughter*, which meant that Larkin's mother had definitely been experiencing some Champagne recently.

"Is your situation under control?" Claire asked.

"Absolutely," Larkin said. She hadn't mentioned the part where Jay had shown up unexpectedly, or the part where she had inadvertently implicated Handy, or the part where Elliott had unlocked the Koningin Suite in under four seconds. She also hadn't mentioned her disappointment at not being able to create a costume with Ed—and she still hadn't told anyone what she had told Adamantine at breakfast that morning, or what she'd have to do over the next five days to make sure Adamantine stayed alive. Larkin was so full of situational management and self-control that she didn't know if she'd have any room for dinner.

"Good," Claire said, "because we're planning on eating with the LGBTQ+ Boomers tonight, and I wanted to make sure you didn't need either of us for anything."

"She'll have her friends," Josephine said. "That's what my daughter has always needed."

"Right," Larkin said, not mentioning the part where Anni and Elliott had made other plans—because that didn't make them *not her friends*, Elliott had broken into a stateroom for her and Anni had left her a headband that played Beethoven on command. They were the best friends a thirty-six-year-old girl could have.

"And she's got love," Josephine said, after swallowing another sip of whatever she was currently drinking. "I wonder, by my troth, what thou and I did 'till we loved?"

"Is that Shakespeare?" Claire asked.

"Of course not," Josephine said, giggling again. "It's John Donne."

"I've got one," Claire said. Larkin heard the crack of an old paperback; the flap and slap as Claire turned the cheaply printed pages. "Most people think of time as a line that always moves forward, and love as a line that extends until it breaks." She took a deep breath. "But time is a circle and love is the point and I am the line, lonely and on my own, until you and I were brought together."

"Is that Shakespeare?" Josephine asked.

"Nope," Claire said. "Adamantine Darcy."

This time Larkin heard the kind of silence that could only mean a kiss.

"All right, you two," she said. "I'll leave you to it."

Then she slipped into the bedroom, slid into her hibiscus dress, spritzed and brushed her hair until it fell, smooth and shiny, underneath Anni's headband—Ed looked at her and smiled—and tucked Adamantine's manuscript into a cruise-branded tote bag.

"Have fun with Grandmaster Trey," she said to her boyfriend, leaning her face next to his as she applied her lipstick. She squeezed his shoulder, since his headphones were too bulky for her to kiss his cheek, and set off for the Main Dining Room.

CHAPTER 11

arkin had spent enough time in the theater to trust what was colloquially known as the *second-night slump*. A person who gave 110% for Opening Night only had 90% to give for the second performance—and even though the nerds she passed on the way to the Main Dining Room might have argued that it was mathematically impossible to give more than a hundred percent, their costumes proved both the theorem and the theory. Nobody looked their best, not on this second descent down the Grand Staircase. Some nerds had already gotten sunburned. Other nerds had already stopped showering. Even though most of the people surrounding her were dressed *as something*—Larkin saw one person wearing cat ears and a blue bathrobe, and another person wearing a rainbow flag pinned around their neck like a cape—there was definitely a ninety-percent-vibe going on.

Which made it very easy for Larkin to complete the last phase of her mission. She showed her badge to the cruise ship employee guarding the dining room door, walked towards the Special Guest section like she belonged there, dropped Adamantine's manuscript under the seat Adamantine had been photographed in at lunch, and went back to the employee holding the tablet.

"Can you get someone to check the Special Guest table?" Larkin asked. The employee, haphazardly matching each nerd's face to the photo associated with their scanned badge, did not look at Larkin. "There's something under one of the chairs."

"Check the Special Guest table," the employee repeated. He was now giving 88% to his job and 2% to Larkin. "Something under one of the chairs."

"I think it might be the manuscript Adamantine Darcy was looking for," Larkin said. The employee turned to look at her—*wrong word, Larkin, you should have said "the manuscript Adamantine Darcy lost"*—and she ducked her tall body behind a nerd dressed in one of those inflatable dinosaur suits. Then she watched the cruise employee continue his two-percent attempt at figuring out who had tasked him with this distracting job before waving over a server and gesturing towards the Special Guest table.

That was it, then; the manuscript would be found, Handy's name would be cleared, and Larkin would have solved another problem. Anni had once suggested that Larkin get business cards that read *Larkin Day: I Solve Everything*—but Larkin had been spared that particular embarrassment by getting hired, last-minute, as the Interim Artistic Director of the Pratincola Summer Shakespeare Festival. Now she only had to deal with the embarrassment of not knowing where to sit at dinner. Most of the nerds she'd passed on the way down had now passed her, filling the four-tops and six-tops in sets they'd already established. The nerds who arrived alone sat alone or hung around the edges of an eight-top until someone offered them one of the empty chairs. Larkin saw Eirwen, who was wearing a medieval chemise and kirtle, but it felt too awkward to walk towards the one nerd whose name she knew and ask if she could sit at her table—so Larkin left the Main Dining Room, crossed the Promenade, and swiped her badge at the ship's glass elevators.

She would have dinner by herself on the Lido Deck. A couple of tacos, some chocolate-vanilla-swirl ice cream out of the serve-yourself machine that Anni had warned her never to use—"I've seen kids stick their tongues right up the spouts"—and one of those cherry-and-orange hurricane drinks that they blended at the poolside bar. It would cost her thirteen dollars, plus tip, but she deserved it.

Except—and Larkin realized it as soon as she stepped out of the air-conditioned elevators and into the wet warmth of a Caribbean evening—she felt like she deserved more than a sticky-sweet drink in a fancy plastic glass. Way more than unsanitary soft serve. Even more than all the tacos she could eat, for free, while looking at a sunset that stretched to infinity and a collection of constellations that would slowly puncture the civil twilight.

"There's no such thing as deserve," Larkin said, pacing around the kiddie pool and trying her best to sound like her best friend. "If you don't get what you want, it means that all of your previous actions have led towards you not getting what you want." Then she decided to sound like herself—the director, not the detective. "Make another choice," Larkin said, softly, her words absorbed by the humid air.

She went to the taco bar. She ordered three shrimp tacos, three carnitas tacos, and three avocado tacos in a to-go box. She asked the server to point her towards the nearest phone. She tucked her tacos under one arm and dialed the Main Office. "Can you connect me to the Executive Suite?" she asked.

The answer was Dutch-accented and brusque. "Do you have business with the Executive Suite?"

"Yes," Larkin said. "Can you connect me?"

"I can leave a message."

"Good enough," Larkin said. She didn't even know if Jay was there, after all. She'd seen the name on the stateroom door before he went in, and she'd figured out the answer to the puzzle he'd set for her. "Please leave the following message. *Geoffrey Holder*."

"Geoffrey Holder," the Dutch cruise employee repeated.

"With a *g*, but it doesn't matter," Larkin said. "And please tell Jay Malhotra that if he wants to talk about Punjab, he has a friend waiting on the port side of the Lido Deck with nine tacos."

There was a pause, and the scratch of a pen—Larkin had forgotten how clear these landlines were, and how easy it was to use them to communicate. The curve of the old-fashioned receiver perfectly matched the space between her mouth and her ear, and she could hear the Dutch cruise employee quietly confirming her message. "And tell him to bring two iced coffees with a shot of bourbon in each," Larkin continued, asking for exactly what she wanted. "Top shelf please, I know he can afford it."

"Would you like me to just connect you to Mr. Malhotra's stateroom?"

"No," Larkin said. "This is much more fun." She looked up, past the stairs at the bow of the ship and into the wide glass windows of the Performers' Lounge. Anni and Elliott were sitting with Daniel and Moira Pennington. She could just make them out—she could wave if she wanted—but Larkin let them be. Everyone was making new friends tonight or remaking old ones. She would too.

"Do you have anything else you'd like me to pass along?"

"No," Larkin said, "but thank you." She wished she had a twenty-dollar bill to send down the telephone wires, although she didn't know if the Dutch employee would be as gracious about receiving it as Handy had been. So she hung up, and walked over to the poolside bar to get herself and Jay each a plastic cup of water, and then arranged herself and her eight tacos—she ate one of the shrimp ones—at a portside table for two.

"Hello, nerds!" It was the all-ship intercom. "I wanted to let you all know that Adamantine Darcy's manuscript has been found! Whew!" Xavier's improvisatory work was slightly less skilled than his scripted banter. "Here I was, thinking that we'd never know what happened to Horatio Bonheur, or, you know, that we had a manuscript thief on board, but the document was in the Main Dining Room the entire time! Let's thank our talented Dutch Cruise International waitstaff for successfully locating the missing manuscript and returning it to Adamantine!" He held, assumedly for applause, and then continued. "And now I want all of you who are on the starboard side of the ship to take a look out of your nearest window, because isn't that sunset something?"

It was, Larkin thought—and so was she. She was a grown woman on a relaxing cruise vacation, she had a plan to keep Adamantine alive, she'd successfully kept Handy from getting into trouble, and she was going to spend the evening getting to know her former nemesis.

The iced coffee was placed in front of her, just as she expected it would be.

"Hello, Larkin," Jay said. "What are you wearing on your head?"

CHAPTER 12

The coffee cups were empty; only half an avocado taco remained untouched. Their conversation had followed its logical path from Anni's Beethoven-playing headband, the eight bars of *Für Elise* barely audible above the Weird Al parodies that soundtracked the Lido Deck like a security blanket—"that one's not Weird Al," Jay corrected, when Larkin commented on the choice of noise, "it's Da Vinci's Notebook"—to Anni and Elliott as roommates, and then Jay and Xavier as roommates, both in the present and in the past, and then the best and worst roommates either of them had ever had.

It was not quite small talk. It was, Larkin thought, a substitute for the apology each of them owed the other. She and Jay had pretended to be friends, each of them operating under false pretenses. Now they might decide to become friends for real.

"Punjab," she finally said, after enough stars had come out for the Lido Deck to switch its background music. No more parodies, and no more lyrics—just a lush hum that Larkin suspected could be purchased, in a CD packaged with a scented candle, at the starboard spa. "You watched *Annie* to see Geoffrey Holder playing Punjab."

"Correct," Jay said. "Imagine me at eight years old, a skinny little brown kid, so desperate to see a character who looked like me that I completely ignored the fact that I was watching a Black man play an Indian man."

"And Punjab was, like, the ultimate stereotype," Larkin said, trying to remember the last time she'd seen the movie. Geoffrey Holder wore a turban and whirled around Daddy Warbucks' mansion before levitating a potted plant.

"Well, sure," Jay said. "But also, you know—"

Larkin didn't know. She waited, quietly, for Jay to tell her.

"He wasn't the other kind of stereotype, right? He didn't program computers or own a convenience store. He didn't do the little head shake"—Jay waggled his head from side-to-side—"and he wasn't the ass-end of the joke."

Larkin watched Jay shift his gaze from her eyes to his fingers. Then she watched him look away from them both. "He was an action hero," Jay said, softly, towards the left-over avocado taco. "He used that helicopter to save Annie when she was dangling from the railroad bridge."

"And that was what you wanted to do," Larkin said. They had had this conversation before, although not quite at this level. Jay had joked about having the kind of mind that could easily figure out how to murder people, so he had decided to put his extensive mental capacities towards saving them instead. Jay was a surgical resident, now—a noble, appropriate career that had pleased both of his parents—but part of him still hoped to become the kind of man who could launch himself from an autocopter to outwit the bad guys.

"It's what I still want to do," Jay said. He ran his hand

through his thick, curly hair before turning to Larkin and affecting a smile. "Not that I'd make a very good bodyguard." He grabbed a fistful of the pudge that pressed against his T-shirt. "I haven't even taken care of the body I have."

"Neither have I," Larkin said, lifting her left arm and letting it jiggle. "Put it all in the ol' brain."

"To brains," Jay said, raising his plastic coffee cup and sipping the centimeter of melted ice that still coated the bottom.

"Braaaaaaains," Larkin said, reaching her arms towards Jay like a zombie—and then pulling away, like a human woman who very definitely had a boyfriend, as soon as her fingers brushed his shoulders. "Sorry," she said, picking up her empty coffee cup and pretending to drink from it. "To brains." *Two brains*, she thought, thinking of Ed. *He would have made a joke about it.*

But Ed was with Grandmaster Trey, turntabling—and as Larkin turned away from the table she was sharing with Jay to see if there was anything else she could do to keep her from getting into the kind of trouble she couldn't get out of, *literally anything*, she could go talk to that family of nerds who were playing handheld video games in a row of deck chairs, or she could go help the three teenage nerds who were trying to figure out shuffleboard, not that she knew anything about shuffleboard herself, or she could tag along with the elderly nerd couple who were wearing matching sweatshirts—*I'm With Smart*—and walking the circumference of the Lido Deck as if it were a track, she heard Jay say "Hello, Ms. McFarlane!"

It was Eliza, dressed for a late-night swim. She registered Jay's voice, categorized him as a stranger, and then noticed he was sitting next to someone she knew. "Hello," Eliza said, nodding briefly at Jay before turning to Larkin.

"We found the manuscript," she said, pulling up a chair. "It was in the Main Dining Room."

Larkin couldn't tell whether Eliza knew how the manuscript had made its way into the Main Dining Room or not, so she kept her mouth shut and waited for Eliza to continue the conversation.

"I'm sorry Adamantine accused you," Eliza said. She looked tired. Her arms and legs were enviably slim, but there was something about her body that suggested she hadn't prioritized regular meals. Her swimsuit gapped when she sat, and the strands of metallic hair trapped under her goggles looked like they were ready to snap. "I tried to tell her you couldn't possibly have taken her book, but she wouldn't listen to me."

Larkin looked at Jay, who knew that she had in fact taken Adamantine's manuscript and waited for him to ruin the moment. He did not. Like Larkin, he seemed much more interested in hearing what Eliza had to say.

"I finally got her to sleep," Eliza continued, her eyes twitching towards the bits of avocado taco that sat in the bottom of the to-go box. Larkin watched Jay raise his hand, issuing a command with the tips of his fingers. It only took a moment for the attendant to appear; Jay gave him both a request and a twenty as Eliza continued talking. "She's still pretty good, most of the time. They call it sundowning, you know. People get more forgetful at the end of the day, probably because they're tired, and it was an extra-tiring day for Adamantine. She finished her final draft this morning."

"And then she lost her manuscript," Jay said.

"And right before she accused me of stealing it," Larkin said, remembering what she had seen in the Gehoorzaal, "the power went out."

"I know," Eliza said. The attendant arrived with a box

of tacos and a glass of white wine. "I can't figure out how that happened."

"Don't power outages just happen?" Larkin asked. "Like, because of weather or whatever?"

"Not if you're on a cruise ship," Eliza said, finishing her first taco in two bites. "There are generators and fail-safes." She took a sip of her wine. "There have been cruise ships that have lost power before, but only after catastrophic events." She reached for another taco. "There was that infamous sailing, you remember, where the engine room caught on fire." Then she took another sip of her wine. "Wow," Eliza said, turning to Jay. "This is an excellent pinot gris."

"I thought you might appreciate it," Jay said. "If you're going to eat fast-food tacos, might as well pair them with a decent wine." Larkin wondered if Jay was flirting with Eliza, or—even worse—doing that thing that didn't even have to be called flirting because it happened so naturally. Making a connection. Bonding.

"What happened to TOM after the power went out?" Jay asked. "I assume Adamantine lost access to her stored data."

"She lost access to her stored memories," Eliza corrected, wiping her fingers on one of the paper napkins that had been shoved into the corner of the taco box. "Adamantine had to rely entirely on what she could recall from her own mind." She held her wineglass to her lips, and then set it down without sipping. "I should have thought of that," she said. "The power outage. We were working off the ship's Wi-Fi network, which meant that TOM was triaging pretty hard. It was storing Adaman-tine's memories in place of its own."

"TOM has memories?" Larkin asked. She still wasn't quite sure how artificial intelligence worked.

"All operating systems have memory," Eliza said. "But they only have a limited amount of local storage, so when Adamantine decides to do something like download fourteen hours of Blythe and Bonnie Cooper's podcast so TOM can sort and summarize every mention of *detective Larkin Day*, the system is designed to overwrite something it considers inessential."

Larkin had been wondering about that. "So Adamantine didn't interview Blythe and Bonnie."

"Not in what you would consider the original use of the term," Eliza said. "She asked TOM a series of questions that she would have liked to ask Blythe and Bonnie, and TOM analyzed the podcast audio until it found the answers they might have given." She fingered the stem of her wineglass, careful not to touch the remaining pinot gris. "That wasn't my idea, not originally. A journalist who was interviewing me brought it up. He said he knew I would give Slate the same basic answers I'd given Vox and Wired, and he wished there was a way he could ask TOM the questions and have it scan my previous work and generate my most likely responses."

"But that ends up taking a lot of data," Jay said. "Which means that TOM has to overwrite some of its other stored data."

"It isn't a big deal," Eliza said, "in most cases." She looked at Larkin and Jay as if what she were about to say should already have been obvious to them both. "In the real world, a person like Adamantine will nearly always have access to fast, reliable Wi-Fi." She considered, one more time, whether she deserved to sip such a good wine. "TOM can upload and download to the cloud, pulling and shelving memories as needed."

"But on a cruise ship—" Larkin began.

"Exactly," Eliza said. "It was the middle of the day, and

the limited Wi-Fi was already overloaded. After the power outage, TOM couldn't maintain a connection long enough to complete its reboot procedures."

"Which is Adamantine's loss," Jay said—*pun intended*, Larkin thought, thinking of Ed—"but your gain." He nudged Eliza's wineglass towards her. "Come on," he said. "Don't punish yourself for thinking of it."

Eliza McFarlane—high-strung, platinum-haired, body like an Ethernet cable—took a careful sip of her wine. "I had two responsibilities on this cruise," she said, before taking another swallow. "One was to Adamantine. That one I failed." She finished the glass. "The other was to TOM, which is to say to myself." Jay raised his hand again and Eliza shook her head. "I successfully identified one of the major problems with taking TOM on a cruise, which should also apply to users who want to take TOM on safari or into low-earth orbit or any of those other bucket-list things that don't come with reliable internet connections. I can fix what went wrong."

"It's a net positive," Jay said, lowering his hand onto Eliza's wineglass-wrapped fingers. Squeezing her thumb. "The shareholders will agree. So will all of the people who might someday use TOM to help them manage their minds." He released his grip and held Eliza's eyes. "They won't need to know what happened to Adamantine, of course—but if it ever got out, they'll be glad you updated TOM, so it won't happen to them."

Eliza nodded. Jay was, as usual, captivating—and Larkin wondered if he were performing his typical manip-ulations, or if he had ulterior motives in mind. She imag-ined Eliza turning left instead of right, entering the Executive Suite instead of the Koningin—and then Larkin decided to change her own course, since she didn't trust herself not to interfere with their collision.

"I'm going to find my boyfriend," she said, standing up and stretching her arms over her head, letting Eliza see her length, width, and depth, not to mention the cheap sundress she was currently wearing, and register her as *no threat*. "He must be done turntabling by now." Larkin glanced up at the Performers' Lounge, hoping she would see Ed behind one of the plate glass windows. Elliott and Anni were still there, as was Daniel Pennington. She didn't see Grandmaster Trey, but she could call the Main Office and ask to send a message to his stateroom. "Give Adamantine my best, when she wakes up," Larkin said, fist-bumping Eliza and then, since Jay refused to hold up his closed hand, aiming her fist into his shoulder.

It landed a little harder than she meant it to—which is to say that it landed exactly as hard as she wanted it to—and then Larkin left, to find the man she was spending the night with and told herself not to look back. Jay was either staring at her or gazing at Eliza, and neither of those decisions would affect what needed to happen next.

CHAPTER 13

"Hello, nerds!"

Larkin was awake even before Xavier made his announcement. She had slept well, her eyes flicking open with the sunrise, her mind called to attention with the ship's horn. Ed, who had covered his eyes with a Howell-branded sleep mask and pressed a pair of flesh-toned foam earbuds into their respective crevices, shifted position but continued to snore.

"Welcome to St. Maarten, where the local time is 6:53 a.m. and the local temperature is 79°F, 26°C, and 299 Kelvins!"

She waited.

"Wow, when you convert things to the Kelvin scale they sure do feel minus thirty-two, multiplied by five, divided by nine, plus 273.15 times as hot, don't they?"

Ed's snore sounded almost like a snicker. She wondered if he was waking up. After the night they'd had, Larkin didn't want to wake him herself—even though she could see the scene in her mind, her dark hair falling over his dark skin, her lips brushing against his cheek, a whisper turning into a kiss. *Good morning, darling*. She'd never called Ed *darling* before, but it seemed like the thing women did, after the kind of encounter that turned a boyfriend into a lover. Larkin had both made and directed that play, too—she didn't think Ed knew, and she hoped he didn't know *why*—and the prompted improvisation had expanded into a narrative and then, for both of them, a climax.

They'd had sex before.

They had never had this kind of sex before.

"But don't worry, if the daystar gets a little too warm for some of you indoor nerds, you can always come back to our climate-controlled cruise ship! The twenty-four hour Game Room will still be open, and I've been told that the Lido Deck will be serving breakfast tacos all day long!"

Larkin immediately imagined a different scene—she and Ed, still in bed, feeding each other egg and chorizo. Leaving Handy a forty-dollar tip, to make up for the mess they left behind. She'd already planned to place a twenty on the nightstand, to thank Handy for changing the sheets. They'd both had to sleep in wet spots, although neither of them had minded.

"If you are taking a scheduled excursion, one of our cruise attendants will guide you to the appropriate location! They'll be scanning every badge as it leaves the dock, and making sure everyone gets to swim with the dolphins or tour Fort Amsterdam or whatever you're hoping to do today! If you still need to schedule an excursion, call or visit the Main Office. We've got a few more snorkels available, for those of you who want to see the underwater pirate ship!"

Anni had told them not to bother with the underwater pirate ship. She'd also warned them against any excursion that involved riding horses into the ocean—"fun fact, horse droppings float"—and suggested they spend their time focusing on the island's history.

Larkin only wanted to focus on the present. She was giving Ed the gift of sleep, and waiting to see what he would give her when he pulled the foam out of his ears and slipped the fabric off his eyes.

It took Ed a while to fully awaken—an interminable interval, during which Larkin distinctly heard Anni and Elliott discuss what they had heard the night before—and the silence of their shared bed only ended when Larkin, who had hoped to hold both her tongue and her bowels, could no longer wait to evacuate. By the time she came out of the bathroom, Ed was not only *up*, but also *at 'em*.

"Good morning," he said, unfolding a pair of seersucker shorts and giving Larkin a kiss that was meant for her cheek but got tangled in her unbrushed hair.

"Good night," Larkin said, hoping to turn the favor into conversation. "Pun intended."

Ed looked at her—or he almost did, anyway, before turning his eyes back towards his clothing. He pulled at a hidden drawer, placing a crisp button-up over the puckered seersucker. "It was a good night, wasn't it?"

"Best we've ever had."

Another hidden drawer revealed a row of rolled-up towels. "Do you mind if I take the first shower? We're doing this Black History tour of St. Maarten, it's this unofficial thing, the Blerds arranged it, Grandmaster Trey's leading it, we're supposed to meet for breakfast in fifteen minutes—"

"Sure," Larkin said. "Go ahead."

"Thanks," Ed said, holding the towel under his arm. He was naked—he'd slept naked, except for his eyeshade and earplugs—and didn't seem to mind. This could have been because he felt comfortable with Larkin. It also could have been because his mind was somewhere else.

"We probably won't be back for lunch, either," Ed said, his shower-capped head popping out of the bathroom door as the water began to steam. "Are you going to be okay hanging out with Anni and Elliott? I'd invite you, but—"

"Of course," Larkin said. "I love you."

He'd gone back to being a boyfriend again—and after he left, kissing Larkin quickly on the top of her disheveled head, Larkin realized that she would be spending the morning, if not the entire day, alone. Anni and Elliott had inserted their earbuds and were tapping at their respective keyboards. Anni had left a note which explained, in more words than might have been necessary, that she and Elliott would be spending the morning putting things in order, that they had seen St. Maarten before and did not need to repeat the tour, *but we hope you and Ed have as much fun as you seem to be having, etc. etc. etc.!* Larkin called Interior 3689, trusting that her mother would say something about how she'd just been thinking of her, and would love to meet up for breakfast and explain exactly what Maarten had done to become a saint, but the phone rang ten times before Larkin replaced the receiver—and so the message, such as it was, was received.

It was unbelievable, but not surprising. Everyone else was being their Best Selves—Ed with the Blerds, Anni and Elliott with their work, and Josephine and Claire with each other.

Which meant that Larkin would need to figure out how to be whoever she was when she wasn't with Ed, or Anni and Elliott, or her mother and Claire.

She hadn't been that person in a very long time.

The first step was, of course, to get a cup of coffee. Not from one of the sunscreen-smeared carafes on the Lido Deck, which served the kind of all-day brew that hotels and cruise lines could afford to give away for free, but from one of the gleaming, buzzing, five-dollar-shot machines on the Promenade. The Coffeeshop—all one word, unlike The Coffee Shop in Pratincola—was covered in wood paneling and silk tulips. It smelled of roasting and grinding and hand sanitizer, and Larkin accepted the squirt of ethanol from the automated dispenser before she took her cup of dark, acidic espresso from an efficient Dutch barista.

It was barely enough for a swallow, but Larkin knew exactly what this kind of coffee could do to a person who usually diluted her drink with milk and sugar. Wake her up; shake her out; send her straight to the nearest bathroom.

That was where she met Eirwen.

"Hello," Larkin said. Eirwen was wearing a turquoise necklace and a ruffled white blouse; her skirt was printed like a bandana and her hair was tied back in one. A tote bag was clamped under her arm; an intimidatingly large book was poking out of the top. "You look like you're ready to explore St. Maarten."

Eirwen glared at Larkin. She ran her hands underneath the automatic faucet, mumbling the alphabet song under her breath.

"Okay," Larkin said. "Clearly I said something wrong. I'm sorry."

She waited for Eirwen to get all the way to Z.

"I just meant that I liked your outfit," Larkin said. "I didn't wear an outfit today. Just clothes."

Eirwen ran her hands under the automatic dryer.

"Sorry," Larkin said again. "I'm, um, just going to leave now."

She pushed her terrycloth-covered hip against the bathroom door.

"You can stay," Eirwen said, her voice loud enough to accommodate the automatic dryer. "If you want."

"I don't really want to stay here," Larkin said. "All of these cruise ship bathrooms smell like rotten vegetables."

"I know, right?" Eirwen said. The automatic dryer finished its cycle, and she finished drying her hands on her skirt. "I've been on three of these cruises and I still haven't figured out what that smell is."

"It's not puke, right?" Larkin asked, holding the door for Eirwen to pass through.

"I don't think so," Eirwen said. "If this sailing had norovirus, we would know by now."

"Does that mean we can start shaking hands again?"

"No," Eirwen said. The two of them were walking, slowly, down the Promenade. "Handshakes are outdated technology. Fist bumps only, on this cruise."

"And hugs," Larkin said. "Unless you have the button that says you don't want hugs."

She looked at Eirwen's lanyard. *SHE/HER*, a trans flag, and a button that read *ASK ME WHAT I'M READING*.

"What are you reading?"

"Electric Quim, mostly," Eirwen said. "It's this new literary journal for trans writers, but it's online only, so I couldn't, like, bring it on the boat. I'll catch up on the updates when we get back."

"What are you reading now?" Larkin gestured towards the enormous volume dominating Eirwen's tote bag.

"*The Once and Future King,*" Eirwen said. She almost looked embarrassed. "You know, T.H. White?"

"I know *Camelot*," Larkin said. "It might be my favorite musical." Now she almost felt embarrassed. "But I never read the book."

"I've read it ten times," Eirwen said. "I mean, I've only read the whole thing, like, three times. But I used to read *The Sword in the Stone* over and over and over."

They were at the fountain; Eirwen knelt down to poke at a tiny rubber duck wearing a tiny wizard's hat. "I used to wish Merlin would help me." She pushed the little wizard forward with her finger, sending it bobbing and bumping into one of the many duck-shaped Time Lords. "Then I figured out that, like, *that was what the whole book was about.*"

"Think, Arthur, think," Larkin said, giving her best David Hurst impression. She sat down on the edge of the fountain, watching Eirwen nudge and rearrange the ducks. "So should I read it?"

"Yeah, if you want," Eirwen said. She appeared to be pointing all of the ducks in the same direction. "I mean, there are probably more important things for you to read right now." The wizard duck had gotten turned around, somehow; Eirwen gently tapped its flank until it was in line with its fellows. "Besides an old white guy book, you know."

"So when you're old, what you write doesn't matter anymore?" Larkin asked. She smiled, even though Eirwen couldn't see it. "Better not tell Adamantine Darcy."

"No," Eirwen said, "the book's what's old. White wrote it when he was young." She paused; her shoulders hunched. "Younger than me. He redefined an entire genre when he was, like, *thirty-two.*"

Larkin remembered their earlier conversation. "Which is what you want to do."

"Yeah," Eirwen said. "I mean"—she turned to Larkin—"that's what you have to do, right?"

"What do you mean, *have to do*?"

"If you want to be, like, *real*." Eirwen pushed herself off her heels and settled on the edge of the fountain. "You can't just copy what's worked before, or everyone will forget you." She looked at her feet; a pair of flowered flip-flops and a row of red-painted toenails. "That's what's going to happen to Adamantine Darcy, you know, as soon as she finally kicks it. You think she's, like, Terry Pratchett? Octavia Butler? Ted Chiang? I mean, Ted Chiang's still alive, I hope he stays alive, but"—Eirwin kicked at the fountain—"did Adamantine Darcy actually do anything to expand the possibilities of sci-fi and fantasy? Is there any reason to remember her after she's gone?"

"I don't know," Larkin said. She had no idea who any of these authors were. "Some people might remember Adamantine, or at least they'll remember how much they liked her books."

"Her books are garbage." Eirwen funneled her face into a sneer. "Adamantine Darcy cranked out a bunch of sexy time-traveler novels right before sexy time-travel became really popular." She pointed her anger at Larkin. "She got lucky."

"Whoa," Larkin said. "I wouldn't say that. You know she's not well."

"Yeah," Eirwen said, "and I know she has access to an exobrain, and Eliza McFarlane walking around with some fake-ass dyed hair like we won't recognize her, taking notes on everything that happens, and Adamantine's probably going to turn it into some kind of posthumous memoir, and I can't even get a single one of my stories into Electric Quim."

"Okay," Larkin said. She didn't know what to say next,

so she looked out towards the Promenade—and saw Anni, at the photo kiosk, writing something on what appeared to be a sign-up sheet. Larkin decided it was a sign. "Let's go ask my friend Anni about it." She stood up. "She's a writer."

"She's, like, a *finance* writer." Eirwen stood up, reluctantly. "She does *content*."

"And she's content with it," Larkin said, "pun intended." She waved at Anni and smiled at Eirwen. "Plus, she's the smartest person I know. If anyone can figure out how to get magazines to pay attention to your stories—"

Then Larkin stopped.

"Wait. Maybe I'm the smartest person I know, at least for today."

"Why?"

Larkin sat down again. "Because I figured it out. The real problem, and the real solution." She patted the part of the fountain next to her, and Eirwen lowered herself to the rim. "You shouldn't be writing for this Electric Whatever-it-is."

"Yeah, I should," Eirwen said. "It's the biggest outlet right now for trans writers."

"Okay, great, but still." Larkin looked at the woman sitting next to her. "I saw your manuscript. It's very high tech, I think that's the right word for it, there were plenty of words I didn't understand, but most of it was, like, computers and sex toys."

"Trans is tech," Eirwen said. "That's Electric Quim's tagline."

"Okay, great," Larkin said again, "but it seems to me like you're writing a bunch of stuff you're not really interested in."

"I'm not really interested in being trans?" Eirwen

twisted her face again, turning it away from Larkin. "Tell that to my medical bills."

"This has nothing to do with—" Larkin knew she had to choose her words carefully. "You like the Arthurian legends. You like that story about the young girl who disguises herself as a knight and goes into the forest to learn how to be brave. You probably love the Narnia books."

"I liked *The Magicians* better," Eirwen said. "Especially the TV series."

Anni, at this point, had joined them. "Hello, Larkin. Hello, Eirwen. I assume you were waving me over?"

"I was," Larkin said, "and I want to ask you a question about writing." She stood up, wiped a stray drop of water off the edge of the fountain, and gestured for Anni to sit next to Eirwen; Anni inspected Larkin's handiwork, nodded in approval, and sat. "Let's say that you've been submitting a bunch of stories to a magazine that isn't accepting your work. Is there any reason to continue submitting stories to this magazine?"

"There are many reasons to continue submitting stories," Anni said, "whether you are interested in improving your craft or interested in gaining status as a writer by association with this particular publication."

This wasn't how Larkin had expected Anni to answer—so she asked a different question. "But what if these stories aren't what you really want to write?"

"What do you mean?"

"What if—just as an example—you're really into fantasy and the magazine only accepts sci-fi?"

"Then you take the aspects of fantasy writing that most appeal to you and reconstruct them within a science-fiction paradigm," Anni said. "There are plenty of storytellers who have successfully integrated the two genres, *Star Wars* being the classic example."

"Original trilogy only," Eirwen said.

"Obviously," Anni agreed.

"Okay," Larkin said, "but *Star Wars* is also a terrible example—and I can't believe I know this, because I am *not a nerd*—but didn't they start focusing on all kinds of crap that didn't have anything to do with the story, like, let's shove everything a computer can do at the original trilogy, because everything is better with computers, and let's make a movie that has something for the kids and something for the superfans who are really into intergalactic senate meetings, and let's take the one thing everyone wanted to see happen and, like, *take it away from them*, because surprise endings are way more interesting, even though anyone who's studied storytelling in any form knows that *the most satisfying ending is the one you see coming*?"

Eirwen laughed. "How are you not a nerd?"

"Larkin's a theater geek," Anni said. "She doesn't think that's the same thing."

"The point is"—Larkin had forgotten what the point was, but she knew she needed to make one—"I don't think Eirwen should write stories about teledildonics. Not because I'm anti-sex or anything. It's just that all of the writing I saw in that manuscript was incredibly cynical, it painted the future as this terrible place where everyone would be miserable all the time, with only sad robot dogs and cranky robot dildoes to keep them company"—and then Larkin remembered the point, and looked directly at Eirwen to deliver it—"and I think that you should write about heroes and bravery and *what it means to be a person*, since that's really what you're interested in, and that's really what's going to interest other people, *no matter what the future is like,* and leave the angry beep-boop stuff to someone else."

Eirwen looked carefully at Larkin, the lines in her fore-head wavering between distrust and hope. "I will take your advice under consideration," she said. Then she turned, swiping one hand under her eyes, and began re-organizing the rubber ducks.

"I really liked your story about the boy and the moon," Anni said. "I thought it was your best one, of all the ones you shared to the cruise forums last year. You should read it at the talent show. There are still plenty of slots, or at least there were when I signed myself and Elliott up." She gestured towards the sheet of paper next to the photo kiosk. "Larkin, your mom and Claire signed up too. They're doing some kind of dramatic reading."

This, unbelievably, did not surprise Larkin. Her mother and Claire seemed to be having exactly the kind of relaxing cruise vacation they had all been promised—and she'd have to ask them about it the next time she saw them, which might not be until Disembarkation Day.

Until then, it might be time for her to see just how nerdy she actually was—and how good she was at making new friends.

"Are none of us going to explore St. Maarten?" Larkin asked. "I've never been."

"I've been seven times," Anni said, "but I'll go with you if you want."

"Good," Larkin said. "You can be our tour guide. Are you in, Eirwen?"

Eirwen, who was still getting her ducks in a row, shrugged. "I don't want to leave the ship. I might not be, you know, *welcome.*"

"St. Maarten is one of the most LGBTQ-friendly destinations in the Caribbean," Anni said. "That's why the cruise keeps it on its port list."

"Yeah," Larkin said, "but what does it keep on its starboard list?" She both pantomimed and beatboxed a rimshot, and then she bent over the rim of the fountain to pluck out the rubber duck that was dressed as a tiny wizard.

"Here you go," Larkin said, wiping the duck off on her terrycloth shorts before handing it to Eirwen. "Keep that as a reminder of my good advice, whether or not you end up taking it." She turned to Anni. "I need to go back to the stateroom and get my big floppy hat, and probably a bottle of water, and maybe a thing of sunscreen."

"I already have sunscreen," Anni said, "and two bottles of water in my bag."

"Then I'll get one more, for Eirwen," Larkin said, "and I'll meet you all back here in five minutes. Let's go see Fort Amsterdam!"

———

Larkin thought, as she made her way back to Verandah 213, that her Best Self had turned out to be a pretty good person—with or without her friends and family and boyfriend. She could help a famous writer; she could help a future famous writer; she could make the kinds of choices that allowed people like Jay to connect with people like Eliza, instead of the kinds of choices that trapped herself and Jay and Ed in some kind of titanic love triangle. She could even hold her own with the nerds, as long as they stuck to subjects like *the most popular film series ever made.*

She could also wink, knowingly, at Handy—because there he was, in the stateroom, finishing up his portion of the housekeeping—and apologize for leaving the bedroom the way she and Ed had left it.

"Thank you for changing the sheets and cleaning everything up," Larkin said, sliding her suitcase from underneath her bed. She shook out her floppy hat and fished through her purse for a five. "Ours was the worst stateroom you've seen today, right?" She held the folded bill in Handy's direction. "The biggest mess?"

"It was nothing, Miss Day," Handy said, taking both the money and the bait. "You should have seen the mess they left in the Koningin Suite this morning! Everything was out of order." He smiled, conspiratorially. "You will keep this between us? I had to request a new set of sofa pillows. The ones in Miss Darcy's stateroom were no longer in an acceptable condition."

"Unbelievable," Larkin said—even though she was, for the third time that day, not surprised.

In fact, it was exactly what she wanted to happen.

What she had hoped for.

Now all she had to do was prevent what Adamantine feared.

CHAPTER 14

Adamantine Darcy's seminar on artificial intelligence in sci-fi and fantasy—the one Claire had called "AI 'n' SF 'n' F"—took place not in the Main Theater, but in the kind of cruise ship conference room that included a smartscreen, four rows of folding chairs, and the ever-present cash bar.

Larkin, arriving early enough to secure five consecutive seats—Ed and Anni had elected to remain in Veranda 213 with their respective instruments; Eirwen, after the success of the St. Maarten field trip, had voted herself into the group—had immediately dubbed the room "the Gehoorsmaal."

"That would be *small* with two *a*s and one *l*," Larkin said. "Like Gehoorzaal, except, you know. *Smaller.*" Then she thought of what Ed might say, if he were there. "It's only a little joke."

"Yeah, and if you have to explain it, it doesn't count," Claire said, grinning.

Josephine, who had enjoyed a mimosa at breakfast, a French 75 at lunch, and was in the process of experiencing a kir royale, giggled. "I understood it without the explanation!"

"Sit down, you two," Larkin said. "It took all of my problem-solving skills to convince Adamantine to let you attend this seminar, and I will not have you kicked out of it."

"Technically," Elliott said, "since our badges are already inside the room, Adamantine would be the one who would be physically prevented from entering. If TOM works the way I think it does, the door won't open for her." He looked at Larkin—and Larkin realized that meant he thought she was the person most likely to understand what he was saying. "It's an obvious flaw in the system. If TOM is tasked with preventing two badges from being in the same place at the same time, then the first badge to enter the space always wins."

"That makes it zero-sum, right?" Eirwen asked. She had tied her hair back with another of her many wide ribbons and was wearing a T-shirt that read *You look like you've never seen a woman before.*

"Yes," Elliott said. "More importantly, it turns it into a game." He looked at Larkin again. "The game theory kind, not the kind they're playing in the twenty-four hour Game Room."

Larkin nodded. She was aware that game theory existed—although she didn't know how it was different from understanding how to play *Settlers of Catan*—and she was also aware that Elliott was saying to her what he might have said to Anni. She and Elliott were figuring out who they were when their better halves weren't around. The answer seemed to be *friends.*

That was when Jay entered the room—and Larkin's brain told her stomach to curl itself around her heart, because it knew that she and Jay could have been *more than friends*.

If she hadn't had a boyfriend.

If he hadn't had a fiancée.

Which he didn't, anymore—but he might have Eliza McFarlane, by the end of the cruise, and that would not be a terrible thing. *It would be a good thing*, Larkin thought, as Jay waved, and she waved back. *It would be the best thing*, she told herself, as Jay took a seat in the front row.

"I didn't realize Sahil's son was on the cruise," Josephine said, leaning over Claire to talk to Larkin. Her voice would have been a whisper if she hadn't been on her third Champagne cocktail. "He looks lonely."

"His engagement fell apart," Larkin said, keeping her voice as quiet as her mother hadn't. "I think he's here as a distraction."

"That's what I think, too," Josephine said. She looked, concernedly, at Larkin. "I like Ed better."

"So do I," Larkin said. Her stomach succeeded at choking her heart, this time—and Larkin suddenly felt seasick. "Excuse me." She stood up, pushed herself past Elliott and Eirwen, and made it out of the Gehoorsmaal just in time to smack into Eliza.

"I am so sorry," Larkin said. The thin, anxious genius had been standing in the hallway before Larkin pushed her way through the conference room door, but the zero-sum rules that were applied to artificial intelligences did not apply to humans. Larkin knocked Eliza not only off balance, but onto the cruise ship carpet. "You must think all of us Iowans never watch where we're going," she said, holding out a hand and helping Eliza up. "That's why you have to fly over us. Pun intended."

"I don't think that's a pun," Eliza said.

Larkin wondered what Ed would think. He hadn't

been making a lot of puns lately. She couldn't remember the last one. "Are you going in to sit with Jay?"

"No," Eliza said. "I'm going in to give the presentation." She was wearing a pair of extremely skinny jeans, topped by a T-shirt that advertised some kind of research institute. Larkin wondered if it was the one she worked for —or, more likely, founded. "I'm just waiting for Xavier to show up, so he can give the introductions and the apology."

"The apology?"

"You know, the whole *we regret that Adamantine Darcy cannot*," Eliza said, "*but aren't you in for a treat, because Eliza McFarlane can.*"

Eliza did not look like anyone's idea of a treat. Nor did she look like she was enjoying anything remotely close to a relaxing cruise vacation. Many of the nerds, including Larkin—who had not applied Anni's sunscreen as assiduously as she ought to—had come back from their St. Maarten excursions with pink-and-red splotches on their shoulders and noses. Eliza's shoulders were covered, but her face was uncomfortably pale. The skin under her eyes alternated dark and silver, like the edges of her salon-enhanced hair.

"Is Adamantine all right?" Larkin asked.

"Are you asking if she's still alive?"

Larkin was, in fact—but that was when Xavier arrived, his beautifully symmetrical face bronzed but not burned, his feet bounding against the carpet as if each step were hitting a Like or Subscribe button. "Hello, Eliza! Are we ready to get a bunch of people excited about artificial general intelligence?"

"AGI is still only hypothetical, Xavier," Eliza said. She had switched on; he, it seemed, never switched off. "I'll be speaking—on behalf of Adamantine, of course—of both the realistic and fictional possibilities of the artificial intelligences we currently have."

"Outstanding," Xavier said. "I am so ready to learn. Are we going to talk about Skynet? You know you can't have an AI seminar without at least one reference to Skynet, right?"

The two of them left, entering the Gehoorsmaal and beginning the seminar. Larkin could hear Xavier's voice through the hallway wall; she could hear Eliza thanking him for the introduction and beginning her speech; she could hear a set of very familiar footsteps—slightly off-cadence, but undeniably recognizable—approaching the door.

"Are you all right?" Josephine had never been the type of mother to get overly concerned about Larkin's whereabouts—she knew enough about statistics to understand that Larkin would probably turn up safe and, more importantly, that there was nothing she could do to prevent an obscure or rare scenario—but the day-drinking had gone to Dr. Day's head. "Did somebody get murdered?"

"No," Larkin said. It was the second lie she'd told her mother that morning. "I was just feeling a little nauseous."

"You mean *nauseated*," Josephine said. Now she sounded more like the mother Larkin had grown up with. "You don't suppose it's norovirus?"

"No," Larkin said again. "If this sailing had norovirus, we'd know by now. Can you send Elliott out here, just for a minute? He has some of Anni's seasickness pills."

"Oh!" Josephine said. She giggled, again, for no apparent reason. "Anni has everything, doesn't she! I've never met someone so completely prepared!" She paused, considering this. "You know, it's kind of annoying. You'd think she'd leave something for the rest of us to do."

"You can go get Elliott," Larkin said. "That's a thing you can do."

"I shall!" Her mother slipped back into the Gehoorsmaal and Elliott, in due time, slipped out. He pulled the ponytail holder off his wrist and wrapped it around his gray-and-ginger hair; then he put his hands in his pockets and took out a roll of wire and a cruise-branded lanyard.

"I assume we're breaking into the Koningin Suite again?"

The lanyard, which included the badge they'd need for ninth-floor access, was Jay's.

———

The two of them made it back to the conference room before the seminar was over—but not before the queue of nerds had started to fill the hallway.

"Line ends back there," one of the nerds said, pointing to a cruise-uniformed employee holding a sign that read END OF LINE.

"Yeah, we know," Larkin said, "but we're trying to catch the end of the seminar."

"They closed it," another nerd said, "to ensure that people like you didn't get ahead of people like us."

Larkin looked at the nerd, who was carrying two *Time Tangent Gentleman* hardcovers under each arm. "Is this line for the Adamantine Darcy signing?"

"Yes," the nerd said.

"Has Adamantine shown up?"

"She's giving the seminar," the nerd said, gesturing towards the closed conference room doors. Two of the books started to slide out from underneath a sweaty armpit; the nerd stopped them with one hand and dropped the two books on the opposite side. Larkin bent down to pick them up. "Careful," the nerd said. "Those are first editions."

The books, which had each been wrapped in plastic—to protect them from nerd residue, Larkin presumed—were identical copies of *How Now, Horatio*. The original title of Adamantine's first book, before she knew she was writing a series. Larkin glanced at the nerd's other arm as she handed them back; those two were *How Nows* as well. "Have you read these books?" she asked. "Or are you just planning on reselling them?"

"The prediction markets suggest that there's a ninety percent chance that the value of signed first editions of *How Now, Horatio* will increase by one hundred twenty-five percent after Adamantine Darcy's death," the nerd said, wiping his hand under his nose to collect the snot. Larkin picked up the other two books as they fell to the ground. "I paid $201.95 in total for these four copies, which means that I stand to make, I don't know—"

"Fifty bucks," Elliott said, quietly. Then he went to the conference room door and began knocking. One short, three long. "Jay," he said to Larkin, repeating the sequence a second time—and then Jay opened the door.

"Was she there?" he asked, as the three of them walked past the *END OF LINE* sign and sat, together, on a faux-wooden bench next to a freestyle soda machine that chirped, excitedly, until it figured out that none of them were going to give it any money. Larkin wondered whether it was tracking their badges the way TOM had, and whether it was aware that none of them had used any of its services thus far, and whether that meant the machine would put less effort into trying to convince them that now was the time to mix every available flavor together and call it—

But that was a word she would not allow into her mind, not now.

She would think of *literally anything else*, even if it meant focusing on the way it felt to sit, thigh-by-thigh, with Jay.

"The suite was empty," Elliott said, passing Jay's lanyard and badge over Larkin's lap. "No sign of Adamantine."

"She left her manuscript, though," Larkin said. "On the bed." The print copy of *The Yet Unknowing World* had included a handwritten note, on its title page—*Final draft for publication, AD.*

"She also left an envelope," Elliott said.

"To be opened in case of death?" Jay asked.

"Yeah," Larkin said. "We didn't open it."

Jay held his breath. Then he exhaled and looked carefully at Larkin. His eyes were unbearably earnest; whomever he had been before that moment, he no longer was. "What are we doing next, Detective Day?"

Larkin, looking back at Jay, was also no longer herself; she never would be, ever again, and she knew that Jay and Elliott knew it. "I figure we'll see if Adamantine shows up for her signing, and we'll see if Eliza has anything to say about any of this."

She didn't know whether Jay and Eliza would end up together. She didn't know whether she and Jay would end up together. She was pretty sure that she and Ed *wouldn't*, because he had never looked at her the way Jay had just looked at her, and she was going to spend the rest of her life looking for someone who could look at her, in that way, *for the rest of her life.*

"And then I should pay a visit to my new friend Artie, right?"

It was Jay, but not Jay. His voice was the same, his

inflections echoing his previous insouciance, but his face was absolutely sincere. He'd figured out how to change, he wanted to know how to help, and he was asking Larkin to see—no, *validate*—no, *love*—the person he had decided to become.

"Yeah," Larkin said. "And then you should pay a visit to your new friend Artie."

———

Adamantine did not appear.

Eliza had nothing to say. Larkin let Jay interview her first, hoping it would give her a way out of her dilemma—Elliott saw this, and nodded with approval—but all Eliza had to offer was fatigue and obfuscation. "Adamantine wasn't feeling well last night," she repeated, just as she had done two nights ago. "She must still be in her stateroom."

Jay and Larkin both knew this wasn't true. Neither of them knew if it was a lie, so they allowed Eliza to elide and leave—and then Larkin, using a line she had learned during her first murder investigation, followed Eliza into the cruise ship restroom and asked if she could borrow a tampon.

"Sorry," Eliza said. "I use one of those digi-cups. It's got a sensor that monitors fluid level and notifies your phone or smartwatch when it's full."

"Okay," Larkin said. "Gross."

"You are aware of what they make tampons out of, right?" Eliza asked, before entering the furthest stall.

"I never did look it up," Larkin said. "My friend Anni would probably know. She knows everything. Finance, productivity, how many times you need to shuffle a deck of cards before it's fully randomized, that kind of thing.

She even helped me create my first will last year. Or, you know, maybe it'll be my Last Will."

Larkin waited for a laugh; she got a flush instead.

"I asked her if I should put it in an envelope marked To Be Opened in Case of Death."

Then she just waited.

Eliza exited the stall.

She stalled, at the sink, just long enough to soap her hands thoroughly and sing what appeared to be the entire Periodic Table set to a melody from *The Pirates of Penzance*.

She eyed the hand dryer, and then wiped her hands on her jeans.

"So you know," Eliza said, calmly. "I assume Handy told you."

"I'm tired of people assuming Handy is anything less than professional," Larkin said, less calmly. "I found out on my own. I have sufficiently advanced technology at my disposal, after all." She waggled her fingers in front of Eliza's face. "*Magic*."

"Did you seriously just quote Arthur C. Clarke?"

"No," Larkin said, "I quoted my friend Elliott. He didn't do the finger-waggle thing, though. He's not that kind of a nerd." She took a deep breath and expanded her body until it blocked the doorway; Eliza, in response, crossed her wiry arms across her chest. "The thing about friends," Larkin said, "is that they're kind of like an exobrain or an artificial intelligence assistant or whatever it is that you're trying to build. Good friends—and good family too, if you're lucky enough to have them—are way better than TOM, because they're real, and that's why Adamantine asked me to help her, because I'm real, and *you know it*."

Larkin put her hands on her hips, feeling a bit like a superhero.

Unfortunately, she didn't know enough about superheroes to know which one.

"And now I'm here to help."

Eliza nodded, her cropped hair sparkling under the fluorescent restroom lights.

"Fine," she said. "Then we begin Phase Two."

"I'm one step ahead of you," Larkin said, pushing the restroom door open and gesturing for Eliza to pass through. "Jay is in the process of notifying the ship's Chief Security Officer, and I expect we'll meet the two of them in Adamantine's stateroom."

"Fine," Eliza said again, stepping past Larkin's outstretched arm—and walking straight into Claire's square shoulders.

"Careful, ma'am," Claire said. She had switched into Officer Novak mode, stabilizing Eliza and defusing the situation. "A lot of people don't assess their surroundings when they walk through doors." She held Eliza in place, managing to make the grip appear friendly. Then she grinned at Larkin. "Elliott told me that you were getting law enforcement involved."

Perfect, Larkin thought. "Great!" she said aloud. "I'm sure Eliza McFarlane won't mind if you accompany us to the Koningin Suite."

"Who are you?" Eliza asked, gently withdrawing her arm from Claire's grasp.

"You know who I am," Claire said. Both of them knew that she could have easily prevented Eliza from pulling away. "Your AI took my name and badge on Embarkation Day and used that information to prevent me from having full and unobstructed access to the vacation I paid for. I don't believe I consented to that, and if I decide to press the issue, you might have a problem."

"My lawyers are ready to argue that using TOM to

block a doorway is no different from using a human friend to prevent an unwanted guest from entering a party," Eliza said. "Nor is it different from a friend telling a person to stay away from a party because someone they don't want to see might be there."

"I look forward to reading about the lawsuits," Claire said. She kept both eyes on Eliza while turning her voice to Larkin. "Are we ready to begin investigating the potential homicide?"

Larkin kept her eyes on Eliza as well.

Phase Two.

"Yes," she said. "Let's go."

CHAPTER 15

The scene played exactly as a professional theater director might have staged it—

Dr. Jaipal Malhotra in quiet conversation with Chief Security Officer Aart Van der Voort.

Eliza McFarlane, companion to Adamantine Darcy, standing just far away enough to pretend she wasn't listening.

Larkin Day, amateur maritime detective, observing the interactions.

Claire Novak—well, Larkin hadn't planned for Claire to be there, but there she was, *oh well*—staring carefully at the envelope on Adamantine's bed and announcing, to everyone around her, "You know we can't open this."

"Why not?" Eliza asked.

Larkin, just as a detective might have done, raised one suspicious eyebrow.

"Because we don't know for sure that she's dead."

"She has a point," Officer Van der Voort said. Claire had introduced both herself and her credentials, and Artie was delighted to have an American colleague. "What would you do if we were in—how did you say it? *Pratin-cola, Iowa?*"

"I'd find Ms. Darcy," Claire said. "This ship is a contained space, which means that all we've got to do is search it." She turned to Eliza. "Ms. McFarlane, is there any possibility of tracking Ms. Darcy through her artificial intelligence assistant?"

"TOM maintains the privacy of its clients at all times," Eliza said.

"Does that mean we would need a warrant?"

"Technically, you'd need a legal ruling," Eliza said. "Take us to court, make your case, and see if Podunk, Iowa can beat the best minds in Silicon Valley."

"Podunk?" Artie asked. "Is that how you say it?"

"I'd prefer to locate Ms. Darcy as quickly as possible," Claire said, "and I believe that Officer Van der Voort and I can do that on our own."

This was the role that Larkin had planned to play—but she realized, almost immediately, that Claire would do a better job of it. The two of them were already putting their minds together, turning training and protocol into plans and actions. Officer Van der Voort had taken a hand-held walkie-talkie off his hip, and Claire had picked up the stateroom phone to leave a message for Josephine.

"Hoping we can get this done by Formal Dinner, love," she said—Larkin had not heard that particular intimacy before, not between her mother and Claire, and found it unexpectedly comforting—"because I've been looking forward to seeing you in that dress for a long time."

"You're taking Eliza to Formal Dinner," Larkin said, as she and Jay descended the length of the ship, their faces reflected in the glass-front elevator. He was looking at her. She was looking at the elevator's interpretation of his eyes.

"If you want to help me—

"I do—"

She had not told Jay about *Phase Two*. She was trusting him to trust her, even though she could see, upon reflection, that he knew she could not trust herself. "Ask Eliza out."

"I doubt she'd consider a romantic entanglement," Jay said. "Not while the woman who is physically entangled with her life's work is missing, presumed dead." The elevator stopped; the doors opened. "Presumed murdered?"

"We don't know anything yet," Larkin said, the two of them exiting onto the loud and brightly-lit Promenade, explorers adapting to the atmosphere in breath and tone and pitch, "except that you have a way with pretty much every heterosexual woman I've ever seen you interact with—"

"With whom you've ever seen me interact—"

"Nope," Larkin said, "that's an Ed joke, we're not doing Ed jokes, you're taking me—sorry, you're taking *Eliza* to Formal Dinner, and you're going to make her believe you are absolutely into her, and then you are going to get as much information out of her as you can."

"To see if her tongue will slip like yours?"

That was a Jay joke—and Larkin paused, her lips pressing together in an attempt to keep herself from smiling. The two of them were passing in front of a store that sold swimwear, their bodies floating through the columns of mirrors that separated the headless mannequins in bikinis and board shorts. A man and a woman; he looking at her, and her looking at them. Larkin looked away—but that was even worse, because then it was their shadows faintly staining the gleaming tile, a man and a woman, two faces with a vase in between, the allusion of the tarot card that Adamantine had told Larkin to take to heart. She could not remember which card it was. She could only remember the future it had promised.

"Where will I meet you afterwards?" Jay asked.

"I don't know," Larkin said. She never knew, with Jay—and he knew she never knew it. "But one of us will find the other."

"I'm sure we will," he said, and then he turned and walked back to the elevator—because of course he would, he had only ridden down to the Promenade as an excuse to talk to her, and now he had to ride back up to the ninth floor and make an excuse to talk to Eliza—with his hands in his pockets, his sandals slapping at the soles of his feet, whistling a melody that Larkin was not at all surprised to recognize.

It was from *Titanic*, of course.

The love song.

She was pretty sure he meant it ironically—but, as he knew, she didn't know.

———

Larkin knew she should return to Verandah 213, to ask Ed how his afternoon had gone and begin dressing for the evening that was to come, but—since she was already on the Promenade, and since she could see the bench where they had sat from where she was standing—she detoured to the closed doors of the conference room where Adamantine had been scheduled to speak and then sign.

There was a significant amount of nerd noise, on the other side of those doors—and a not-insignificant amount of nerd stench, when Larkin pulled them open.

"All right!" Xavier was saying. "How many of you are willing to put twenty points towards a future in which Adamantine Darcy spreads norovirus to sixty percent of the ship?"

Seven hands went up, each holding a corresponding lanyard.

"Let's get those identities secured, okay?" Xavier asked, as Elliott slipped in and out of the rows of folding chairs and held his phone in front of each nerd's badge. Her mother, leaning comfortably against the cash bar, was holding a glass of what Larkin hoped was sparkling water.

"What's going on?" Larkin whispered. Whatever her mother was drinking did not appear to include umbrellas, lemon wedges, or swizzle sticks, which was probably a good sign.

"Xavier's running a prediction market," Josephine said. Her diction was exceptionally precise, which was probably a bad sign. "They're taking bets on why Adamantine didn't appear for her signing, and then they're making all of these side bets on what might happen next." She laughed, the *ha* turning into a cough and then back into a laugh again. The umbrella that might have been in her cocktail glass was balanced carefully on a damp napkin. "I don't even know if I said it right. Side bets? Is that what they're called?"

"I don't know," Larkin said. "Isn't all of this, like, illegal?"

"Oh, you know," her mother said, giving Larkin's shoulder a tipsy nudge that tipped her into the edge of the faux-wooden bar. "Maritime law, right? Everything's different when you're at sea!"

"Hey, Larkin," Elliott said, as Xavier asked the nerds to consider how many points they wanted to put towards the possibility that Adamantine's artificial intelligence assistant would end up taking control of the entire ship. "You've figured out what's going on?" The room cacophonized as clusters of nerds discussed strategies; Larkin could barely hear her own voice as she responded with the obvious joke: "I leave you alone for five minutes and you set up a gambling ring?"

"Nobody's betting money," Elliott said. "We're using a point system, and the winner gets to have dinner with the Special Guests on the last night of the sailing." He nodded his ponytailed head towards the front of the room. "That was Eirwen's idea."

"Of course it was," Larkin said. "Good for her."

"It's good for you, too," Elliott said. "We've been doing this for an hour, and do you know what scenario has never, ever, ever come up?"

Now Larkin understood what was really going on. "Does it start with an *M*?"

"Yep," Elliott said. His left hand was tapping, excitedly, against the cash bar. A thin strand of gray hair had come loose from its elastic, and his right hand kept pushing it out of his eyes. He looked happier—and nerdier—than Larkin had ever seen him. "We put every single idea into their heads *except* that one."

Larkin did not let herself ask if any of those ideas had started with an *S*.

"We even got them to bet on the possibility that Adamantine Darcy cryogenically froze her own brain to prevent further neural degeneration."

Larkin knew that there was always another person on the other side of someone's *we*—and in this case, the person might have to be incorporated into *Phase Two*. "You mean you and Xavier?"

"No," Elliott said. "Me and Eirwen." He nodded his

head, again, towards the front of the room. "She gave up the opportunity to win the game in order to run it."

Now Larkin noticed that Eirwen was writing, rapidly, in a paper notebook—and then passing each torn-off page to Xavier, who glanced at it just long enough to learn his lines. "So she's on the team, now."

"Yeah," Elliott said. "She's great. If anyone can help us figure out who M-dashed Adamantine Darcy, it'll be her."

"It'll be Larkin!" Josephine said. "My daughter, the detective!"

"It'll be all of us," Larkin said, "working together. It has to be."

Elliott, whose phone was needed to photograph badges, nodded and left.

"Why does it have to be?" her mother asked. "Why can't it be just you?"

"Because the last time I tried to do it on my own," Larkin said, "two people died."

CHAPTER 16

"You look amazing," Ed said, as Larkin emerged from the shared bathroom.

"So do you," Larkin said. It was not a lie. Ed, resplendent in suit and suspenders, looked as he had when Larkin first imagined their happily-ever-after. She had kissed him, then, in front of all of their friends. He, for reasons she was finally starting to understand, had been surprised.

He was surprised by this kiss as well. "Is everything okay?"

"Yeah," Larkin said. She turned away from the man who did not yet know that he was no longer her boyfriend —*stop thinking about it that way, Larkin, you can sort it out after you save Adamantine*—and stared carefully at herself in the vanity mirror. She was wearing the delicate, shimmering evening gown that had been purchased for her last summer, last minute, so she could be appropriately dressed for the Shakespeare Festival's Preview Night Gala. A dead body had been discovered in her cabin; the costume designer had been obliged to provide her with new clothes.

"You don't look okay," Ed said. "I mean, you look beautiful, Stanley knew what he was doing when he bought that dress, but you look—"

Larkin watched Ed watch her watch herself in the mirror.

"Sad," he said.

"I was just thinking about this summer," Larkin said. That was also not a lie. "Can you believe that you and I have, like, witnessed three murders? In the past year?"

"We only witnessed one murder," Ed said. "The other two we found after the fact—or, you know, after the act." He put his hand on Larkin's shoulder and gave it a soft squeeze. "Pun intended."

Larkin suddenly realized that Ed only made puns when he felt uncomfortable. She couldn't believe she'd missed that. The two of them had missed everything, together. They'd looked through eyes occluded by ideas, unable to see beyond the dazzling afterimage of the imagined future.

They'd missed each other.

She would miss him, but it would be worth the truth. If she could say it *right now*, as they stared into the shared mirror—but she had to save it, for three more days, to save Adamantine.

"You know what I mean," Larkin said, instead. "It's incomprehensible. Preposterous. Other big words that fail to adequately communicate the enormity of the situation."

She watched Ed watch her.

He did know.

He didn't know.

He didn't know if he wanted to know—because he, like Larkin, had something else he wanted more.

"How did the practice session go?" she asked.

"Great," Ed said. "How's the mystery you're not telling me about going?"

He knew.

"I think it's going to be my best one," Larkin said. "There are a few pieces left to put into place. Elliott knows some of them. Claire and Eirwen are helping, too."

"Who's Eirwen?"

"A new friend," Larkin said. She wondered, like Ed had when they were discussing Wendy Carlos, whether she should mention that Eirwen was a trans woman. "She's a writer. Short stories. You'll meet her at dinner."

Then she kissed him—because it was still all right to kiss him, there was nothing about what they were currently sharing-and-not-sharing that could be hurt by a kiss—and squeezed the firm fabric of his suit jacket.

"Shall we?"

Ed offered his arm, just as he'd done the first time they'd gone out together. "We shall." It had been a Halloween party, and he had dressed as the Phantom and she had dressed as Christine, and she had told her mother that the two of them were just really good friends who liked music and theater a whole lot. *Don't worry,* she'd said. *Christine and the Phantom aren't endgame.* Then she'd had to explain to her mother what *endgame* was.

It had been amazing how much they'd known, even from that very first date.

It had been amazing how much they'd ignored since then.

"Let's go," they said, the words overlapping like their arms, the laughter pushing the sadness out of their hearts for just long enough.

———

Elliott had done his share of pieces-moving—it was really what he was best at, whether he was writing code or playing chess or making cards appear and disappear—and when Larkin and Ed walked into the main dining room, they found Handy waiting for them.

"Miss Day! Mr. Jackson! Please come with me!" Handy smiled; Larkin could only imagine how much Elliott had paid him. "You are our special guests this evening," he continued, escorting them through the crowded dining room and into the reserved section. "Here we are!"

Handy gestured delightedly towards a long table—it was actually two six-tops pushed together and covered with a trio of tablecloths—and indicated that they should take their seats. "See, your names have already been written down!"

Larkin Day and *Ed Jackson* were next to *Elliott Fox* and *Annilee Morgan*.

Claire Novak and *Josephine Day* were on Larkin's other side.

The cards on the opposite side of the table read—from left to right—*Daniel Pennington, Moira Pennington, Jaipal Malhotra, Eliza McFarlane, Walter Johnson Murray III,* and *Xavier Torres.*

"You invited Trey," Ed said, noting Grandmaster Trey's given name. "Thanks."

Eirwen Wald was at the foot of the table.

Adamantine Darcy was at the head.

"The other guests are getting their photographs taken," Handy explained, carefully pouring water into Ed and Larkin's glasses. "Your friend Elliott Fox, the magician, asked Ismael to prioritize them."

"Should we have gotten our picture taken?" Ed asked. Larkin had hurried them past the crowds of nerds forming a queue at the foot of the Grand Staircase, hoping to enter the Main Dining Room early enough to watch the other guests arrive. "Would Ismael have let us cut the line?"

"Probably," Larkin said. "I can only imagine how much money I'll owe Elliott before this thing is over." She squeezed Ed's hand under the table. "You understand why I'm not telling you precisely what's going on, right?"

"Because you want me to play a specific role, and it'll be better if I don't know my lines in advance?"

"Pretty much," Larkin said. Then she glanced at Handy. "Would you ask Ismael to photograph all of us, at our table, once he finishes with everyone else?" She squeezed Ed's hand for the second time. "See? We'll get ours too, don't worry." Then she kissed him, carefully, on the cheek. "You look too good not to be memorialized."

"Interesting choice of words," Ed said. Then he stood up. "Hey, there's Trey!"

While Ed waved at his new mentor and welcomed him to the table, Larkin turned her mind and her eyes towards the other invited guests. Daniel and Moira Pennington were first, the magician pairing his porkpie hat with a pinstripe suit. Moira wore flat shoes and a shapeless dress; knitting needles speared the ball of yarn poking out of her patterned craft bag.

"I don't believe we've met," Daniel said, holding out his hand to Ed.

"I believe we have," Moira corrected, nodding politely at Larkin.

As Ed introduced himself, Eirwen slipped quietly into her seat. She was wearing a high-waisted, lace-edged gown that Larkin might have approved for a production of *As You Like It*, *Arcadia*, *Into the Woods*, or—if her career didn't go the way she hoped it would—*Spamalot*. Eirwen was thrilled to be there and terrified to speak. By the time Anni and Elliott joined them, she had already splashed water down the front of her dress.

"Don't worry, miss," Handy said, handing Eirwen an extra napkin. "You look beautiful." Eirwen, who had tucked her lanyard into her cruise-branded tote bag, looked euphoric.

"I saw you put your name on the talent show sign-up list," Anni said, fist bumping Eirwen as Handy filled her and Elliott's water glasses. "Thank you, Handoyono." She looked at the place cards in front of her and Elliott's chairs, then swapped them and sat down. "How did the prediction market go?"

Larkin knew Elliott had told Anni about the plan—she'd asked him to, after all—and Anni was doing her best to optimize it, engaging Eirwen in a conversation about predictions and equations and something that had to do with a rational rewrite of *Harry Potter*. This put Elliott next to Ed, allowing him to exchange pleasantries with Daniel and Moira as Ed leaned over Larkin's place setting to share what he had learned about turntabling with Grandmaster Trey.

"You don't mind?" Trey asked, smiling at Larkin before standing up and swapping his place card with Jay's. Larkin did mind—she had wanted Jay and Eliza next to Moira and Daniel—but she couldn't stop him, now that Anni had set the precedent.

"Thank you, Handy," she said, as he picked up the Grandmaster's water glass and placed it in front of his new seat. "Why don't you two tell me what you've been up to?" she asked, brightly. It would be the only chance she'd have to feign interest, so she might as well make the most of it.

As Ed and his mentor explained what they had been exploring—"it's all about the discipline of organizing sound," Ed said, excitedly—Larkin watched her mother and Claire take the seats next to hers. "Watch out," Trey warned, laughing, "your woman's distracted."

"She's not my woman," Ed said, squeezing Larkin's hand under the table. Letting the double meaning pass between them, as clearly as if he had tapped it out in Morse Code. "She is, however, one of the smartest women I've ever met. Next to her mother, of course."

"Pun intended," Larkin said, smiling first at Ed and then at Josephine. Her mother was going to be so disappointed—once she sobered up enough to realize what was going on.

"We're getting apéritifs, right?" Josephine said, twisting from side to side to find a server. "Hello, Handy! Are you taking care of us this evening?"

"It is my pleasure, Dr. Day," Handy said. "Would you like me to start you off with a glass of Champagne?"

"It would be rude to drink alone," Josephine replied, smiling. "Would it be possible to order Champagne for the entire table?"

"Of course, madam," Handy said. He looked quickly at another cruise-uniformed attendant, who nodded and went to fetch the bottles. "May I put this order on the Verandah 213 account?"

"You betcha," Josephine said, raising her water glass towards Anni and Elliott. "If I'd known what a decade of cruise loyalty points can getcha"—she laughed, startlingly, at her unexpected rhyme—"I would have started taking these vacations ten years earlier."

Larkin leaned over the back of her mother's chair. Claire, equally alert, pushed her own chair back to meet her. "Does Anni know she's covering Mom's newfound thirst for cheap sparkling wine that probably came from southern California?"

"Yep," Claire said. "She transferred her complimentary unlimited booze package over to us, the day Officer Van der Voort took you into custody. Jo said she needed a drink, and Anni said she had a few to give away."

"More than a few," Larkin said, looking at her mother —who had unfolded her swan-fold napkin and was attempting to reverse-engineer it into shape. "Are you keeping an eye on her?"

"You know I am," Claire said. "And don't worry. If anyone deserves to spend the week buzzed on bubbly, it's your mother. She's had a rough year."

"Who hasn't?" Larkin asked, because she didn't want to ask how much of her mother's rough year had to do with the murders her daughter had failed to prevent—and then they were interrupted, loudly, by the next guest to join the table.

"Hello, Formal Nerds!" Xavier Torres had paused, microphone in hand, to address the crowd. "Don't we all look good?" The room filled with whoops and applause. "Tonight's dinner is always one of my favorite parts of the cruise, and I can hardly wait for the concert afterwards. Who else is excited to see Grandmaster Trey, live and onstage?" The applause was equally loud, perhaps to overcome the lack of whoops. "I've got the Grandmaster himself, right here," Xavier said, turning to Trey and gesturing for him to stand. "Want to say a few words?"

He held his microphone in front of the musician.

"Don't skip my gig," Grandmaster Trey said, sitting down before Xavier could ask any follow-up questions.

"You heard it straight from Grandmaster Trey," Xavier said. "You are not going to want to miss his performance!"

"I shouldn't tell you this," Ed whispered, his voice

close enough to block out Xavier's, "but there's going to be a surprise during tonight's show."

Larkin was about to guess the surprise—she was sure it had something to do with Ed playing a set, or guesting on a fourth turntable, or doing something that reflected the results of all the practicing he'd done in front of the mirror—but her eyes were drawn, inevitably, towards the last guests to join the party.

Jay and Eliza.

Jay wore crimson, a square-cut tunic draping over loose trousers, the silk interwoven with threads that caught the light. Eliza wore silver, a sheath dress with a slit cut, the satin slightly darker than her hair.

"Sorry we're late," Eliza said, as Jay pulled out her chair. Everyone watched her sit; they were probably wondering how she was going to manage it. Her legs were under the table before anyone could see how much she was likely to reveal.

"So let's give a hand to all of our special guests," Xavier continued, concluding whatever he had been announcing before Jay and Eliza arrived, "and another hand to everyone at Dutch Cruise International who is doing so much work to ensure we have the best cruise ever!"

Larkin applauded.

They all did.

"Will Adamantine be joining us?" Moira asked Eliza, as the applause died. The Champagne had arrived; the glasses were set. A server who wasn't Handy uncorked and poured.

"I don't know," Eliza said. "I haven't seen her all day."

Moira glanced at Daniel. A question passed between them; Daniel answered by asking. "Isn't that a little unusual? I mean, isn't it part of your job to, you know, watch Adamantine?"

"I think you mistake the nature of my job," Eliza said, emphasizing the syllable as if it were distasteful. "What Adamantine Darcy does with her time is independent of my research."

"Not completely independent," Daniel said. He seemed insistent on being right, for some reason. "Don't you need Adamantine's body? Like, literally?"

"Does Jony Ive need yours?" Eliza said, nodding towards Daniel's smartwatch. "Like, literally?" She picked up her glass of Champagne.

"Wait!" Josephine said, stopping Eliza before she sipped. "He's got to sit"—that was Xavier, who was handing his microphone to a server and signing an autograph for a nerd—"and we've got to toast."

Jay stood up. "Xave," he said, "they need you to sit down."

"Now I need both of you to sit down," Josephine said, laughing again. "That is a lovely ensemble, Dr. Malhotra. Is that what you call a kurta pyjama?"

Jay was comfortable in his crimson silk. More comfortable than he'd been in his worn-out T-shirt and clunky sandals, neither of which flattered his build or his bearing. "In my family, Dr. Day," he said, settling himself in his chair, "we just call them *clothes*."

Then he looked at Larkin. "You also look remarkable."

"Thank you." Larkin had not planned to speak during this dinner, and now that she'd gotten started, she planned to speak as little as possible. "Everyone does, really."

"Absolutely," Jay said. He ensured that Xavier was secure in his chair, and then turned to Josephine. "Should we toast to that?"

"To clothes?"

"No," Jay said. He looked around the table, once again establishing himself as the head—even though Larkin had placed him, deliberately, in the center. "To being remarkable." She watched him meet every separate pair of eyes. "Daniel, you had an impressive career as a neuroscientist before becoming the kind of magician who gets booked on these kinds of cruises. Moira, you taught high school biology at my alma mater. Me, of course—well, it would be rude to talk about my own accomplishments, so let's move to Eliza. We all know what this truly intelligent woman is trying to do with artificial intelligence, and how many people might benefit once her work proves successful. Xavier, well, he's one of my oldest friends, and he ends up running this place. Look at him!"

They all looked at Xavier, which stopped them from looking at the empty chair next to him. *Well played, Jay,* Larkin thought. *We both know how to get people to do what we want.*

"Then across from Xavier we've got Officer Claire Novak—who, along with her partner Dr. Josephine Day, have done significant work bringing social justice to small-town Iowa."

Larkin wondered if Jay was referring to her mother's decision to resign from her position as Dean of Howell College, in order to pass the opportunity to someone who could more cohesively serve the needs of Howell's diverse student body. She wondered how he knew about that. It had definitely been part of Josephine Day's *rough year.*

"And then, of course, there's Larkin."

Everyone looked at her in a way that Larkin had never, ever expected to be seen.

"What can I say about Larkin? I mean, she's a brilliant director, she can make a better cappuccino than anyone I've met—I mean, don't you hate it, when you ask for a cappuccino and they give you a latte with foam on top?" He waited, just long enough for Moira and Xavier to nod. "I probably can't share what I know about her future, because it's privileged information that I only have access to because I kind-of-maybe poked around my father's office until I found out, but he and the Board of the Pratincola Shakespeare Festival have made their final decision about whom to hire as the full-time Artistic Director, and let's just say that knowing that information would make Larkin's—"

He looked at Ed, inviting him to finish the sentence.

"Day," Ed said. "Pun intended."

He only says that when he's uncomfortable.

Unfortunately, Ed was also next in line to be toasted, and Larkin watched as everyone shifted their gaze towards a man who did not want anybody looking at him. "When you hear Ed with his community choir," Jay began and then paused. "You know, I've never heard it. But I've heard good things."

Wrong move, Larkin thought—and she thought about interrupting him, telling the table that Dr. Ed Jackson was one of the smartest and kindest men she knew, he could bring a group of people from across the Iowa Creative Corridor into a cramped church basement and teach them how to sing a masterwork like Beethoven's Ninth, he could walk onstage after a tenor soloist had confessed to murder and sing the solo perfectly, he could help a friend compose an opera and help another friend come out to her parents and help his brother's kids sit still as his niece graduated from sixth grade.

She could have said all of that.

She should have.

But she had already committed to staying as quiet as possible.

"Then we've got Elliott Fox, whom you may know as Scarbo, but trust me—he hates it when people call him that."

Elliott shrugged, his shoulders brushing against the ends of his hair. "It is what it is, Jay. I own my mistakes, and I love the life I've pulled out of them."

"Like a rabbit from a hat," Jay said, "or a woman from a single-axis replicator."

That was meant for Anni, and she was clearly the only person at the table who understood it. "Jay came to our house this summer and asked me how a person can change," she said. "I told him that all change derives from love, which in turn derives from learning something new, which in turn derives from turning a deficit into a credit, which in turn derives from the process of going from guessing to knowing."

Jay laughed. "I think she said exactly those words."

"So if you want to know how he's remarkable, it's because he asked," Anni said, "and now I will speak to Eirwen Wald, since Jay doesn't really know her, but I've read some of Eirwen's stories, and I'd say that one of the guest authors on the cruise should take a look at her work and offer some advice, but Elliott and I know from experience what can happen when you take advice from someone you meet on a cruise."

Anni rarely weaponized language—but she rarely missed her targets. Daniel Pennington flinched, and the Ace of Spades fluttered, slowly, from his left-hand jacket sleeve. Handy picked it up and handed it to him.

"Is this your card?" he asked.

"Yes, you idiot, of course it's my card," Daniel said, as Eirwen tried not to laugh, and Josephine didn't bother trying. "Come here, you genius," she said, waving to

Handy and opening her handbag. "I'm sure I have a dollar in here somewhere for that."

Larkin let Claire be the one to put her hand on Josephine's arm. "Sir," she whispered, as Handy accepted his tip, "do you think it might be possible to, um, expedite the dinner service? Get us some bread for the table, or something?"

"Of course, Miss Novak," Handy said. "I will begin the service immediately."

"We still have to toast," Josephine said, picking up her Champagne glass for the second time. "I mean, we have to do the part of the toast where we drink." She squinted at the bubbles that were fizzing at the top of the flute. "My sparkling wine is beginning to dull."

"Sure," Jay said, continuing the charge he had already taken. "To being remarkable—"

"Wait," Eirwen said. It was her one line, and she delivered it like a pro. "Adamantine Darcy isn't here."

This was the moment at which at least one of the faces should have registered surprise.

Concern.

Anything.

They didn't even look at Adamantine's empty seat. Daniel looked at Moira, who looked at Eliza, who looked at Larkin. Xavier looked at Eirwen and then Jay. Anni looked at Eliza—it was what she had been tasked to do, as part of the plan—while Elliott and Claire watched everybody. Ed waited. Grandmaster Trey thanked Handy for serving him a poppyseed-covered dinner roll.

Josephine went ahead and drank—and then she spoke.

"Well, we all know she's been murdered, right?"

That had the necessary effect—on Xavier, Eliza, Daniel, and Eirwen. Moira thanked Handy for serving her an oatmeal-covered dinner roll.

"That's why we're all here," Josephine continued. "My daughter, the detective, thinks one of you did it."

Everyone looked at Larkin again—her mother, Xavier, Daniel, Eirwen, and Grandmaster Trey first, followed by Elliott, Claire, and Eliza, whose eyes followed the crowd, and Jay, whose eyes met Larkin's in a way that suggested he was enjoying this more than he had expected to. Maybe exactly as much as he had expected to. Anni finally caught on that she was supposed to turn her head in Larkin's direction, and Ed finally stepped in and saved her.

"What if your detective daughter thinks you did it?" he said, jovially, to Josephine.

"Me?" Josephine said. "I couldn't have done it! I had an alibi the entire time, if a drink counts as an alibi." She took another sip of Champagne. "Anyway, you all saw me. During the book signing that turned into a prediction market when Adamantine didn't appear. That was when she was murdered, right?"

Now Xavier looked confused—as did Moira and Eliza. "Nobody told me I was covering up for a murder," he said. "I thought I was doing a solid for one of my favorite authors. I knew from Embarkation that she wasn't going to be able to fulfill her obligations to the cruise, but I wasn't going to turn her away. I've loved her books since I was eleven years old."

Eirwen thanked Handy for serving her a parmesan-covered dinner roll.

"I read her blog," Xavier continued. "I know Adamantine isn't well. But we didn't know, when we booked her, that she would decline so quickly. I'm surprised she's still here at all."

Larkin waited.

Somebody say it, she thought. *Tell us what Adamantine might have done.*

Anni and Elliott thanked Handy.

Everyone else remained silent.

Perhaps they thought it was their right.

Then Ed, on her left, stepped in for the second time.

"Thank you, Handy," he said. "Xavier, I assume you're referring to—

"Yes," Xavier said. "I mean, well—"

He looked into the faces of everyone at the table. Larkin understood why Xavier and Ed—teachers, online and off—were avoiding the word. She'd posted her own lists of trigger warnings, when she was a grad student assisting three sections of Theater 101. *Murder* was never on the list, but this word was.

"Thank you!" Josephine said. "Are those sesame seeds?"

"You wondered when Adamantine Darcy would choose to die with dignity," Moira said, calmly. "I do not blame you. Adamantine and I talked about it, several times." Claire, Xavier and Eliza thanked Handy; Jay broke off a piece of his roll and buttered it. Moira picked up her knife, holding it as precisely as one of her knitting needles. "In fact, I am amused that all of your minds went immediately to *murder*. Perhaps she chose this sailing as her opportunity to say farewell."

This time Larkin didn't have to wait for people to speak. All she had to do was watch.

"Why would she end her life on the ship?" Xavier asked.

"Many cruise ship sailings have at least one death," Anni answered, speaking quickly and without emotion. "It is nearly always an elderly passenger in poor health and is often brought on by a drastic change in diet and alcohol consumption. These deaths, while unfortunate on the individual level, happen often enough that cruise ships have a protocol for handling the remains. If a person like Adamantine wanted to quietly end her life without starting a lengthy nerd-driven conversation about whether other people should make the same choice, and whether authors owed it to their fans *not* to make that choice, and whether—" Anni paused. "I do go on." She buttered a piece of her roll. "Imagine that times 1,163 nerds, and you can see why Adamantine might have preferred to make her death look like an accident."

"Hold up," Claire said. Handy had begun serving salads. "We still don't know for sure that Adamantine Darcy is dead. From my perspective, and from the perspective of Chief Security Officer Aart Van der Voort, she's a missing person."

"So you have to wait, what, twenty-four hours?" Daniel asked. He put his fork immediately into his salad and raised a large bite towards his mouth. "Or is it forty-eight?"

"You've been watching too much television," Claire said. "You should report a missing person to your local law enforcement team as soon as possible, which is exactly what Ms. McFarlane did."

"And you're saying we should let the professionals handle this one," Eirwen said, after thanking Handy for serving her, "and not spread any rumors about what might have happened to Adamantine."

"Bingo," Claire said, grinning.

"That's why we ran the prediction market the way we did," Eirwen said, picking up her fork and then putting it down again. "We didn't want any hot goss, you know, so we kept the predictions completely ridiculous, you know, like Adamantine's AI assistant taking over the entire ship."

She laughed. Grandmaster Trey did not. "So you're saying this is all real?"

He looked at Ed and got his answer without having to ask. "I thought this was some kind of nerd nonsense," Trey continued. "I know you all like your role-playing games, and I heard that some of you were making bets on what had happened to Adamantine, and I just assumed—"

He looked at Larkin. "And you're really a detective?"

"Not really," Larkin said.

"Yes really!" her mother corrected.

"She's an amateur detective," Moira said. "Like Father Brown."

"And Adamantine Darcy is really missing?"

"Yes," Ed said, quietly.

"And somebody really did cut the power to the main theater on Monday?"

Xavier leaned over his salad plate. "You saw it too? I thought I was going mad, I mean nuts, I mean—I don't even know what word to use." He shrugged. "I thought it was just me."

"I saw it," Elliott said. He looked at Eliza. "The power outage caused TOM to reset itself, right?"

Eliza nodded, not wanting to meet Elliott's eyes. "It was a failure of anticipation on my part. We'll correct that in the next version."

Jay picked up his fork and set them on course. "So whatever Adamantine was thinking or planning before TOM power cycled, well—her mind could have literally changed."

"Not literally," Eliza said quietly.

She hated him in that moment, Larkin could tell.

So could Jay—who could also tell how Larkin felt about the interaction.

"This is a delightful salad," Moira said. "Is that chervil?"

"Sure tastes like it," Ed said. "Pun intended."

So could Ed.

So could Eirwen, who read what she saw and rewrote the scene. "Maybe the salads are poisoned."

"Maybe the Champagne is poisoned!" Josephine said, her laugh louder than ever. "I'll be the next to go!"

"One of us will be the next to go," Moira said, her voice quieter than ever. "Thirteen at the table."

There was a pause, while everyone counted heads.

"Well, I'll be damned," Daniel said. "I suppose one of us is doomed to die."

"We're all doomed to die," Anni said, "actuarially speaking."

Jay smiled at Anni. He liked her, nearly as much as Larkin did, and Larkin gave herself just enough time to imagine the four of them—herself and Jay and Anni and Elliott—sitting comfortably in the living room of Anni and Elliott's farmhouse. Then she saw Jay watching her. "I know what you're thinking, Detective Day," he said. "We're all going to die, but are any of us going to be murdered?"

Another pause. Handy began to clear the salad plates.

"We still don't have any proof there's a murderer on board," Claire said.

"If there's a murderer on board," Xavier said, pressing the end of the butter knife into his thumb, "that's it for the cruise."

"There might be a murderer on board, and you're worried about the cruise?" That was Grandmaster Trey, his voice overlapping Daniel's, who was saying, "We can start a new cruise. Rebrand. You won't be on it, of course, but there are oceans of possibility here."

"Oh," Xavier said, "so you'd sacrifice thirteen years of my life to help you book a few more of your quotidian magician gigs."

"Quotidian magician," Josephine said. Someone had refilled her Champagne flute when Larkin wasn't watching. "That's good."

"I think more people would come on the cruise if they knew it was a murder cruise," Eirwen said. "You'd get the true crime market."

"Or you could run it as a murder mystery cruise," Jay suggested, winking at Larkin, "on an ocean liner where someone had actually been murdered."

"So that's what's become of us," Eliza said, quietly. She seemed to be saying it to Jay. "So much mental capacity wasted on jokes and status. We could be putting our minds towards Adamantine's disappearance, but we've spent the entire evening drinking and laughing and asking each other whether Adamantine was murdered." Now she looked at Larkin. "We deserve to be replaced by artificial intelligences. Every last one of us."

Josephine reached out her hand, across the table, to pat Eliza's arm.

Elliott made his final—and most important—move.

"Then let's use your artificial intelligence to solve this," he said. "It'll tell us exactly where Adamantine is, and where she's been, and what she's been thinking about. There will be video and audio. Give us TOM's data, and we'll know what happened to Adamantine Darcy."

"No," Eliza said. "I can't. If we set that precedent now, TOM fails. Our clients have to believe that their information will be completely secure."

"No information is completely secure," Trey said. "You know that."

"I said *believe*," Eliza corrected. "The rest can be sorted out in the Terms and Conditions."

This time everybody looked at Eliza—and none of them noticed the cruise-uniformed man who was quietly approaching their table.

Which meant it was finally Larkin's turn to speak. "Ah, yes," she said. "Terms and Conditions. We all signed them, didn't we, when we agreed to join this cruise?"

"She's making a speech," Josephine said. "Just like a real detective."

"Nothing like a real detective," Claire corrected.

"In those Terms and Conditions, it states that your likeness can be photographed at any time. Is that not correct?" Larkin looked at Xavier, who nodded. "That's correct."

"And any photographs taken by Dutch Cruise International may be considered the property of Dutch Cruise International, to be used for marketing materials and/or any other purposes they deem necessary and appropriate?"

"Something like that," Xavier said.

"And all photographs taken by Dutch Cruise International are taken on film, ensuring a series of corroborating negatives that cannot be deepfaked and must be treated as an accurate assessment of reality?"

"Sure," Xavier said. He'd calculated what was coming, and he approved. "I know some people think that photography distorts reality, since a limited amount of information fits within the frame and an infinite amount of information is left out, but I can't offer any opinions on that. I'm a math guy."

"You're a professional," Larkin said, "and so is everyone who is employed by Dutch Cruise International. That's why we don't need TOM." She looked at Eliza. "We have our own intelligence system, a human one, and he's been collecting data—all of which *can* and *will* immediately be turned over to Chief Security Officer Aart Van der Voort—this entire time."

She gestured towards the ship's photographer.

"Call him Ismael."

Ismael held up his camera and took a picture of the group.

Finally, they all looked surprised.

CHAPTER 17

After the plates were cleared, Larkin met with Handy and Ismael.

"Thank you," she said. "You both performed exactly as I hoped you would."

"I have always wanted to be an actor," Handy said. He had led them to a quiet table in the corner of the Main Dining Room, and poured cups of steaming, sweet, milky tea. "My daughter shares this dream."

"Well," Larkin said, "I hope she gets the chance to pursue it."

"Would you like to see a picture?" While Handy reached into his pants pocket to pull out a well-loved snapshot, Larkin thought about everything that still had to be done before the case was closed. This was the second secret meeting she'd had that day—the first, of course, had been with Elliott and Eirwen—and she hoped it could be the last. Ever since she'd had breakfast with Adamantine, she'd been arranging meetings and rearranging information like so many deck chairs. By the time they all sat down for Formal Dinner, she was not at all sure she could keep her plans afloat—but here they were, Handy's photo in his hand and Ismael's on his camera.

"She's lovely," Larkin said. "What's her name?"

"Melati," Handy said. "She will be so proud of her father."

"She should be," Larkin said. She wondered, briefly, if she would ever have children—it was a thought that passed through her mind, these days, nearly every time she saw one—and then turned to Ismael. "What did you notice from the photographs?"

"If you wanted to make your guests uncomfortable, you were enormously successful," Ismael said. "The two most uncomfortable guests were the man sitting next to you and the man sitting across from you."

This was not what Larkin was expecting to hear.

"Dr. Jackson and Dr. Malhotra," Handy whispered, helpfully.

"Yes, thank you," Larkin said. She had thought Jay was enjoying himself. Once again, she'd looked at a man she wanted to love and missed everything. "What else did you notice?"

"Two pairs of guests were secretly communicating with each other throughout the meal."

"Yep," Larkin said, "Anni and Elliott and Daniel and Moira."

"Nope," Ismael said, delighted to know something Larkin didn't. "Daniel and Moira Pennington were supremely unsuccessful at communicating with each other. It was Xavier Torres, our cruise director, and the woman seated next to him."

"Xavier and Eliza," Larkin said. This had not occurred to her. It had clearly occurred to *them*, and they'd occluded it from everyone else. "Interesting."

"I will show you the photographs once the film is

developed," Ismael said, "and I will also show you the series of photographs you asked me to collect from our previous days at sea. I am not sure whether you will find what you are looking for, but I hope that it will be helpful to the investigation."

"You've been helpful already," Larkin said. "Both of you." She reached into the right-hand pocket of her sparkling dress—because Stanley, the Shakespeare Festival costume designer, had made sure her gown had pockets—and pulled out four twenty-dollar bills. The Promenade had an onboard ATM, and it had cost her another ten dollars in fees just to get the cash. "Thank you—from me and from Adamantine Darcy."

"Whom I hope is still alive!" Handy said, smiling.

"Me too," Larkin said—and then she saw Officers Novak and Van der Voort walking quickly towards her. "Excuse me."

She knew what they were going to say before they said it. So did Ismael and Handy.

"We've found what appears to be Adamantine's body."

———

Larkin followed Claire and Artie into the hallway where she had been taken for her earlier interrogation. They passed Officer Van der Voort's office. They passed a dismal, windowless door—Larkin wondered if it led to *the brig*—and paused in front of an open doorway.

"We checked this room, of course," Claire said, "the first time we searched the ship." She gestured for Larkin to go inside. "But we didn't check the lockers."

They were in the ship's morgue. It was the size of a galley kitchen; a corpse-sized counter on the right, and two corpse-sized lockers on the left. Upper and lower bunk, with long rectangular metal doors.

The body was in the upper. Larkin saw the feet first; a pair of sensible shoes, a pair of old-lady pantyhose. Tan, of course—darker than Adamantine's skin had ever been. The dress covered the rest, from knees to wrist to neck, and that was when Larkin turned around and looked at Claire and Artie, waiting for them to explain what she had just seen.

Or—more specifically—*not seen*.

"Yes," Officer Van der Voort said. He almost smiled. "The figure is missing its head."

———

"You missed the concert," Ed said.

He was standing outside of the Coffeeshop, waiting for her.

She hadn't known he'd be there, but she knew he'd be somewhere—and it was thoughtful, really, for Ed to have remembered how much she loved coffee. The kind of thing you'd expect from a sort-of-maybe-boyfriend who hadn't yet been officially broken up with. Almost sweet.

Ed, however, looked mostly sour.

"I'm sorry," Larkin said. "I lost track of time, I didn't bring a watch, phones don't work, it's not like there are a bunch of analog clocks around here, we're supposed to forget what time it is, we're on vacation."

She let her voice carry towards the Promenade fountain, where a group of nerds were gathered around the unicycling ukulelist. He was balancing his unicycle on the edge of the fountain, cycling back and forth just fast enough to advance catastrophe.

"So what were you doing, while you were *on vacation*?" Ed asked. "Were you with—"

"No," Larkin said.

He knew.

He didn't know.

It didn't matter.

"I was with Officer Van der Voort," Larkin said, speaking loudly enough to cover the whirr of the espresso machines and the careful plucks of a ukulele being tuned. "They found Adamantine Darcy's body."

The ukulelist stopped tuning. She hoped he wasn't going to start playing.

"Good for them," Ed said. "Did they need you to be there? Or did you just want to be a part of the mystery? Is there something about the death of Adamantine Darcy that a Chief Security Officer hired by Dutch Cruise International needs an amateur detective to solve?"

"Yes," Larkin said. She could sense that the unicycling ukulelist and his fountain fanbase were watching her. She waited for the barista to take his shot—and then she took hers. "Adamantine's body was missing its head!"

She heard the splash as the unicyclist unbalanced.

She looked at Ed, hoping he'd understand.

He didn't.

"You missed the concert," he said, again. Ed spoke quietly, keeping his voice aimed directly at Larkin. "I know you've got something going on, and I know you have this whole plan, and I know that I'm not supposed to know about the plan, and that's fine. But you could have included Grandmaster Trey's concert in your plan. You could have taken a ninety-minute break from whatever it is you're doing, and you could have watched Trey and me put on the best show I've ever been a part of."

"I'm sorry," Larkin said. She meant it. "It's just—"

"No, it isn't," Ed said. "I've seen you make rehearsal schedules. I've seen you adjust and cut and reprioritize. You can fit everything in that needs to fit, and you chose not to fit me in."

Larkin did not know what to say. She could hear the nerds, behind her, spreading the news. She could hear the barista, in front of her, speaking in rapid and excited Dutch.

"So it was a good show?"

"I don't want to talk about it," Ed said. "I'm going up to the Performers' Lounge, and then I'm going back to our stateroom, and I don't want you following me or waiting for me." He considered what he was about to say and decided to accept the consequences. "Find somewhere else to sleep tonight."

"I'll ask Mom and Claire," Larkin said.

"I'm sure you will," Ed said before walking away.

———

Larkin did, in fact, ask her mother and Claire if she could sleep in Interior 3689—if calling the stateroom and then knocking on the door counted as asking. She imagined Claire with Officer Van der Voort, discussing the headless dead body, and her mother with the LGBTQ+ Boomers, drinking her seventh glass of Champagne.

Then she called the Executive Suite.

Jay met her at the top of the stairs.

"I wouldn't ask," Larkin said, "except—"

She was crying.

She hadn't expected to be crying.

Neither had Jay.

"You know how I'm the best amateur detective in Prat-incola, Iowa?" Larkin said. She felt Jay put his arms around her. His touch was hesitant; the two of them stood in the hallway with a full six inches between them, like they were at a middle-school dance. "Well, I figured out Xavier and Eliza."

"Good for you," Jay said. Ed had said something like that, but he'd made it sound like Larkin was the worst person in the world—which made Larkin sob even harder. "Good for you," Jay said again. He made it sound like Larkin was maybe all right.

"And I know that Eliza isn't going to be sleeping in her cabin anymore, since it's kind of a murder scene, so they've put her in some empty stateroom, and I know that's where Xavier's sleeping tonight, because that's where I'd be sleeping if someone I cared about had just gotten kicked out of their cabin because of a dead body." Ed had done something like that, back when they'd done the Pratincola Shakespeare Festival together. He'd been such a good boyfriend, and she could have gone to his show, and she should have, and now she was crying so hard that Jay was pulling her close, her snot and her dress pressed against his skin, his hands in her long, dark hair, the two of them accepting each other as they were without asking themselves what they might become.

"And you need somewhere to sleep tonight," Jay said, stroking the back of Larkin's head. "Because you were so busy amateur-deducing that you forgot about Grandmaster Trey's concert."

Larkin sniffled, then swallowed. "Were you there?"

"Yeah," Jay said. "It was one of the best shows I've ever seen."

"Then I really am sorry I missed it."

Jay let go of Larkin's hair and took her hand. "You're in luck," he said. "The cruise ship has, like, eight television channels, and one of them's just, like, terrible old movies, and another one is non-stop advertising for the cruise line, and I think one of them shows news via satellite, but at least two of them run footage of mainstage programming over and over and over."

He led Larkin towards the Executive Suite door.

"We can sit up until we see it again."

CHAPTER 18

arkin sat, once again, with Anni. It was morning. They were both in cruise-branded bathrobes. Larkin's bathrobe had a tiny Executive Suite emblem stitched into the front pocket, which Anni noted with a nod. They both knew Larkin hadn't slept in Verandah 213 last night.

"So is that the private island?" Larkin asked. The ship was closing in on the kind of Caribbean coastline that had previously only existed in Larkin's imagination. Gleaming white sand, glittering blue water, rows of cabanas and a line of multi-colored kayaks. Palm trees. Thatched roofs. Steel drums. "We get to spend the entire day, like, *there*?"

It wasn't as if Larkin hadn't ever seen a beach before. She'd lived in Los Angeles, which practically required her to have opinions on Santa Monica vs. Venice; she'd grown up on the Puget Sound, where the ocean met rocks instead of sand. She'd spent a semester in London, which meant taking the obligatory trip to the White Cliffs of Dover. She'd put her feet in both the Atlantic and the Pacific, wearing swimsuits or sweaters as appropriate. It was just that she had never seen any beach, *anywhere*, that looked like this.

They were close enough for Larkin to read the banner: *Welcome to Dutch Cruise International's Paradise Isle.*

"Yes," Anni said. "I'll give you the tour, if you want."

It was left unsaid—because neither of them needed to say it—that Larkin and Ed would not be exploring the private island together. Larkin had not seen Ed that morning. She had woken up next to Jay, and she had slipped a note under the door of her former stateroom letting Anni know that she was on her way to the Lido Deck. The rest—

"Okay," Larkin said, "but I don't want to talk about what happened."

Anni pulled her knees up to her chest. "I like Jay," she said, "and I like Ed." She looked at Larkin. "I like you best."

"Thanks."

That was when the two of them saw Larkin's mother, also bathrobed, with an enormous glass of water in each hand. "Good morning," Josephine said, in a voice that suggested her morning had been less good than she was expecting. "May I join you?"

"Of course," Larkin said, getting up and pulling a third deck chair closer to the other two. "How are you doing?"

"You know how I'm doing," Josephine said. "I'm hungover." She took a drink of water. "I haven't been hungover in thirty-eight years." She took another drink. "Unlike Champagne, the experience does not improve with age."

Larkin twitched her nose at her mother. "Don't worry," she said, "we'll take care of you."

"But I came up here to take care of you!" Josephine said, twitching her nose back at Larkin. It was one of their oldest forms of communication. "I saw that you had tried to call our stateroom, so I called your stateroom, and Anni told me not to worry." She took another drink of water. "And then I called again this morning, and Elliott told me I could find you here."

"Did they tell you anything else?"

"No," Josephine said. "Is there something else I need to be told?"

"No," Larkin said. The ship swayed, slightly, as it settled into the dock. "I mean, yes."

She looked at her mother.

"Do you know already?"

Josephine set one of her water glasses on the arm of her deck chair and squeezed Larkin's hand. "I think you need to tell me anyway."

Larkin looked at Anni, who reached out and squeezed Larkin's other hand. This was the least-Anni-like thing she had ever done—Anni hated touching people, especially spontaneously—but if Anni could change, and Jay could change, then Larkin could change too.

"Ed and I—"

She almost started crying, but she let her mother and her best friend hold her together.

"Ed and I are ending things."

Josephine squeezed as hard as she could. "I'm sorry," she said. "Not because I feel any particular way about you and Ed, I've always admired him as a teacher and I enjoyed seeing the two of you together, but you're my daughter and you get to choose who you spend your life with." Larkin squeezed back, as hard as she could. "I'm sorry because I know this kind of transition can be enormously painful, and I do not like to see my daughter in pain, but it's part of the process, and I can't stop it."

She let up on the squeeze and turned towards her daughter. "I'm also sorry because I can tell you're exhausted. You've done so much since you moved to Iowa. You gave up on your dissertation. You started working those early-morning shifts at The Coffee Shop. You stepped in, last-minute, to direct a Shakespeare Festival. You began financially contributing to a household that had just lost its primary earner. Then you had to go through a lengthy interview process for the job you'd just proved you could do, better than anyone in the tri-state area if you ask your mother's opinion, and as soon as you get a break, your first vacation in years, you break up with your boyfriend."

"Wow," Larkin said, trying to laugh because she did not want to cry. "I really have been through a lot."

"You've also been taking high-intensity fitness classes twice a week," Anni said, "and singing in community choir, and working with Ben on his opera, and helping Elliott and me move into our farmhouse."

"Right!" Larkin said. "I've been doing, like, *everything*."

"I told you that should have been your business card," Anni said. She had, back when the two of them were trying to figure out if Larkin should start a private detective business. "Larkin Day: I Solve Everything."

"Doing everything isn't the same as solving everything," Larkin said.

"I know," Anni said.

Larkin thought of what Adamantine had said about Anni and Elliott. *If he is more than his failures, it is because she is doing everything she can to give him something else to be.* She wondered if Anni was as exhausted as she was. Larkin held Anni's hand as tightly as she could, hoping her friend would understand the message. She really should have learned Morse Code. If Jay could do it—

"Good morning, nerds!"

It was the voice of Xavier Torres, broadcasting across the entire ship.

"I would like to welcome you to Dutch Cruise International's Paradise Isle! I don't know about you, but I hope that pair of dice is twenty-sided!"

"Where does he get these jokes?" Josephine asked. "Are they the same ones every cruise?"

"Most of them," Anni said. "Nerds like knowing what's going to happen next."

"So do theater geeks," Larkin said. When she'd been a grad student in Los Angeles, she'd spent more time and money than she could afford driving down to Disneyland with her classmates. They'd crowded into the Haunted Mansion, chanting the patter along with the Ghost Host. Part of the reason she loved working in the theater was because you not only knew what was going to happen—every word, every cue—but could also control the way in which it happened. Maybe she was more of a nerd than she realized.

"We're going to be spending the entire day at this beautiful private island, so I hope you've set aside a little time to leave the comforts of the ship and soak up some of the most beautiful scenery you're likely to see in your life!"

"He's right about that," Josephine said. "I don't know if I've ever seen a more beautiful island." She turned to Anni. "I assume I shouldn't ask too many questions about the island's maintenance."

"Probably not," Anni said. "If you feel badly, tip well."

"You can relax in one of our many comfortable cabanas, enjoy live music, take a guided tour—or, since we know you're all nerds, spend the entire day in the outdoor game room! The snack stations are ready and waiting, so all you have to do is get out of bed and get on board!"

"Wait for it," Anni said.

"I'm waiting," Larkin said.

"Did I just say *get on board*? I meant *get off board*!" Xavier concluded, laughing at his own joke. "See you there!"

The three women sat, in their nearly matching bathrobes, still holding each other's hands.

"We'll spend the day together," Josephine said.

"Of course we will," Anni said.

Larkin, surrounded by love, no longer felt its absence.

"Who's going to take care of Ed?" she asked.

"Elliott, obviously," Anni said. "We talked about it this morning."

———

By the time the three of them had breakfast, made their way back to their respective staterooms, and put on clothing that wasn't bathrobes, it was nearly—well, only Anni knew exactly what time it was, and she told them she wasn't telling.

"We're on vacation," she said, leading the way down the gangplank. "For at least one day, on this cruise, all of us should be on vacation."

"So you didn't practice the piano this morning?" Larkin asked.

"No," Anni said. She was wearing a T-shirt that read *I like big books and I cannot lie.* "But I'll practice tomorrow."

"Good," Larkin said. "I don't want you to change *too* much."

Anni looked nonplussed, in both senses of the word.

"Okay, fine," Larkin said, "you can change exactly as much as you want."

"Everyone changes exactly as much as they want," Anni said—and that was when they passed the second clump of nerds who were talking about Adamantine Darcy. Larkin knew it because they behaved exactly like the first clump of nerds they'd passed, at the top of the gangplank; a quick turn of the head towards Larkin, who had allowed the news to spread and was therefore irrevocably linked to it, and then a quieter discussion about Adamantine's missing one.

"We're on vacation," Anni said again, pulling Larkin past the conversation.

The three women scanned their badges as their feet sank in the sand. Larkin was wearing flip-flops. Anni was wearing pink plastic clogs with little holes in them. Josephine had a pair of casual flats with thick rubber soles, and she immediately took them off and dangled them from the ends of her fingers.

"We can go barefoot when we're on vacation, right?"

"I would recommend not," Anni said, reaching into her ever-present canvas bag and offering Josephine a pair of flip-flops to match Larkin's. "Do you have any idea how many dice get lost in this beach every year?"

"At least a pair of them," Josephine said, laughing. It was a sober laugh—the one Larkin had grown up with. "See, I'm starting to become one of you! What do I need to do next?"

"Well," Anni said, "you could get your hair braided, or you could go for a kayak ride or a hot-air balloon ride, or we could visit the dolphin preserve, but all of that stuff costs money. We could go play a board game, which is free, or we could put our feet in the ocean, which is my favorite thing to do while we're here."

"Let's do that," Josephine said, and they did—or at least they started to. Larkin stopped, just long enough to say hello to Ed, who had just finished scanning his badge.

Elliott stood a respectful distance away, giving them the illusion of privacy.

"I watched the recording of your show." She wanted Ed to know that, even if they never spoke to each other again. "It was really good."

"Yeah, it was," Ed said. His face was tight, and his eyes were tired. "I'm glad you saw it."

"I'm sorry I missed the real thing. I really am."

Ed nodded, and then neither of them said anything, and then Larkin turned and ran to catch up to her mother and Anni. Her flip-flops were slippery and awkward in the sand, but she didn't look back to see if Ed was watching her.

"Is he all right?" Josephine asked.

"Yep," Larkin said. "Let's go put our feet in the ocean."

It didn't take long for the three of them to stand, side by side, with waves cresting as high as their knees. Anni, who was considerably shorter than Larkin and Josephine, was soaked almost to the waist—and she kept running forward to meet the next wave, jumping up and down and shouting with excitement.

"I think Anni wants to put her entire body in the ocean," Larkin whispered.

"Let her have her fun," Josephine said. Another nerd had joined Anni, and the two of them faced down a wave that was as high as Anni's shoulders. "You can go splash around with her, if you want."

"No," Larkin said. She took her mother's hand, again. "I want to stay here with you."

"Good," Josephine said, "because I want to stay here with you, too." She twitched her nose at Larkin.

Larkin twitched back. Then she asked her mother the question she'd always wanted to ask, ever since she was old enough to put question marks at the ends of sentences. "Did my dad, um, not want to stay with you? Or did he not want to stay with me?" She squeezed her mother's hand. "It's all right if it was me, I don't mind, I've just always wanted to know."

Her mother considered this.

"You know, your father got back in touch with me a few weeks ago," she said. "He wants to see you."

"I don't know if I want to see him." The last time Larkin had seen her father, he'd told her to lie about her age in order to get a twelve-and-under discount. Larkin had been eleven—a tall eleven, she was always tall for her age, but he should have known. She hadn't corrected him, which meant they had both spent the day being dishonest with each other.

"It was me more than it was you, if that's what you're asking," Josephine said. "Not that you helped, but our problems were in place before you were born." The two of them watched Anni and her new friend welcome a third nerd into their wave-cresting game. "Sometimes I wish I'd married a different man, but then I would undoubtedly have had a different daughter, or maybe no daughter at all." She squeezed her hand and twitched her nose at the same time. "And what would I do without you?"

"I cannot believe my own mother indulged in a cliché," Larkin said, twitching her nose back.

Josephine laughed again. "This cruise is all about indulgence," she said. "But if you want me to say it in my own words, then—"

Larkin watched her mother think.

She'd grown up watching her mother think.

In many ways, it was how she'd learned to do it.

"We get to choose who we invite into our lives," Josephine said. "I chose you."

The nerds splashed; the steel band began; the hot air balloon hung, like a second sun, over the ocean.

"Wow," Larkin said. "I definitely have salt water in my eyes."

———

There were, of course, multiple themed restaurants, all of which accepted cash, credit, or crypto—but their all-inclusive cruise package promised them three meals per day, and by noon the majority of the nerds had gathered around a Dutch Cruise International branded tent, ready to take advantage of hamburgers, cheeseburgers, veggie burgers, hot dogs, and some kind of vegan cylindrical foodstuff that Larkin immediately dubbed a *not-dog*.

"Don't ever try to roast one of those things over a fire pit," Anni advised. "They melt."

"Fair enough," Larkin said. She could tell, by the way the nerds in front of them paused when they heard her voice, that they had been talking about Adamantine. Everyone seemed to know that the famous author had been decapitated, which was exactly what Larkin was hoping for.

"Is everything going as planned?" It was Elliott, hands in his pockets, hair in its ponytail, cutting the line without apology. "Except for the whole Ed thing, I mean."

"How's he doing?"

"He's having lunch in Café Afrikaans with the Blerds," Elliott said, gesturing one shoulder in Ed's presumed direction. "How are you doing?"

"I'm about to get a free hot dog on a paper plate," Larkin said, "so I'm doing just fine."

The line moved forward; the four of them received

their cruise-branded lunches and retreated to one of the empty cabanas.

"Don't you have to pay for these?" Josephine asked, arranging herself in a low, cushioned chair. "Wait, don't tell me—it's another Super Elite Status perk."

Anni nodded. "A lot of people don't realize just how much these loyalty programs have to offer, if you're willing to put in the financial and time commitment up front. This is the least money I've ever spent on this trip, and I'm in the best stateroom I've had so far, but I had to pay for five cruises before I got Elite Status and another five cruises before I started getting Super Elite benefits." She read the ingredient list on her bag of cruise-branded potato chips and then tossed it to Larkin. "The math doesn't really work out, it's not like the money I'm saving on this trip makes up for the money I spent on all of the other trips, but if you like a certain kind of vacation and you think you'll want to take it every year, sign up for the loyalty program. At a certain point, you'll be spending less every year instead of more." She opened up her hamburger bun and used her napkin to carefully wipe away the chopped onion. "Unless, of course, you're the kind of person who takes what they would have saved and puts it right back into the vacation. Dolphin excursions, restaurants on port days, that kind of thing."

Larkin, who had heard Anni talk about this kind of thing before, turned her attention to Elliott—who was watching a crowd of nerds gather at the cabana in front of them. She spotted Eirwen's hair ribbon and Daniel Pennington's porkpie hat. "What's going on?"

"It's Daniel and Moira's cabana," Elliott said. "She's doing tarot readings."

"Meh," Larkin said. "She did mine on the first day. Told me that everything I loved would fall apart, or something like that." She couldn't remember any of the cards Moira had read; she could only remember her Shadow Card, which she'd interpreted herself—and which had, in both fantasy and fact, come true. Larkin wondered if she would have ended up in Jay's room last night if she hadn't seen him staring at her on the Two of Cups. Then she tucked that thought deep into the squiggles of her brain, so she wouldn't have to answer her own question.

"I'm not close enough to see for sure," Elliott said, "but I think she's forcing the cards."

He stood up. "Anyone got any trash?" Anni handed over her onion-covered napkin. Josephine passed Elliott her empty potato chip bag. Once he'd collected everything, he walked calmly towards the nearest trash can. Larkin waited for his head to turn towards the Penningtons' cabana, but it never did.

"He's good," she said to Anni.

"Best I've ever known," Anni said, "and he keeps getting better."

"So you're not, like—" Larkin wanted to ask Anni about what Adamantine had said, about Elliott's failures and her overcompensation, but she watched Anni watch Elliott and understood that it was an impossible question to ask. It wasn't that Anni was giving Elliott something more to be; it was that she was part of a partnership in which both of them could become who they were, over and over again. "You really love each other, don't you."

"We've always loved each other," Anni said. "It is the great luckiness of our lives."

Elliott returned. "She's definitely forcing the cards," he said.

"That's awful," Anni said.

"Why does it matter," Josephine asked. "Isn't tarot all made-up anyway?"

This was Elliott's area of expertise, but this time Anni provided the explanation. "It matters because she's choosing which cards people see, instead of allowing them to choose their own," she said. "If you believe that you have agency in your own life, then tarot becomes an exercise in expectation management. You choose the cards, you observe how you react to them, you ask yourself if any negative feelings associated with the cards indicate a potential error in your thinking or behavior, you ask yourself if any positive feelings associated with the cards indicate an opportunity for positive change, and then you adjust your behavior accordingly."

"But if Moira's choosing for you," Elliott said, "then she's manipulating the emotions you get from the cards."

"Which means she's manipulating your behavior," Larkin said. She thought, again, of the reading Moira had done for her. *If you continue on your current path, you will lose everything.* She'd only lost Ed, so far, but they still had a full day at sea. There was plenty that could still go wrong, and Moira knew it.

No—Moira *had* known it.

She'd seen it, in Larkin, when they'd met in the Performers' Lounge.

"You're good at reading people, right?" Larkin asked Elliott.

He shrugged. "I'm a magician. It's kind of part of the deal."

"What do you see when you look at me?"

She waited for Elliott to look at her, but he kept his eyes on the horizon. "I see a woman who is trying very hard to be everything to everybody around her," he said. "I also see a woman who wants to become a talented artist, and I think she could be, but right now she's preoccupied by what she believes to be her obligations to other people."

"So why would you give me a tarot reading in which you told me I would lose everything?"

"I wouldn't," Elliott said. "If I were the kind of magician who forced cards, I'd probably draw the Seven of Wands, for you. The artist who cannot create because she is out of balance with the world around her."

"I can't even take a vacation," Larkin joked. "Here we are on the most beautiful beach I've ever seen, and we aren't even enjoying it."

"I'm enjoying it." Elliott reached down, took a handful of sand, and let it tumble between his fingers. "I've found this week to be extremely interesting—but I'm not stuck under the Seven of Wands."

"Okay, then get me unstuck," Larkin said. "What card would you draw next?"

"The Death card."

Larkin kicked the sand, which got stuck between her foot and her flip-flop. "Always with the Death card."

"It doesn't really mean death—"

"I know it doesn't really mean death!"

"But it does mean that you need to let something go."

"I know," Larkin said. "I will." She looked at Elliott. "I promise."

"You don't have to promise me," Elliott said. "The cards already know." He finally turned his head to look at Larkin. "Check your pocket."

"You are fucking kidding me," Larkin said, reaching into the pocket of her terrycloth shorts and pulling out a single tarot card. "The Magician."

"The artist who has mastered their craft," Elliott corrected, "and lives in balance with the needs of the world." He stood up. "That's who you could become—if you don't make the same mistake I did."

"Convincing yourself that you should do a television

show when you really wanted to do in-person close-up magic?"

"No," Elliott said, over his shoulder, as he left Larkin with the card in her hand. "Listening to Daniel and Moira Pennington."

———

As the afternoon waned—Claire stopped by the cabana, Josephine took a much-needed nap, Anni went to put her feet in the ocean for the second time—Larkin considered what Elliott had suggested. She watched him, belted and ponytailed, battle other nerds with orange-tipped foam swords. Someone had stamped a ring into the sand, and the game seemed to involve thrusting and parrying until one of the combatants stepped outside of the boundary. Elliott was undefeated, but he also wasn't rude; he stepped aside, after four rounds, to give another pair of nerds a chance.

I need to step aside too, Larkin thought. *Just for a little while.* She had a Shakespeare Festival to direct, after all—if what Jay had said at the Formal Dinner had been true, and the job really was hers, but whether or not she should trust Jay was another one of those thoughts that she tucked away, behind the ledge of her imagination. *Don't try to solve the Jay problem right now,* she told herself. *You haven't even seen him, like, all day, and you'd think—*

That was when Larkin spotted him. She hadn't been watching for Jay, but her eyes went immediately to his curly hair, his open, eager smile, and the foam sword he was holding in his hand. Jay was going to play the game, whatever it was, and as he sword-swiped awkwardly at the nerd in front of him it became obvious that he wasn't very good at it. The other nerd quickly pushed him outside of the boundary, and Jay held up his hands—and the foam sword—in surrender.

He was still smiling.

Then he wasn't, and Larkin stood up and began running towards the makeshift arena, because Ed had a foam sword pressed between Jay's shoulder blades and was walking him into the center of the circle.

"You are not seriously telling me you demand satisfaction?" Jay was trying to laugh; Ed was not. "Come on, you already know you can kick my ass."

"We will fight like gentlemen," Ed said. "That is what one does, in a matter of honor."

"If I'd done anything dishonorable, I'd be willing to let you foam sword fight me over it." Jay saw Larkin; Ed didn't. "But my behavior has been above reproach. Ask anyone you like."

"I loved her," Ed said.

"This is ridiculous," Jay said.

"*En garde,*" Ed said.

"Oh, shit—"

They fought, sort of. Jay dropped his sword almost immediately and held up his hands to protect his face from the blows he feared would come—but Ed played fair and pressed his sword into the space above Jay's heart.

"Concede," Ed said.

"Concede what?"

"That you have wronged me," Ed said, "as a gentleman." He lowered his sword. "And as a friend."

"I did nothing wrong," Jay said.

He took a step forward, and Ed took a step backward, and everyone around the boundary got very quiet.

"You were the one who turned her away."

Another step, from each of them.

"After leaving her alone for most of the cruise."

That was true, in a way that Larkin hadn't realized until Jay said it. Ed had ignored her, and Larkin had tried to ignore it, and now all she could see was the man who had met her eyes in the crowd and the man who hadn't.

Then she watched Jay turn his attention back to Ed.

"And we aren't friends."

That was loud enough—and the step was large enough—for Ed to stumble, his heel dipping into the hollow of the boundary. Larkin was not close enough to stop what she knew would happen, and she watched Ed collapse into the sand, his right elbow catching his weight.

"You are out of line," Jay said, picking up his foam sword and standing it, upright, in the center of the circle. "I win."

He looked at Ed, then at the crowd, then at Larkin. Jay hadn't changed, or maybe he'd only changed as much as he wanted to, or maybe Ed had made him so uncomfortable that he'd reverted to a previous version of himself, or maybe he'd thrown his first fight to put Ed off his game, or maybe he'd been the one to suggest picking up the foam swords and stamping out the boundary circle, understanding that Ed would be compelled to challenge him.

He knew.

She didn't know.

"I win," Jay said again. "I always do."

CHAPTER 19

The MS *Kalmerende Zeeën* departed Paradise Isle with a single horn blast. The ship was serving dinner, for anyone who felt like sitting down to another three-course meal—but Larkin felt like sitting, quietly, outside of the Coffeeshop.

Sipping an Americano.

Staring at a shortbread cookie stamped with the Dutch Cruise International logo.

Starting to get up—there had to be something she could do; she could talk to Ismael about the photos he'd collected or see if her mother and Claire wanted to eat tacos on the Lido Deck or find Anni and ask her whether she thought Jay was only pretending to change—and then sitting down again.

"You're supposed to be on vacation."

It was Eirwen. She still had bits of sand sticking to her sandals. Her ribbon was askew, her eyebrows awry. "Did you seriously pay eight dollars for a shot of espresso in a cup of water?"

"Ten plus tip," Larkin said. "But they gave me a free

cookie." She pushed the napkin with the shortbread towards Eirwen. "You want it?"

"Sure," Eirwen said, picking up the cookie and popping it into her mouth. "And if you ever want a decent cup of coffee, come by our suite. We got one of the big ones on Deck Eight, it sleeps twelve, but there are sixteen of us in there." She wiped her fingers on the napkin. "Anyway, it comes with a coffeemaker, and we've got, like, five bags of beans and a coffee grinder."

"You can bring a coffee grinder on a cruise ship?"

"There's nothing in the rules that say you can't," Eirwen said. Her left eyebrow was now wry. "Everything not forbidden is compulsory, right?"

"Sure," Larkin said. She was pretty sure she knew that quote from somewhere, but she couldn't remember where —and she still couldn't remember where she'd seen the quote on Adamantine Darcy's manuscript. *The Yet Unknowing World*. It meant something, or it had meant something to Adamantine, which meant that it should mean something to her.

"You look miserable," Eirwen said. "No offense."

"None taken."

"Can I help?"

Larkin looked at Eirwen, surprised at the offer—and even more surprised at her immediate impulse to accept. The redheaded, recalcitrant nerd she'd sat next to during Opening Ceremonies had somehow become a friend. "Yes."

"Excellent," Eirwen said. "There are a bunch of us setting up a filk circle in one of the conference rooms. Come sing with us." Now her eyebrows looked delighted. "It always makes your spirits rise, according to Arthur and Guenevere."

"According to Lerner and Loewe," Larkin corrected—

but she was on her feet, and she was smiling. "I guess I can go sing, if you want. What's a filk circle?"

Eirwen laughed. "So there was this, like, typo, in this essay, like, back in the 1950s, and they misspelled *folk music* as *filk music*, and from there—"

Her whole face looked delighted.

"Let's just say it's like the best thing ever."

———

The filk circle was forty-odd nerds—or forty *odd nerds*, because these were some of the strangest-looking people Larkin had ever seen in her life—jammed into a window-less conference room. The jamming had begun before Larkin and Eirwen arrived, and they squeezed two more chairs between a nerd wearing a T-shirt that should have been thrown away after its second underarm hole and the nerd who had worn the functional model train around his torso at the first three-course dinner. The train nerd intro-duced himself as Bartholomew and handed Larkin a stapled stack of well-worn paper with a bunch of song lyrics that had looked like they had originally been typed —like, *on a typewriter*—and then photocopied enough times that the edges of the previous pages were still visible.

"You'll know the tunes," he said.

She did. They sang a song about the Starship Enter-prise set to the theme from *Gilligan's Island*, and then they sang a song about *Game of Thrones* set to Don McLean's "American Pie." Much of the singing was nowhere near the pitch, and all of it was way too loud for the room, and there were five guitars going at the same time, and somebody had brought a melodica that they didn't really know how to play, and every breath

Larkin took tasted like tacos and armpits, and she loved it.

"Thank you," she whispered to Eirwen.

"You're welcome," Eirwen whispered back.

After they got a third of the way through Larkin's packet, there was a pause—and an older nerd, draped in a cape that had been crafted out of sci-fi convention programs, said she wanted to do "an original ose."

"That means a song about death," Eirwen whispered. "It comes from *morose*."

"And *even more ose*," Bartholomew whispered, happy to perpetuate what appeared to be a very old joke. Larkin laughed, and not just because she was supposed to. Filking was *fun*.

The woman's song, however, was beautifully, terribly sad.

Adamantine, out of time
Worlds made and then broken
Mind your mind before you lose your head
Bodies hold our thoughts in place
Words may go unspoken
But stories last long after we are dead.

The singer, who had been accompanying herself by slapping one hand against her thigh, held her other hand towards the assembled circle. "Sentences as magical as tangents," she said.

"That's from *How Now, Horatio*," Bartholomew whispered.

"Come away from your watch," another nerd said, "and keep time with me."

"That's from *Unfold Yourself*."

"Time is a circle and love is the point."

"That's from *One with Moderate Haste Might Tell a Hundred*."

The group continued reciting Adamantine Darcy's writing, and Bartholomew continued whispering titles into Larkin's ear. She recognized some of the titles—they were from Shakespeare, and most, or maybe all of them, were from *Hamlet*—and she also recognized a few of the quotes.

"If he is more than his failures, it is because she is trying as hard as she can to give him more to be."

That was what Adamantine had said about Anni and Elliott.

"You are here when you have no reason to be here. That may be the most important thing about you."

That was what Adamantine had said about her.

Then Larkin understood.

"Adamantine trained her AI on her own writing," she whispered to Eirwen. "TOM's been telling her what to say, using her own words."

"Huh," Eirwen whispered back. "That would make a really interesting short story."

"It would make a really interesting *novel*," Larkin said, "but that's not the point. The point is—"

That was when Ismael entered the circle.

"I am sorry to bother you, Miss Day," he said, "but your badge indicated you'd be here."

Larkin had, in fact, swiped her badge when she entered the door. She watched Ismael take in the room and place one hand discreetly over his nose.

"The photos are ready," he said, crouching slightly to speak directly into Larkin's ear. "I think you'll want to see them."

CHAPTER 20

Larkin stood in front of the Performers' Lounge.

She gave the bouncer the passcode.

She went inside.

It was, on the outside, the same as it had been the first night she entered. Dimly lit, comfortably arranged, a cruise-uniformed bartender pouring compliments and beverages. The kind of lounge a performer might imagine, if they were considering whether to accept the invitation to play the sailing. Dark wooden paneling. Tiffany-style lamps. A grand piano, its closed keyboard draped with a fringed scarf. Black-and-white photographs of the most famous people who had spent time in the space, reminding the performers that even though they had been booked on a luxury cruise—and were, at that moment, within the private room designated entirely for their comfort—there were still levels of professionality ahead of them.

Larkin had also increased her level of professionalism, prior to approaching the bouncer. She'd pulled her long dark hair back, clipping it into place with the barrette she'd borrowed from her mother a year ago. Her mother had also chosen the outfit she was wearing; a seafoam dress, streaked with gold, that wrapped carefully around Larkin's hips and settled, gracefully, in a knot at her waist. Larkin had argued that she didn't need another dress; that she felt more comfortable in her scruffy theater clothes; that she had no idea where she'd wear something like this.

The Performers' Lounge, as it turned out.

She walked through the room of people as if she belonged there, not caring whether they paused to look—and stopped, calmly, in front of Grandmaster Trey.

"I owe you an apology," she said. "On the first day of the cruise I told you that I would attend your concert, and I did not."

Trey smiled. "Do you think I really care if some white woman skips my gig?"

"I care," Larkin said, "because I made you a promise and failed to keep it." She looked into Trey's quizzical eyes, watching him realize that she was treating this not as a situation in which she wanted absolution for her behavior, but as an interaction between two working artists. "I think you care too, because I saw your performance on the stateroom television later that evening. It was amazing work, and I should have prioritized it."

Trey held out his hand. "I accept your apology."

They shook.

Larkin nodded.

Then she moved on, walking through the darkened room until she saw Moira Pennington. The magician neuroscientist's wife was sitting—and knitting—in what Larkin understood was her usual spot, her quilted craft bag filling the space that had once been occupied by Adamantine.

The needles paused.

The eyes met.

"I need to talk to you."

This time Moira nodded, and wrapped up her work-in-progress, and followed Larkin towards the door of the Performer's Lounge. They passed Daniel, who was holding an intense conversation with the unicycling ukulelist; they passed Ed, who was entering the lounge as they left it.

"Hello," Larkin said.

"Hello," Ed said.

"Hello," Moira said. "You're Trey's protégé, aren't you? So talented. Loved your set. My husband does bookings, if you're ever interested in that kind of thing." The shoulder that held the craft bag gestured towards the head that wore the porkpie hat. "Talk to him. I'd introduce you, but I'm afraid this lovely woman has already claimed my time."

"Be careful," Ed said with a smile. "She's formidable."

Larkin didn't know if he was saying it to her, or to Moira—but it didn't matter. Nothing about her and Ed mattered anymore. The only thing that mattered was getting Moira Pennington outside.

———

They stood in the same spot where Larkin had first spotted Jay. The sky was darker this time; the air hung heavily around them, obscuring any semblance of starlight. There was salt in every breath; the deck was slightly damp, and Larkin gripped the railing to keep herself from stumbling. It was nearly as difficult to see as it had been the day she boarded the ship.

"Beautiful night," Moira said.

She arranged herself and her craft bag on the nearest

deck chair—the one where Larkin had sat, when Jay was handing her ginger babies—and picked up her knitting needles. "You don't mind?"

"Of course not." Larkin could watch Moira's hands as well as her eyes, and gain information from both. "Do you mind?" She sat on the edge of the next deck chair over; the one Jay had used, when the two of them were interrogating each other.

"Of course not," Moira said, her overly gentle inflection matching Larkin's. "I was expecting this."

Larkin wasn't expecting *that*—but she still had the advantage. Jay had chosen well; her position pinned Moira into a smaller space, giving Larkin the opportunity to control both of their movements. If Moira looked like she was going to stand up and walk away, Larkin could block the path. If Moira looked like she wasn't going to cooperate, Larkin could pull her deck chair closer—or simply stand up, all six feet of her, and take two steps forward.

"Go ahead and ask," Moira said. "I know you want to."

She knew.

So did Larkin.

"Did Adamantine Darcy ask you to help her die with dignity?"

The needles continued, calmly. "Yes."

"Did Adamantine ask you to help her die with dignity on this cruise ship?"

The needles completed another row. "Yes."

"Did Adamantine know that you were planning to preserve her brain?"

The needles paused.

They both knew.

"No."

Larkin waited. Moira would be compelled to speak next; the story would have to be told now that there was someone to whom the magician neuroscientist's wife could tell it.

"We'd talked about it, right at the very beginning," Moira said, her needles clicking a little faster than they had been. "After the diagnosis. Save the mind while it was still predominantly solvent." She met Larkin's eyes, just long enough for Larkin to see what might have been hope. "Adamantine wanted to finish her series first. I argued that the loss she might experience during the writing process would be insurmountable; that she would never be able to come back from it, and that we would never be able to use what was left of her to learn how to help other people."

"So you weren't necessarily trying to, like—" Larkin didn't want to use the words, but there they were. "Reanimate her."

Moira laughed. "You thought we were going to try to revive her?" Her voice was as blunt as the tips of her needles. "We were going to study her."

"You and Daniel." *A neuroscientist and a biologist*, Larkin thought—but she didn't need to say it aloud. "Except Adamantine wanted to finish her book."

"She wanted to complete her series," Moira said, "even though Daniel said that there was much more potential in leaving something unfinished. Mozart's *Requiem*, for example." She looked at Larkin. "Sue Grafton's *Alphabet Series*, since it's clear you like detective fiction." She looked back at her needles. "Think of everything we've been able to do with *The Wheel of Time*."

Larkin didn't know what *The Wheel of Time* was, but it didn't matter. "I bet Sue Grafton would have finished her last book if she could have," she said. "The world would have been better if she had."

"No, it wouldn't have." Moira's needles moved even

more quickly. "Unfinished work increases in value because you never know how good it might have been. It invites people to imagine what they might have done. To engage with other enthusiasts and create their own endings." She glanced up at Larkin, then back down at her work. "Think of all of the people who became mathematicians simply because Fermat didn't have enough space on his paper to prove his theorem."

"I'm only interested in thinking about Adamantine right now," Larkin said, "and she wanted to stay alive long enough to turn in her final draft."

Moira cast off. "And then she got in touch with Eliza McFarlane."

"Yes," Larkin said. She could see, in Moira's hands, how much she hated the woman. "And Eliza offered Adamantine a chance to test an external consciousness."

"I think that's a bit hyperbolic, don't you?" Moira began winding up her work and her worsted. "It's bad enough that we're calling these things *intelligences*. They're programs. Ones and zeroes. They can't do half of what a human mind can do." She looked at Larkin. "They don't count."

Larkin thought of what Ed had said about the MOOG —and about Wendy Carlos. She wished Ed were here to hear her say this. "You're a TERF, aren't you." She didn't give Moira the chance to respond. "Yes, I know, you support trans rights. You have trans friends. But you secretly think you're more of a woman than they are, and you secretly think you're more of a person than Adamantine is, and every time you meet someone who's on antidepressants you secretly judge them for not being able to selectively inhibit their own serotonin."

"I'm not against SSRIs," Moira said.

"But you are against AI," Larkin said, "even though

you saw the way it could help people. You're an AIERF—
yes, I just made up an acronym, nerds do it all the time,
you know what it means—even though Eliza's half-
finished invention literally stopped Adamantine from
killing herself."

"It's not the right solution to the problem," Moira said.
"We need to study the causes of these kinds of deficiencies.
Eliza wants to spackle them over with search engines and
algorithms."

She glared at Larkin.

"Now that the beta-amyloid hypothesis has been
proved false—"

She stabbed her knitting needles into her ball of yarn.

"More than false, *fabricated*—"

She fingered the edge of her quilted craft bag.

"There's an opportunity for someone to finally prove
what happens to us."

Larkin wondered if Moira was counting herself as one
of the *us*. If the magician neuroscientist's wife spent her
spare minutes knitting as an attempt to keep her own
mind from unraveling. She wanted to ask, but there was
something else she needed to ask instead. The question
she had been building towards, ever since Ismael had
shown her a series of photographs that proved where
Moira had been. What Moira had done.

She knew.

"So you murdered Adamantine."

Moira shook her head—slowly, sadly, sympathetically.
"No."

She didn't know.

"I told Adamantine I'd do everything I could to keep
her alive."

Moira hadn't done it.

"Even though it meant changing the plan we'd been working on for a year."

She'd missed something.

"But my husband—"

Larkin saw Moira's eyes lift, looking towards a point beyond Larkin's left shoulder; as Larkin turned, she saw two figures swaying in the shadows. One was walking towards them; the other was being pushed.

"He wanted to go ahead with it."

Daniel Pennington had his hacksaw in his hand.

The blade was held against Ed's throat.

CHAPTER 21

'm going to need you to walk towards the railing."

Daniel's voice was calm.

Confident.

Compelling.

Larkin walked.

"Now put your hands on the railing, where I can see them."

Larkin put.

She did not look at Ed, who was—she knew—still trapped within the grip of Daniel's arm and the gritted teeth of his hacksaw.

"Now climb over."

Larkin placed the sole of her strappy sandal against the lowest rung of the railing.

"Daniel!"

That was Moira.

"Larkin!"

That was Ed.

"It's all right," Larkin said, pressing her other foot against the higher rung and swinging her lower leg over.

"I'm right here." She allowed herself to laugh, as if this were a casual gathering among friends. "Anyway, I'm a theater person. I know how to take a fall."

"It's ten decks!" Ed, again.

"Quiet!" Daniel.

"No it isn't," Larkin said, looking down. "I could almost jump down to the Lido Deck from here. Everything's fine." She was lying. If Daniel forced her to let go, her next contact would be with the white-capped chop of the Caribbean.

"Daniel." Moira, again.

"Damn it, won't you all just stay quiet?"

"Do you need Ed for this?" Larkin asked, ignoring Daniel's command and balancing on the outside of the railing. Letting herself relax into her precarious position, as if it were an everyday way to spend an evening. "You've got me. Why not let him go?"

"I can't let him go," Daniel said. "Your lover is my leverage."

"Actually, we broke up," Larkin said. "You must have missed it." She smiled, trying to meet Daniel's eyes. "But that's okay. I missed a few things too."

She waited.

For the first time in her amateur detective career, nobody filled the silence.

"What did you miss, Larkin?" she asked, pitching her voice slightly higher. Making herself sound incredulous. "Oh, I don't know," she answered. "For starters, I thought it was Moira who wanted to murder Adamantine. She was the one who cut the power in the Main Theater, after all."

She waited, again.

"How did you figure that out, Larkin?" She laughed, or attempted to. "Why, it was easy! I asked the ship's photographer to show me all of the photos he had taken during the Opening Ceremonies. He caught Moira, in the wings, right before the lights went off—and right after they came back up."

Larkin looked at Moira, who was clutching her craft bag to her chest. "Wow, Larkin!" she said, in her higher-pitched voice. "Guess someone didn't know about sightlines!" She laughed again. "Remember, kids—if you can see the audience, they can see you!"

She waited.

Somebody else *had* to say something.

"And you went and confirmed that the circuit breaker was stage right, and that it would have been possible for Moira to flip the breaker for the Main Theater, and that she would have done it specifically to prevent Adamantine's artificial intelligence assistant from functioning properly?" It was starting to get a little uncomfortable on the outside railing. Her hair was blowing into her face, but she didn't dare reach up to push it away. "So Moira wanted to prove to Adamantine that she couldn't rely on TOM, because she wanted Adamantine to go gently into that good night as quickly as possible, and that's why I assumed Moira was the one who did the ol' chop chop on the brainstem, but whoops!" Her left palm was starting to sweat. "Did I ever get it wrong!"

She looked at Daniel, whose eyes were focused on his hacksaw. She looked at Moira, whose eyes were focused on her knitting needles. She still couldn't bring herself to look at Ed.

"See, Daniel used to be a neuroscientist," she said, wrapping her left fingers even more tightly around the railing. "Except now he's a magician, which was kind of cool when he started, but it's been, like, twenty years and he's still doing the same old tricks he's always done. He's on the same cruise, every year, making the same jokes, and every year the audience laughs a little less." Larkin was hoping, at this point, that she was guessing correctly. She couldn't read Daniel's body language, especially now that a clump of her long dark hair had lodged itself in front of her right eye. "And then he and Moira find out that, like, all of the Alzheimer's research from the past ten years had been fabricated? Faked? I don't know exactly what happened there, but I do know that the two of you saw an opportunity. You were going to do the kind of science that would be impossible to do if you did it, like, *scientifically*." She shook her head, trying to knock her hair out of her face, and her sandals slid slightly against the railing. "There's no way you'd get permission to do what you planned to do with Adamantine's brain, so you decided to ask for forgiveness instead."

A light went on at the far end of the deck. Daniel turned; Moira turned; Larkin's left hand slipped completely and she wrapped her elbow around the railing. "Hey!" she called out. "I'm over here, doing the villain's monologue—which is totally your job, but the two of you already screwed up your job, which was to cut off Adamantine's head without anyone finding out! You had the whole thing set up! You brought a real hacksaw on board, knowing that the security team wouldn't care if a magician packed a hacksaw! You had a cooler ready to go, because there's nothing in the cruise ship rules that say you can't bring a medical-grade cooler on board!"

The light began moving. Larkin held on as tightly as she could. "Moira was going to do the dirty work, but she chickened out!" The noise approached before the helicopter did, and Larkin did her best to shout above the sound of the blades. "Except she didn't tell Daniel, and when they found Adamantine's body, he assumed she'd done it!" The wind was blowing her hair into her mouth, now. "And she assumed he'd done it!" She hadn't planned for this—she'd planned for nearly everything else over the past four days, but she hadn't planned for *this*—and she wasn't sure she could hang on. "And your medical-grade cooler felt like it had a head in it, because I got Elliott to swipe a ten-pound weight from the fitness center and shove it in there, but neither of you wanted to open the cooler because you didn't want to risk ruining Adamantine's brain!"

She was going to have to explain everything all over again, she was sure of it—but first, she was going to have to get herself off the railing and onto the ladder that had been dropped from the door of the helicopter. Officer Van der Voort was the pilot; Jay leaned out as far as he could, beckoning and waving.

"I can't reach the ladder!" Larkin called towards him, hoping he could hear her. "I'll fall!"

She watched Jay make his decision.

She watched him descend the ladder and extend his arm.

She watched one of his expensive German sandals come loose, catching in the wind and landing in the sea.

She reached out her right hand and felt Jay's fingers close around her wrist.

She closed her fingers around his.

"Let go! I've got you!"

He did.

Then her feet were on the ladder, and her arms were pulling her upwards, and she was inside, and Claire was wrapping her in a rough gray blanket.

"We've got you, kiddo," she said. "Everything's going to be okay."

Larkin shook her head, pushing aside the blanket and scrambling towards the open doorway. "What about Ed?"

She felt Jay's hand, gripping the fabric of her seafoam dress; she saw, on the deck, Elliott using an orange-tipped foam sword to disarm Daniel. To knock the hacksaw out of place, allowing Ed to run safely towards Anni, who was standing with Handy and Ismael and a pair of cruise-uniformed officers who each held a set of handcuffs.

"Relax," Claire said. "We've got this."

"Woo-hoo!" Officer Van der Voort shouted, banking the helicopter. "This is my first time to be a hero!"

"Mine too," Jay said, holding Larkin's hand.

Mine too, Larkin thought—but she needed to be sure, first.

"Adamantine's all right?"

"Your famous author is alive and well," the Chief Security Officer said, turning the helicopter back towards the helipad. "We have been hiding her in the brig!"

"I don't know where you got the idea to fake her death," Claire said, "but it saved her life."

Larkin wanted to tell them everything—how she'd worked with Elliott to unlock the morgue and steal the headless mannequin from the Promenade; how she'd asked Jay to convince Artie to hide Adamantine and pretend the plastic corpse was real; how she'd given Anni the task of making Adamantine's stateroom look like a crime scene. How Eirwen had helped, without being asked. How Eliza had agreed to play along and look suspicious. How Larkin had kept the entire plan in her head the entire time.

She would tell them everything, eventually.

But now—with Jay and Claire on either side—she would sit in the overwhelming noise of the helicopter and weep.

CHAPTER 22

The knock awakened Larkin.

"Are we relaxed? I brought you some tea."

The cruise-uniformed woman—Sanne, according to her nametag—placed a small tray next to the massage bed. Larkin had been asleep, or close enough to it, for longer than she realized.

"Thank you," Larkin said, pulling her head out of the lavender-scented face cradle. She was naked, or close enough to it, but Sanne didn't mind. The massage therapist was the kind of woman who had seen every kind of body there was to see and cared for them all. "You have a lot of muscle," she'd said, at the beginning of their ninety-minute session. "You're stronger than you look."

"Thanks," Larkin had said, because she hadn't known what else to say.

Larkin had never gotten a massage before. Claire had booked it for her, along with the sixty-minute facial and the thirty-minute foot scrub. "I told you I'd make sure you spent a day in the spa," Claire had said—and Larkin had said "thanks," because she hadn't known what else to say, and then she'd gotten her foot scrub and fallen asleep during her massage and was about to spend an hour wrapped in a bathrobe while Sanne dealt patiently with her pores.

"Have you had a good vacation?" Sanne asked, leading Larkin towards a cushioned chair.

Larkin considered everything that had happened to her over the past five days.

"Yes," she said. "I have."

———

The talent show was that evening. Larkin stood, in the back, next to Eliza and Adamantine.

"You're not going to read from *The Yet Unknowing World*?" she teased, her freshly manicured hand squeezing the octogenarian author's wrinkled one.

"I prefer to keep my final work a mystery," Adamantine said, "at least until publication."

"Anyone who knows *Hamlet* knows exactly what the last *Time Tangent Gentleman* book is going to be about," Larkin said. She didn't tell Adamantine that she had spent part of her morning flipping through a battered Shakespeare in the ship's library. "Horatio Bonheur is going to consider ending his life, and then his friends are going to convince him to stay alive and keep telling stories." She glanced at Eliza, whom she knew had been one of those friends. "Which means there's no way this novel will end up being your final work."

Adamantine laughed. "Do you think I have another book in me?"

"Maybe," Larkin said. "Or maybe your next act will involve helping someone else."

The two of them watched Eirwen as she read, aloud, in

front of the crowded room. The redheaded nerd had wowed them all with her short story about the boy and the moon. Then she'd announced that she wanted to read the first page of a new project.

"This is kind of a fantasy story," Eirwen said, holding a notebook in her hand. "I wanted to write something that felt kind of like the books I used to love, and I'm still figuring out how to put that feeling into words, but here they are."

"I'll get her contact information," Eliza said, quietly.

"Yes," Adamantine agreed. "TOM can arrange a meeting."

Next up was Josephine and Claire, who got plenty of hoots and hollers as they attempted a dramatic interpretation of the climactic scene from *How Now, Horatio*. The nerds had figured out, more or less, that Adamantine had faked her own death—and although they didn't exactly know why, enough of them had won big in the prediction market that everyone was happy.

"It was a marketing stunt," Larkin had heard a nerd argue at breakfast. "She wanted to get more attention for her last book."

"It was a hint," another nerd said, "about what's going to happen to Horatio."

"It was elder awareness activism," a third nerd had insisted. "Many older people are marginalized and made invisible by society. By making herself disappear for a day, Adamantine Darcy reminded us just how important the older generation of Americans really are. Did you know she served in the Korean War? She was a Marine!"

"Good for her," a young nerd had replied, "but we all know that she had to go offline for a day so her AI could update its firmware. Without TOM, she wouldn't be able to talk, or walk, or, like, *do anything*. She's a total cyborg."

"You're all forgetting the part where she apparently lost her head for, like, twenty-four hours," the first nerd said. "Do you really think they had to take her skull off to upgrade her AIA? It was all a marketing stunt. I heard it wasn't even a corpse they found, just a headless mannequin."

"What if she's a mannequin?" the young nerd asked. "Like, they put her brain into TOM and turned her body into an android?"

"Like Data?"

"Totally like Data."

That was where Larkin had left them—since she didn't really feel like mentioning that she had once met Brent Spiner, and it hadn't been at a Star Trek convention, and she'd gotten to ask him all of the questions she'd wanted to ask about working with Stephen Sondheim, and *wow, she really was a nerd*—and now she found herself watching Ed and the Blerds perform a hip-hop history of the Caribbean. Ed was at his turntables, and as he both kept and manipulated the beat, Larkin realized that Ed had not only changed in the past week, but he'd also had a novel's worth of new experiences that she didn't know about. She'd fallen in love with Ed, back when the two of them were working together to solve their first murder, in part because they'd shared a story. Now they didn't—and although they could, if they wanted to, Larkin suspected that both she and Ed wanted to move on.

Anni and Elliott, on the other hand—well, they began their act by explaining, in both words and a surprisingly sophisticated slide deck, exactly what Elliott meant by *a scalable, pattern-based tutoring system with an emphasis on 1:1 knowledge transfer*. Then Elliott proved his system by demonstrating how he had taught Anni a deceptively complex card trick and proved it again by inviting a nerd onstage and using the same patterns to quickly and efficiently transfer the information. Once the nerd had mastered the trick—which took, as far as Larkin could tell, approximately four minutes—Anni informed the audience that it worked for other disciplines too.

"I taught Elliott, who had never played the piano before in his life, the prima part to a simple Debussy duet," she explained, as Elliott wheeled the digital keyboard onto the stage. "It's called *En Bateau*, which could mean *on a boat* but is more often translated as *sailing*."

The two of them sat, side by side, on the bench.

They began playing, Anni's hands running up and down the keyboard while Elliott played a slow, beautiful melody.

Then Anni's hands stopped.

"Elliott," she said, turning towards him. "How did you—"

She held up her left hand. Her ring finger caught the light and sparkled.

"Magic," Elliott said.

He looked happier than Larkin had ever seen him. So did she.

"Will you marry me?" Elliott asked.

"Obviously," Anni answered.

There was applause, and a few cheers, and the Debussy was abandoned as Elliott and Anni kissed in a way that Larkin hadn't known either of them were capable of. As she watched—was she crying?—she felt Jay put his hand on her shoulder.

"Is someone jealous?"

"No," Larkin said, not knowing whether she should sniff her snot back into her nose or wipe it on her forearm.

"I'm not losing a best friend; I'm gaining a close-up magician."

"They're lucky to have you," Jay said. Then he asked, with intent—"Am I?"

"I don't know," Larkin said, and meant it. "Is it okay if I don't know?"

"It has to be," Jay said. "It would be ungentlemanly to argue otherwise."

"You're not a gentleman."

"No, I'm not," Jay said, "and as you might recall, I play to win."

"So do I."

"No you don't," Jay said. "Not yet. So far I've only seen you play to make other people happy. You're very good at it, my father adores you, you earned your way into that Shakespeare Festival job, but—"

His voice was soft, almost seductive, against Larkin's ear.

"I look forward to seeing who you become when you decide to play for yourself."

———

"Good morning, nerds!"

Larkin, who had been awake even before Xavier began his announcement, smiled.

"I know that for most of us it's a less-than-good morning, first because it's the day we have to leave the ship and second because it is—by the ship's clock—6:45 a.m., but I know that we can have just as good of a time today as we've had all week!"

Larkin had said goodbye to both Xavier and Eliza the night before, as they'd all gathered for a party that began on the Lido Deck and ended in the Performers' Lounge. Ed had been there, too. She'd danced with him when the DJ played Walter Murphy's "A Fifth of Beethoven." They'd bought each other drinks, toasted each other's success, and then come back to their shared bedroom—where the double bed had been separated and remade as two singles.

Anni had left a note on each of their pillows.

Larkin—I know you'll say this isn't necessary but separating and/or joining beds is part of the standard cruise package and I thought you might both be a little more comfortable this way. I already tipped Handy, but if you pretend you don't know that, he'll be thrilled.

Larkin leaned over the edge of her bed and felt around in her purse until she found her wallet. There had to be at least one twenty left over—and if there were two, Handy would get them both. She'd also give him her email address, just in case either he or his daughter wanted advice on how to break into the theater business.

"We're going to disembark based on the flight information you provided the cruise line, so those of you with the earliest flights will be leaving the ship first! If you haven't already checked your stateroom for your color-coded departure ticket, now's the time—because the Blue Team is going to disembark in exactly forty-five minutes!"

Larkin had no idea where her color-coded departure ticket was. She wasn't even sure when their flight was leaving.

"Don't worry," Ed said, his sleep mask still covering his eyes. "We're Yellow Team. We've got another two hours."

She loved him. More than ever, now that her love didn't come with obligations—and she'd love watching whatever Ed did next, from whatever distance or closeness they agreed was comfortable.

"Thanks," Larkin said. "What would I do without you?"

"Save Adamantine Darcy's life," Ed said. "Probably the best thing you've ever done."

"For now," Larkin said, thinking of what Jay had told her.

She continued thinking about Jay's advice—*play for yourself*—as she packed her first bag and ate her last breakfast taco and stopped by Eirwen's stateroom for the promised cup of coffee. The sixteen nerds crammed into the deck eight suite were Green Team, last to leave the ship, and most of them hadn't even gotten dressed yet.

Eirwen had. "I got invited to the Koningin Suite for breakfast," she told Larkin, tying a blue bandana around her red hair. "Adamantine Darcy wants to help me with my novel."

"It's going to be a novel?" Larkin asked. She did not remind Eirwen that at the beginning of the week, she'd been dismissive of the Special Guests and the work they'd done to become who they were. Eirwen had also done her work, on the ship, and she'd become the kind of person who could appreciate Adamantine's offer. "Not a short story to send off to Electric Quim?"

"Electric Quim can stick itself up its own itself," Eirwen said. "My project is way bigger than any website."

"Good," Larkin said, because there wasn't much else to say, and then she wished Eirwen the best and warned her that Adamantine would probably eat the butter straight off the dish. "So if you want to butter your toast, get your knife in there before she puts her fingers in."

They hugged, sort of, and promised to keep in touch.

On her way back to the stateroom, Larkin stopped by Aart Van der Voort's office. The Chief Security Officer was delighted to see Larkin and poured her a warm cup of

Dutch cocoa while explaining how he'd had more fun in the past week than he'd had in years.

"I loved your idea," he said, "to put the dummy in the morgue!"

Larkin didn't tell him that it was where Adamantine and the Penningtons had planned to stash her actual corpse, back when Adamantine had boarded the ship believing she'd never leave it. As far as Artie knew, Adamantine was a famous author who needed to be hidden, in the brig, until the two people who had agreed to murder her both assumed the other one had done it. That was the plan Larkin and Adamantine and Eliza had created, the day Adamantine had asked Larkin for help— and although Adamantine had forgotten the precise way in which Larkin needed to be introduced to the ship's Chief Security Officer, in part because Moira had deliberately crashed her system, the business with the missing manuscript had worked just as well.

"I'm just glad you were willing to play along," Larkin said. "Not everyone would have been so enthusiastic about the job."

Officer Van der Voort laughed. "On this cruise, anything can happen! The last time we sailed, they invited me to play a giant video game in the Main Theater. Something about the stars, and spaceships, and they wanted me to play the role of the ship's security officer, and I ended up getting them all killed by aliens." He held up his hands. "I could not push the buttons fast enough!"

"But you can fly a helicopter," Larkin said, "and I bet nobody else on this ship can do that."

Artie smiled. "It was my first time getting to use that helicopter. We train regularly, so I remember how, but most sailings do not require its services." He raised his gold-rimmed teacup and tapped it, gently, against Larkin's. "I was proud to use it to save you."

When Larkin finally made it back to the stateroom—giving herself a generous fifteen minutes to throw her toiletries and any extraneous pieces of clothing into her suitcase—she found Anni, Elliott, Ed, Josephine, and Claire all staring at their phones.

"What's going on?" Larkin asked.

"We have internet now," Elliott said.

"Free internet," Anni corrected.

"We didn't miss anything, though," Claire said. "The world is in the same place it was when we left it."

"For you, maybe," Josephine teased. Then she held her phone towards Larkin. "One of the small liberal arts colleges in the Corridor is looking for an Interim Provost. Should I apply?"

"You should absolutely apply," Larkin said. "Provosts are like deans, right?"

"Not precisely," Josephine said, "but—"

"Hey," Ed interrupted, his voice quietly excited. "I heard back from Howell College. The music department has agreed to grant me tenure and promote me to Associate Professor."

"Wow," Larkin said. "Congratulations." She knew how much it meant to him—and how much the application process had taken out of him over the past year. "Guess you'll be sticking around, then."

"Yeah," Ed said. "Pratincola will have to be big enough for the both of us."

"We're going to be just fine," Larkin said. "You're still going to do the music for the Shakespeare Festival, if you want to, and I'm still going to sing in the community choir, if you'll have me, and next year both of us may end up on this cruise, because as soon as we disembark I'm going to make an account with Dutch Cruise International and begin the process of working my way towards Super Elite Status."

"Do it now," Anni said, her eyes still on her phone. "You get a ten percent discount if you open a loyalty account and book your next cruise while you're still physically on the ship."

Larkin looked towards her still-open suitcase. "Mom, will you help me pack all of this up? I guess I gotta make an account right now, or something."

Josephine stood up, gave Larkin the biggest hug she'd ever received, and walked quickly into the stateroom. "My daughter just asked for my help! Do you know how long I've been waiting for her to let me help her?"

"Yes, Jo," Claire said.

"Nearly two years!" Josephine continued, as Larkin opened up her phone and ignored her email—including an email with the subject line *Shakespeare Festival Artistic Director Decision*—so she could get her loyalty account set up before it was the Yellow Team's turn to disembark. "My daughter spent all this time living in my house, telling me she could handle everything on her own, insisting she didn't need her mother's help, and I had to stay out of the way and stay quiet, and now, *finally*—"

"We got it, Jo," Claire teased.

"I love you too," Larkin said. Then she put her phone away. "All right, it's done. Dutch Cruise International has my loyalty, I got my ten percent discount, and I am officially booked for next year's Nerd Cruise. Cheapest stateroom class, roommate TBD"—she glanced at Ed and then at Anni, both of whom understood—"and only four more cruises to go before I attain Elite Status."

"Does that mean you're officially a nerd?" Elliott asked. "I told Anni you were one of us."

"I'm not sure what I am, but—" Larkin began, thinking of all of the roles and responsibilities she had taken on over the past year—and knowing that before she could learn how to *play for herself*, she'd have to figure out exactly who she was and what she wanted. It was more than just trying to be a professional. It was more than what she could do for other people. Identity was a complicated thing, and Anni had solved the problem one way and Eirwen had solved it in a different way, and Elliott and Ed had both learned how to code-switch, and her mother had spent the past year learning who she was when she wasn't a college dean, and Larkin—

She knew she didn't know.

She also knew it would be all right in the end.

"Yes," Larkin concluded. "I'm a nerd, and that's cool, and I'm ready for whatever comes next."

AUTHOR'S NOTE

If you ever get the chance to write four novels, back-to-back, over two years—

Well, I'd suggest you take it.

In fact, I'd suggest you give yourself the opportunity, if novel-writing is something that interests you. Don't wait for a publisher to contact you, as Shortwave contacted me. Set aside an hour a day, Monday through Friday, and try to write five hundred words during every writing session. That'll get you two sixty-thousand-word drafts by the end of a year, with two weeks left over for vacation. (I wrote one thousand words an hour because I needed to both *draft* and *revise* my novels within the same limited time frame, but you may not be ready to write at that capacity yet. Start with five hundred words and work from there.)

You'll also want to set aside a little extra time to think about the plot and the characters, and to plan what might happen next—but if novel-writing is something that interests you, that time will set itself aside without your having to schedule it. Your book will be *the thought that occupies your thoughts,* as I once wrote in my now-defunct blog.

When your book is no longer the thought that occupies your thoughts, it may be time to start working on something new.

Even if you don't finish your four novels—even if you don't finish a single sixty-thousand-word draft—you'll have learned something that you can put towards your subsequent projects.

What I learned from Larkin—

Well, it's pretty much what she learned, book by book.

And I'm ready for whatever comes next.

ACKNOWLEDGMENTS

I wrote these books for my parents.

I wrote these books for Alan Lastufka and Shortwave Publishing.

I wrote these books for Larry Finley, the great love of my life.

I wrote these books for you.

I couldn't have done any of this without your support, and I couldn't have finished this book in particular without assistance and insight from Thera Heller, Paul Sabourin, Swamp Qat (assisted by Morgan Wallace), Lila Herbst, Maggie Stiefvater and the Galahad Group, Beth Dieker, Jim Jones, and—of course—Alan and Larry and my family.

<3, you nerds.

ABOUT THE AUTHOR

Nicole Dieker is a writer, teacher, and musician. She began her writing career as a full-time freelancer with a focus on personal finance and habit formation; she launched her fiction career with *The Biographies of Ordinary People*, a definitely-not-autobiographical novel that follows three sisters from 1989 to 2016.

Dieker maintains an active freelance career; her work has appeared in Vox, Morning Brew, Lifehacker, Bankrate, Haven Life, Popular Science, and more. Dieker spent five years as writer and editor for The Billfold, a personal finance blog where people had honest conversations about money.

Praise from Kirkus Reviews: "Dieker excels at depicting how real people think and act."

Dieker lives in Quincy, Illinois with the great love of her life, his piano, and their garden.

A NOTE FROM SHORTWAVE PUBLISHING

Thank you for reading Larkin's fourth mystery! If you enjoyed *Murder on the Nerd Cruise*, please consider writing a review. Reviews help readers find more titles they may enjoy, and that helps us continue to publish titles like this.

For more Shortwave fiction, free-to-read Magazine stories, newsletters, author events, limited editions, and more, please visit us online…

OUR WEBSITE

shortwavepublishing.com

on TWITTER and INSTAGRAM

@ShortwaveBooks

EMAIL US

contact@shortwavepublishing.com

www.ingramcontent.com/pod-product-compliance
Lightning Source LLC
Chambersburg PA
CBHW032028310726
48972CB00002B/583